PENGUIN BOOKS

DANCE OF
THE HAPPY SHADES

Alice Munro was born in Wingham, Ontario, and went to the University of Western Ontario. She thinks she began writing things down when she was about twelve, and at fifteen she declared she would soon write the great novel, 'But I thought perhaps I wasn't ready so I would write a short story in the meantime.' She has been writing stories ever since and is now thought to be foremost amongst Canadian authors. For many years her work was published only in literary magazines but in 1968 her first collection, *Dance of the Happy Shades*, was published and won that year's Governor-General's Award for Fiction. Since then she has published four other volumes of stories. *Something I've Been Meaning to Tell You* (Penguin, 1985), *The Beggar Maid* (Penguin, 1980; originally published in North America as *Who Do You Think You Are?*), which was nominated for the Booker McConnell Prize in 1980, *The Moons of Jupiter and Other Stories* (Penguin, 1984), and *The Progress of Love* (1987), and a novel, *Lives of Girls and Women* (Penguin, 1982).

Almost all of Alice Munro's stories take place in rural and semi-rural southern Ontario, the landscape of her childhood, and where she now lives. Described by one of her peers as going around with a 'delicate, rueful smile and a wicked pen', she says of herself: 'I guess that maybe as a writer I'm kind of an anachronism ... because I write about places where your roots are and most people don't live that kind of life any more at all. Most writers, probably, the writers who are most in tune with our time, write about places that have no texture because this is where most of us live.'

ALICE MUNRO

DANCE OF THE HAPPY SHADES

AND OTHER STORIES

PENGUIN BOOKS

PENGUIN BOOKS

Published by the Penguin Group
Penguin Books Ltd, 27 Wrights Lane, London W8 5TZ, England
Penguin Books USA Inc., 375 Hudson Street, New York, New York 10014, USA
Penguin Books Australia Ltd, Ringwood, Victoria, Australia
Penguin Books Canada Ltd, 10 Alcorn Avenue, Toronto, Ontario, Canada M4V 3B2
Penguin Books (NZ) Ltd, 182–190 Wairau Road, Auckland 10, New Zealand

Penguin Books Ltd, Registered Offices: Harmondsworth, Middlesex, England

First published in Canada by The Ryerson Press 1968
First published in the United States of America by
McGraw-Hill Ryerson Limited 1968
First published in Great Britain by Allen Lane 1974
Published in Penguin Books 1983
7 9 10 8

A number of the stories (some in slightly different form) were originally
published in magazines: 'The Peace of Utrecht' and 'Thanks for the Ride'
in *Tamarack Review*; 'Dance of the Happy Shades', 'Boys and Girls', 'An
Ounce of Cure' and 'The Office' in *The Montrealer*; 'The Time of Death'
and 'Sunday Afternoon' in *The Canadian Forum*. 'Day of the Butterfly'
appeared as 'Goodbye Myra' in *Chatelaine*. 'The Shining Houses' and
'A Trip to the Coast' first were read on the CBC programme *Anthology*.

Printed in England by Clays Ltd, St Ives plc
Set in Baskerville

FOR ROBERT E. LAIDLAW

Contents

Walker Brothers Cowboy

After supper my father says, "Want to go down and see if the Lake's still there?" We leave my mother sewing under the dining-room light, making clothes for me against the opening of school. She has ripped up for this purpose an old suit and an old plaid wool dress of hers, and she has to cut and match very cleverly and also make me stand and turn for endless fittings, sweaty, itching from the hot wool, ungrateful. We leave my brother in bed in the little screened porch at the end of the front verandah, and sometimes he kneels on his bed and presses his face against the screen and calls mournfully, "Bring me an ice cream cone!" but I call back, "You will be asleep," and do not even turn my head.

Then my father and I walk gradually down a long, shabby sort of street, with Silverwoods Ice Cream signs standing on the sidewalk, outside tiny, lighted stores. This is in Tuppertown, an old town on Lake Huron, an old grain port. The street is shaded, in some places, by maple trees whose roots have cracked and heaved the sidewalk and spread out like crocodiles into the bare yards. People are sitting out, men in shirt-sleeves and undershirts and women in aprons—not people we know but if anybody looks ready to nod and say, "Warm night," my father will nod too and say something the same. Children are still playing. I don't know them either because

my mother keeps my brother and me in our own yard, saying
he is too young to leave it and I have to mind him. I am not
so sad to watch their evening games because the games themselves are ragged, dissolving. Children, of their own will,
draw apart, separate into islands of two or one under the
heavy trees, occupying themselves in such solitary ways as I
do all day, planting pebbles in the dirt or writing in it with
a stick.

Presently we leave these yards and houses behind, we pass a
factory with boarded-up windows, a lumberyard whose high
wooden gates are locked for the night. Then the town falls
away in a defeated jumble of sheds and small junkyards, the
sidewalk gives up and we are walking on a sandy path with
burdocks, plantains, humble nameless weeds all around. We
enter a vacant lot, a kind of park really, for it is kept clear of
junk and there is one bench with a slat missing on the back, a
place to sit and look at the water. Which is generally grey in
the evening, under a lightly overcast sky, no sunsets, the
horizon dim. A very quiet, washing noise on the stones of the
beach. Further along, towards the main part of town, there is
a stretch of sand, a water slide, floats bobbing around the safe
swimming area, a life guard's rickety throne. Also a long dark
green building, like a roofed verandah, called the Pavilion,
full of farmers and their wives, in stiff good clothes, on Sundays.
That is the part of the town we used to know when we lived at
Dungannon and came here three or four times a summer, to
the Lake. That, and the docks where we would go and look
at the grain boats, ancient, rusty, wallowing, making us wonder
how they got past the breakwater let alone to Fort William.

Tramps hang around the docks and occasionally on these
evenings wander up the dwindling beach and climb the shifting, precarious path boys have made, hanging onto dry bushes,
and say something to my father which, being frightened of
tramps, I am too alarmed to catch. My father says he is a bit
hard up himself. "I'll roll you a cigarette if it's any use to you,"

he says, and he shakes tobacco out carefully on one of the thin butterfly papers, flicks it with his tongue, seals it and hands it to the tramp who takes it and walks away. My father also rolls and lights and smokes one cigarette of his own.

He tells me how the Great Lakes came to be. All where Lake Huron is now, he says, used to be flat land, a wide flat plain. Then came the ice, creeping down from the north, pushing deep into the low places. Like *that*—and he shows me his hand with his spread fingers pressing the rock-hard ground where we are sitting. His fingers make hardly any impression at all and he says, "Well, the old ice cap had a lot more power behind it than this hand has." And then the ice went back, shrank back towards the North Pole where it came from, and left its fingers of ice in the deep places it had gouged, and ice turned to lakes and there they were today. They were *new*, as time went. I try to see that plain before me, dinosaurs walking on it, but I am not able even to imagine the shore of the Lake when the Indians were there, before Tuppertown. The tiny share we have of time appalls me, though my father seems to regard it with tranquillity. Even my father, who sometimes seems to me to have been at home in the world as long as it has lasted, has really lived on this earth only a little longer than I have, in terms of all the time there has been to live in. He has not known a time, any more than I, when automobiles and electric lights did not at least exist. He was not alive when this century started. I will be barely alive—old, old —when it ends. I do not like to think of it. I wish the Lake to be always just a lake, with the safe-swimming floats marking it, and the breakwater and the lights of Tuppertown.

My father has a job, selling for Walker Brothers. This is a firm that sells almost entirely in the country, the back country. Sunshine, Boylesbridge, Turnaround—that is all his territory. Not Dungannon where we used to live, Dungannon is too near town and my mother is grateful for that. He sells cough medicine, iron tonic, corn plasters, laxatives, pills for female disorders, mouth wash, shampoo, liniment, salves, lemon and orange and raspberry concentrate for making refreshing drinks, vanilla, food colouring, black and green tea, ginger, cloves and other spices, rat poison. He has a song about it, with these two lines:

> And have all linaments and oils,
> For everything from corns to boils. . . .

Not a very funny song, in my mother's opinion. A pedlar's song, and that is what he is, a pedlar knocking at backwoods kitchens. Up until last winter we had our own business, a fox farm. My father raised silver foxes and sold their pelts to the people who make them into capes and coats and muffs. Prices fell, my father hung on hoping they would get better next year, and they fell again, and he hung on one more year and one more and finally it was not possible to hang on any more, we owed everything to the feed company. I have heard my mother explain this, several times, to Mrs. Oliphant who is the only neighbour she talks to. (Mrs. Oliphant also has come down in the world, being a schoolteacher who married the janitor.) We poured all we had into it, my mother says, and we came out with nothing. Many people could say the same thing, these days, but my mother has no time for the national calamity, only ours. Fate has flung us onto a street of poor people (it does not matter that we were poor before, that was a different sort of poverty), and the only way to take this, as she sees it, is with dignity, with bitterness, with no reconciliation. No bathroom with a claw-footed tub and a flush toilet is going to comfort her, nor water on tap and sidewalks past the house and milk in bottles, not even the two movie theatres and the Venus Restaurant and Woolworths so marvellous it has live birds singing in its fan-cooled corners and fish as tiny as fingernails, as bright as moons, swimming in its green tanks. My mother does not care.

In the afternoons she often walks to Simon's Grocery and takes me with her to help carry things. She wears a good dress, navy blue with little flowers, sheer, worn over a navy-blue slip. Also a summer hat of white straw, pushed down on the side of the head, and white shoes I have just whitened on a newspaper on the back steps. I have my hair freshly done in long damp curls which the dry air will fortunately soon loosen, a stiff large hair-ribbon on top of my head. This is entirely different from going out after supper with my father. We have not walked past two houses before I feel we have become objects of universal ridicule. Even the dirty words chalked on the side-walk are laughing at us. My mother does not seem to notice. She walks serenely like a lady shopping, like a *lady* shopping, past the housewives in loose beltless dresses torn under the arms. With me her creation, wretched curls and flaunting hair bow, scrubbed knees and white socks—all I do not want to be. I loathe even my name when she says it in public, in a voice so high, proud and ringing, deliberately different from the voice of any other mother on the street.

My mother will sometimes carry home, for a treat, a brick of ice cream—pale Neapolitan; and because we have no refrigerator in our house we wake my brother and eat it at once in the dining room, always darkened by the wall of the house next door. I spoon it up tenderly, leaving the chocolate till last, hoping to have some still to eat when my brother's dish is empty. My mother tries then to imitate the conversations we used to have at Dungannon, going back to our earliest, most leisurely days before my brother was born, when she would give me a little tea and a lot of milk in a cup like hers and we would sit out on the step facing the pump, the lilac tree, the fox pens beyond. She is not able to keep from mentioning those days. "Do you remember when we put you in your sled and Major pulled you?" (Major our dog, that we had to leave with neighbours when we moved.) "Do you remember your sandbox outside the kitchen window?" I pretend to remember far less than I do, wary of being trapped into sympathy or any unwanted emotion.

My mother has headaches. She often has to lie down. She lies on my brother's narrow bed in the little screened porch, shaded by heavy branches. "I look up at that tree and I think I am at home," she says.

"What you need," my father tells her, "is some fresh air and a drive in the country." He means for her to go with him, on his Walker Brothers route.

That is not my mother's idea of a drive in the country.

"Can I come?"

"Your mother might want you for trying on clothes."

"I'm beyond sewing this afternoon," my mother says.

"I'll take her then. Take both of them, give you a rest."

What is there about us that people need to be given a rest from? Never mind. I am glad enough to find my brother and make him go to the toilet and get us both into the car, our knees unscrubbed, my hair unringleted. My father brings from the house his two heavy brown suitcases, full of bottles, and sets them on the back seat. He wears a white shirt, brilliant in the sunlight, a tie, light trousers belonging to his summer suit (his other suit is black, for funerals, and belonged to my uncle before he died) and a creamy straw hat. His salesman's outfit, with pencils clipped in the shirt pocket. He goes back once again, probably to say goodbye to my mother, to ask her if she is sure she doesn't want to come, and hear her say, "No. No thanks, I'm better just to lie here with my eyes closed." Then we are backing out of the driveway with the rising hope of adventure, just the little hope that takes you over the bump into the street, the hot air starting to move, turning into a breeze, the houses growing less and less familiar as we follow the short cut my father knows, the quick way out of town. Yet what is there waiting for us all afternoon but hot hours in stricken farmyards, perhaps a stop at a country store and three ice cream cones or bottles of pop, and my father singing? The one he made up about himself has a title—"The Walker Brothers Cowboy"—and it starts out like this:

> Old Ned Fields, he now is dead,
> So I am ridin' the route instead. . . .

Who is Ned Fields? The man he has replaced, surely, and if so he really is dead; yet my father's voice is mournful-jolly, making his death some kind of nonsense, a comic calamity. "Wisht I was back on the Rio Grande, plungin' through the dusky sand." My father sings most of the time while driving the car. Even now, heading out of town, crossing the bridge and taking the sharp turn onto the highway, he is humming something, mumbling a bit of a song to himself, just tuning up, really, getting ready to improvise, for out along the highway we pass the Baptist Camp, the Vacation Bible Camp, and he lets loose:

> Where are the Baptists, where are the Baptists,
> where are all the Baptists today?
> They're down in the water, in Lake Huron water,
> with their sins all a-gittin' washed away.

My brother takes this for straight truth and gets up on his knees trying to see down to the Lake. "I don't see any Baptists," he says accusingly. "Neither do I, son," says my father. "I told you, they're down in the Lake."

No roads paved when we left the highway. We have to roll up the windows because of dust. The land is flat, scorched, empty. Bush lots at the back of the farms hold shade, black pine-shade like pools nobody can ever get to. We bump up a long lane and at the end of it what could look more unwelcoming, more deserted than the tall unpainted farmhouse with grass growing uncut right up to the front door, green blinds down and a door upstairs opening on nothing but air? Many houses have this door, and I have never yet been able to find out why. I ask my father and he says they are for walking in your sleep. *What?* Well if you happen to be walking in your sleep and you want to step outside. I am offended, seeing too late that he is joking, as usual, but my brother says sturdily, "If they did that they would break their necks."

The nineteen-thirties. How much this kind of farmhouse, this kind of afternoon, seem to me to belong to that one decade in time, just as my father's hat does, his bright flared tie, our car with its wide running board (an Essex, and long past its prime). Cars somewhat like it, many older, none dustier, sit in the farmyards. Some are past running and have their doors pulled off, their seats removed for use on porches. No living things to be seen, chickens or cattle. Except dogs. There are dogs, lying in any kind of shade they can find, dreaming, their lean sides rising and sinking rapidly. They get up when my father opens the car door, he has to speak to them. "Nice boy, there's a boy, nice old boy." They quiet down, go back to their shade. He should know how to quiet animals, he has held desperate foxes with tongs around their necks. One gentling voice for the dogs and another, rousing, cheerful, for calling at doors. "Hello there, Missus, it's the Walker Brothers man and what are you out of today?" A door opens, he disappears. Forbidden to follow, forbidden even to leave the car, we can just wait and wonder what he says. Sometimes trying to make my mother laugh he pretends to be himself in a farm kitchen, spreading out his sample case. "Now then, Missus, are you troubled with parasitic life? Your children's scalps, I mean. All those crawly little things we're too polite to mention that show up on the heads of the best of families? Soap alone is useless, kerosene is not too nice a perfume, but I have here—" Or else, "Believe me, sitting and driving all day the way I do I *know* the value of these fine pills. Natural relief. A problem common to old folks, too, once their days of activity are over—How about you, Grandma?" He would wave the imaginary box of pills under my mother's nose and she would laugh finally, unwillingly. "He doesn't say that really, does he?" I said, and she said no of course not, he was too much of a gentleman.

One yard after another, then, the old cars, the pumps, dogs, views of grey barns and falling-down sheds and unturning windmills. The men, if they are working in the fields, are not in any fields that we can see. The children are far away, following dry creek beds or looking for blackberries, or else they are hidden in the house, spying at us through cracks in the blinds. The car seat has grown slick with our sweat. I dare my brother to sound the horn, wanting to do it myself but not wanting to get the blame. He knows better. We play *I Spy*, but it is hard to find many colours. Grey for the barns and sheds and toilets and houses, brown for the yard and fields, black or brown for the dogs. The rusting cars show rainbow patches, in which I strain to pick out purple or green; likewise I peer at doors for shreds of old peeling paint, maroon or yellow. We can't play with letters, which would be better, because my brother is too young to spell. The game disintegrates anyway. He claims my colours are not fair, and wants extra turns.

In one house no door opens, though the car is in the yard. My father knocks and whistles, calls, "Hullo there! Walker Brothers man!" but there is not a stir of reply anywhere. This house has no porch, just a bare, slanting slab of cement on which my father stands. He turns around, searching the barnyard, the barn whose mow must be empty because you can see the sky through it, and finally he bends to pick up his suitcases. Just then a window is opened upstairs, a white pot appears on the sill, is tilted over and its contents splash down the outside wall. The window is not directly above my father's head, so only a stray splash would catch him. He picks up his suitcases with no particular hurry and walks, no longer whistling, to the car. "Do you know what that was?" I say to my brother. "*Pee*." He laughs and laughs.

My father rolls and lights a cigarette before he starts the car.

The window has been slammed down, the blind drawn, we never did see a hand or face. "Pee, pee," sings my brother ecstatically. "Somebody dumped down pee!" "Just don't tell your mother that," my father says. "She isn't liable to see the joke." "Is it in your song?" my brother wants to know. My father says no but he will see what he can do to work it in.

I notice in a little while that we are not turning in any more lanes, though it does not seem to me that we are headed home. "Is this the way to Sunshine?" I ask my father, and he answers, "No ma'am it's not." "Are we still in your territory?" He shakes his head. "We're going *fast*," my brother says approvingly, and in fact we are bouncing along through dry puddle-holes so that all the bottles in the suitcases clink together and gurgle promisingly.

Another lane, a house, also unpainted, dried to silver in the sun.

"I thought we were out of your territory."

"We are."

"Then what are we going in here for?"

"You'll see."

In front of the house a short, sturdy woman is picking up washing, which had been spread on the grass to bleach and dry. When the car stops she stares at it hard for a moment, bends to pick up a couple more towels to add to the bundle under her arm, comes across to us and says in a flat voice, neither welcoming nor unfriendly, "Have you lost your way?"

My father takes his time getting out of the car. "I don't think so," he says. "I'm the Walker Brothers man."

"George Golley is our Walker Brothers man," the woman says, "and he was out here no more than a week ago. Oh, my Lord God," she says harshly, "it's you."

"It was, the last time I looked in the mirror," my father says. The woman gathers all the towels in front of her and holds on to them tightly, pushing them against her stomach as if it hurt.

"Of all the people I never thought to see. And telling me you were the Walker Brothers man."

"I'm sorry if you were looking forward to George Golley," my father says humbly.

"And look at me, I was prepared to clean the hen-house. You'll think that's just an excuse but it's true. I don't go round looking like this every day." She is wearing a farmer's straw hat, through which pricks of sunlight penetrate and float on her face, a loose, dirty print smock and running shoes. "Who are those in the car, Ben? They're not yours?"

"Well I hope and believe they are," my father says, and tells our names and ages. "Come on, you can get out. This is Nora, Miss Cronin. Nora, you better tell me, is it still Miss, or have you got a husband hiding in the woodshed?"

"If I had a husband that's not where I'd keep him, Ben," she says, and they both laugh, her laugh abrupt and somewhat angry. "You'll think I got no manners, as well as being dressed like a tramp," she says. "Come on in out of the sun. It's cool in the house."

We go across the yard ("Excuse me taking you in this way but I don't think the front door has been opened since Papa's funeral, I'm afraid the hinges might drop off"), up the porch steps, into the kitchen, which really is cool, high-ceilinged, the blinds of course down, a simple, clean, threadbare room with waxed worn linoleum, potted geraniums, drinking-pail and dipper, a round table with scrubbed oilcloth. In spite of the cleanness, the wiped and swept surfaces, there is a faint sour smell—maybe of the dishrag or the tin dipper or the oilcloth, or the old lady, because there is one, sitting in an easy chair under the clock shelf. She turns her head slightly in our direction and says, "Nora? Is that company?"

"Blind," says Nora in a quick explaining voice to my father. Then, "You won't guess who it is, Momma. Hear his voice."

My father goes to the front of her chair and bends and says hopefully, "Afternoon, Mrs. Cronin."

"Ben Jordan," says the old lady with no surprise. "You haven't been to see us in the longest time. Have you been out of the country?"

My father and Nora look at each other.

"He's married, Momma," says Nora cheerfully and aggressively. "Married and got two children and here they are." She pulls us forward, makes each of us touch the old lady's dry, cool hand while she says our names in turn. Blind! This is the first blind person I have ever seen close up. Her eyes are closed, the eyelids sunk away down, showing no shape of the eyeball, just hollows. From one hollow comes a drop of silver liquid, a medicine, or a miraculous tear.

"Let me get into a decent dress," Nora says. "Talk to Momma. It's a treat for her. We hardly ever see company, do we Momma?"

"Not many makes it out this road," says the old lady placidly. "And the ones that used to be around here, our old neighbours, some of them have pulled out."

"True everywhere," my father says.

"Where's your wife then?"

"Home. She's not too fond of the hot weather, makes her feel poorly."

"Well." This is a habit of country people, old people, to say "well", meaning, "is that so?" with a little extra politeness and concern.

Nora's dress, when she appears again—stepping heavily on Cuban heels down the stairs in the hall—is flowered more lavishly than anything my mother owns, green and yellow on brown, some sort of floating sheer crepe, leaving her arms bare. Her arms are heavy, and every bit of her skin you can see is covered with little dark freckles like measles. Her hair is short, black, coarse and curly, her teeth very white and strong. "It's the first time I knew there was such a thing as green poppies," my father says, looking at her dress.

"You would be surprised all the things you never knew,"

says Nora, sending a smell of cologne far and wide when she moves and displaying a change of voice to go with the dress, something more sociable and youthful. "They're not poppies anyway, they're just flowers. You go and pump me some good cold water and I'll make these children a drink." She gets down from the cupboard a bottle of Walker Brothers Orange syrup.

"You telling me you were the Walker Brothers man!"

"It's the truth, Nora. You go and look at my sample cases in the car if you don't believe me. I got the territory directly south of here."

"Walker Brothers? Is that a fact? You selling for Walker Brothers?"

"Yes ma'am."

"We always heard you were raising foxes over Dungannon way."

"That's what I was doing, but I kind of run out of luck in that business."

"So where're you living? How long've you been out selling?"

"We moved into Tuppertown. I been at it, oh, two, three months. It keeps the wolf from the door. Keeps him as far away as the back fence."

Nora laughs. "Well I guess you count yourself lucky to have the work. Isabel's husband in Brantford, he was out of work the longest time. I thought if he didn't find something soon I was going to have them all land in here to feed, and I tell you I was hardly looking forward to it. It's all I can manage with me and Momma."

"Isabel married," my father says. "Muriel married too?"

"No, she's teaching school out west. She hasn't been home for five years. I guess she finds something better to do with her holidays. I would if I was her." She gets some snapshots out of the table drawer and starts showing him. "That's Isabel's oldest boy, starting school. That's the baby sitting in her carriage. Isabel and her husband. Muriel. That's her room-mate with her. That's a fellow she used to go around with, and his car. He was working in a bank out there. That's her school, it has eight rooms. She teaches Grade Five." My father shakes his head. "I can't think of her any way but when she was going to school, so shy I used to pick her up on the road—I'd be on my way to see you—and she would not say one word, not even to agree it was a nice day."

"She's got over that."

"Who are you talking about?" says the old lady.

"Muriel. I said she's got over being shy."

"She was here last summer."

"No Momma that was Isabel. Isabel and her family were here last summer. Muriel's out west."

"I meant Isabel."

Shortly after this the old lady falls asleep, her head on the side, her mouth open. "Excuse her manners," Nora says. "It's old age." She fixes an afghan over her mother and says we can all go into the front room where our talking won't disturb her.

"You two," my father says. "Do you want to go outside and amuse yourselves?"

Amuse ourselves how? Anyway I want to stay. The front room is more interesting than the kitchen, though barer. There is a gramophone and a pump organ and a picture on the wall of Mary, Jesus' mother—I know that much—in shades of bright blue and pink with a spiked band of light around her head. I know that such pictures are found only in the homes of Roman Catholics and so Nora must be one. We have never known any Roman Catholics at all well, never well enough to visit in their houses. I think of what my grand-mother and my Aunt Tena, over in Dungannon, used to always say to indicate that somebody was a Catholic. *So-and-so digs with the wrong foot*, they would say. *She digs with the wrong foot*. That was what they would say about Nora.

Nora takes a bottle, half full, out of the top of the organ and pours some of what is in it into the two glasses that she and my father have emptied of the orange drink.

"Keep it in case of sickness?" my father says.

"Not on your life," says Nora. "I'm never sick. I just keep it because I keep it. One bottle does me a fair time, though, because I don't care for drinking alone. Here's luck!" She and my father drink and I know what it is. Whisky. One of the things my mother has told me in our talks together is that my father never drinks whisky. But I see he does. He drinks whisky and he talks of people whose names I have never heard before. But after a while he turns to a familiar incident. He tells about the chamberpot that was emptied out the window. "Picture me there," he says, "hollering my heartiest. *Oh, lady, it's your Walker Brothers man, anybody home?*" He does himself hollering, grinning absurdly, waiting, looking up in pleased expectation and then—oh, ducking, covering his head with his arms, looking as if he begged for mercy (when he never did anything like that, I was watching), and Nora laughs, almost as hard as my brother did at the time.

"That isn't true! That's not a word true!"

"Oh, indeed it is ma'am. We have our heroes in the ranks of Walker Brothers. I'm glad you think it's funny," he says sombrely.

I ask him shyly, "Sing the song."

"What song? Have you turned into a singer on top of everything else?"

Embarrassed, my father says, "Oh, just this song I made up while I was driving around, it gives me something to do, making up rhymes."

But after some urging he does sing it, looking at Nora with a droll, apologetic expression, and she laughs so much that in places he has to stop and wait for her to get over laughing so he can go on, because she makes him laugh too. Then he does various parts of his salesman's spiel. Nora when she laughs

squeezes her large bosom under her folded arms. "You're
crazy," she says. "That's all you are." She sees my brother
peering into the gramophone and she jumps up and goes over
to him. "Here's us sitting enjoying ourselves and not giving
you a thought, isn't it terrible?" she says. "You want me to
put a record on, don't you? You want to hear a nice record?
Can you dance? I bet your sister can, can't she?"

I say no. "A big girl like you and so good-looking and can't
dance!" says Nora. "It's high time you learned. I bet you'd
make a lovely dancer. Here, I'm going to put on a piece I
used to dance to and even your daddy did, in his dancing days.
You didn't know your daddy was a dancer, did you? Well, he
is a talented man, your daddy!"

She puts down the lid and takes hold of me unexpectedly
around the waist, picks up my other hand and starts making
me go backwards. "This is the way, now, this is how they
dance. Follow me. This foot, see. One and one-two. One
and one-two. That's fine, that's lovely, don't look at your feet!
Follow me, that's right, see how easy? You're going to be a
lovely dancer! One and one-two. One and one-two. Ben, see
your daughter dancing!" *Whispering while you cuddle near me
Whispering where no one can hear me. . . .*

Round and round the linoleum, me proud, intent, Nora
laughing and moving with great buoyancy, wrapping me in her
strange gaiety, her smell of whisky, cologne, and sweat. Under
the arms her dress is damp, and little drops form along her
upper lip, hang in the soft black hairs at the corners of her
mouth. She whirls me around in front of my father—causing
me to stumble, for I am by no means so swift a pupil as she
pretends—and lets me go, breathless.

"Dance with me, Ben."

"I'm the world's worst dancer, Nora, and you know it."

"I certainly never thought so."

"You would now."

She stands in front of him, arms hanging loose and hopeful,

her breasts, which a moment ago embarrassed me with their warmth and bulk, rising and falling under her loose flowered dress, her face shining with the exercise, and delight.

"Ben."

My father drops his head and says quietly, "Not me, Nora."

So she can only go and take the record off. "I can drink alone but I can't dance alone," she says. "Unless I am a whole lot crazier than I think I am."

"Nora," says my father smiling. "You're not crazy."

"Stay for supper."

"Oh, no. We couldn't put you to the trouble."

"It's no trouble. I'd be glad of it."

"And their mother would worry. She'd think I'd turned us over in a ditch."

"Oh, well. Yes."

"We've taken a lot of your time now."

"Time," says Nora bitterly. "Will you come by ever again?"

"I will if I can," says my father.

"Bring the children. Bring your wife."

"Yes I will," says my father. "I will if I can."

When she follows us to the car he says, "You come to see us too, Nora. We're right on Grove Street, left-hand side going in, that's north, and two doors this side—east—of Baker Street."

Nora does not repeat these directions. She stands close to the car in her soft, brilliant dress. She touches the fender, making an unintelligible mark in the dust there.

On the way home my father does not buy any ice cream or pop, but he does go into a country store and get a package of licorice, which he shares with us. *She digs with the wrong foot,* I think, and the words seem sad to me as never before, dark, perverse. My father does not say anything to me about not mentioning things at home, but I know, just from the thoughtfulness, the pause when he passes the licorice, that there are things not to be mentioned. The whisky, maybe the dancing. No worry about my brother, he does not notice enough. At most he might remember the blind lady, the picture of Mary.

"Sing," my brother commands my father, but my father says gravely, "I don't know, I seem to be fresh out of songs. You watch the road and let me know if you see any rabbits."

So my father drives and my brother watches the road for rabbits and I feel my father's life flowing back from our car in the last of the afternoon, darkening and turning strange, like a landscape that has an enchantment on it, making it kindly, ordinary and familiar while you are looking at it, but changing it, once your back is turned, into something you will never know, with all kinds of weathers, and distances you cannot imagine.

When we get closer to Tuppertown the sky becomes gently overcast, as always, nearly always, on summer evenings by the Lake.

The Shining Houses

Mary sat on the back steps of Mrs. Fullerton's house, talking—
or really listening—to Mrs. Fullerton, who sold her eggs. She
had come in to pay the egg money, on her way to Edith's
Debbie's birthday party. Mrs. Fullerton did not pay calls
herself and she did not invite them, but, once a business pretext
was established, she liked to talk. And Mary found herself
exploring her neighbour's life as she had once explored the
lives of grandmothers and aunts—by pretending to know less
than she did, asking for some story she had heard before; this
way, remembered episodes emerged each time with slight
differences of content, meaning, colour, yet with a pure reality
that usually attaches to things which are at least part legend.
She had almost forgotten that there are people whose lives
can be seen like this. She did not talk to many old people any
more. Most of the people she knew had lives like her own, in
which things were not sorted out yet, and it is not certain if
this thing, or that, should be taken seriously. Mrs. Fullerton
had no doubts or questions of this kind. How was it possible,
for instance, not to take seriously the broad blithe back of Mr.
Fullerton, disappearing down the road on a summer day, not
to return?

"I didn't know that," said Mary. "I always thought Mr.
Fullerton was dead."

"He's no more dead than I am," said Mrs. Fullerton, sitting up straight. A bold Plymouth Rock walked across the bottom step and Mary's little boy, Danny, got up to give rather cautious chase. "He's just gone off on his travels, that's what he is. May of gone up north, may of gone to the States, I don't know. But he's not dead. I would of felt it. He's not old neither, you know, not old like I am. He was my second husband, he was younger. I never made any secret of it. I had this place and raised my children and buried my first husband, before ever Mr. Fullerton came upon the scene. Why, one time down in the post office we was standing together by the wicket and I went over to put a letter in the box and left my bag behind me, and Mr. Fullerton turns to go after me and the girl calls to him, she says, here, your mother's left her purse!"

Mary smiled, answering Mrs. Fullerton's high-pitched and not trustful laughter. Mrs. Fullerton was old, as she had said— older than you might think, seeing her hair still fuzzy and black, her clothes slatternly-gay, dime-store brooches pinned to her ravelling sweater. Her eyes showed it, black as plums, with a soft inanimate sheen; things sank into them and they never changed. The life in her face was all in the nose and mouth, which were always twitching, fluttering, drawing tight grimace-lines down her cheeks. When she came around every Friday on her egg deliveries her hair was curled, her blouse held together by a bunch of cotton flowers, her mouth painted, a spidery and ferocious line of red; she would not show herself to her new neighbours in any sad old-womanish disarray.

"Thought I was his mother," she said. "I didn't care. I had a good laugh. But what I was telling you," she said, "a day in summer, he was off work. He had the ladder up and he was picking me the cherries off of my black-cherry tree. I came out to hang my clothes and there was this man I never seen before in my life, taking the pail of cherries my husband hands down to him. Helping himself, too, not backward, he sat down and ate cherries out of my pail. Who's that, I said to my husband, and he says, just a fellow passing. If he's a friend of yours, I said, he's welcome to stay for supper. What are you talking about, he says, I never seen him before. So I never said another thing. Mr. Fullerton went and talked to him, eating my cherries I intended for a pie, but that man would talk to anybody, tramp, Jehovah's Witness, anybody—that didn't need to mean anything."

"And half an hour after that fellow went off," she said, "Mr. Fullerton comes out in his brown jacket and his hat on. I have to meet a man downtown. How long will you be, I said. Oh, not long. So off he goes down the road, walking down to where the old tram went—we was all in the bush then—and something made me look after him. He must be hot in that coat, I said. And that's when I knew he wasn't coming back. Yet I couldn't've expected it, he liked it here. He was talking about putting chinchillas in the back yard. What's in a man's mind even when you're living with him you will never know."

"Was it long ago?" said Mary.

"Twelve years. My boys wanted me to sell then and go and live in rooms. But I said no. I had my hens and a nanny goat too at that time. More or less a pet. I had a pet coon too for a while, used to feed him chewing gum. Well, I said, husbands maybe come and go, but a place you've lived fifty years is something else. Making a joke of it with my family. Besides, I thought, if Mr. Fullerton was to come back, he'd come back here, not knowing where else to go. Of course he'd hardly know where to find me, the way it's changed now. But I always had the idea he might of suffered a loss of memory and it might come back. That has happened.

"I'm not complaining. Sometimes it seems to me about as reasonable a man should go as stay. I don't mind changes, either, that helps out my egg business. But this baby-sitting. All the time one or the other is asking me about baby-sitting.

I tell them I got my own house to sit in and I raised my share of children."

Mary, remembering the birthday party, got up and called to her little boy. "I thought I might offer my black cherries for sale next summer," Mrs. Fullerton said. "Come and pick your own and they're fifty cents a box. I can't risk my old bones up a ladder no more."

"That's too much," Mary said, smiling. "They're cheaper than that at the supermarket." Mrs. Fullerton already hated the supermarket for lowering the price of eggs. Mary shook out her last cigarette and left it with her, saying she had another package in her purse. Mrs. Fullerton was fond of a cigarette but would not accept one unless you took her by surprise. Baby-sitting would pay for them, Mary thought. At the same time she was rather pleased with Mrs. Fullerton for being so unaccommodating. When Mary came out of this place, she always felt as if she were passing through barricades. The house and its surroundings were so self-sufficient, with their complicated and seemingly unalterable layout of vegetables and flower beds, apple and cherry trees, wired chicken-run, berry patch and wooden walks, woodpile, a great many roughly built dark little sheds, for hens or rabbits or a goat. Here was no open or straightforward plan, no order that an outsider could understand; yet what was haphazard time had made final. The place had become fixed, impregnable, all its accumulations necessary, until it seemed that even the wash-tubs, mops, couch springs and stacks of old police magazines on the back porch were there to stay.

Mary and Danny walked down the road that had been called, in Mrs. Fullerton's time, Wicks Road, but was now marked on the maps of the subdivision as Heather Drive. The name of the subdivision was Garden Place, and its streets were named for flowers. On either side of the road the earth was raw; the ditches were running full. Planks were laid across the open ditches, planks approached the doors of the newest houses. The new, white and shining houses, set side by side in long rows in the wound of the earth. She always thought of them as white houses, though of course they were not entirely white. They were stucco and siding, and only the stucco was white; the siding was painted in shades of blue, pink, green and yellow, all fresh and vivid colours. Last year, just at this time, in March, the bulldozers had come in to clear away the brush and second-growth and great trees of the mountain forest; in a little while the houses were going up among the boulders, the huge torn stumps, the unimaginable upheavals of that earth. The houses were frail at first, skeletons of new wood standing up in the dusk of the cold spring days. But the roofs went on, black and green, blue and red, and the stucco, the siding; the windows were put in, and plastered with signs that said, Murry's Glass, French's Hardwood Floors; it could be seen that the houses were real. People who would live in them came out and tramped around in the mud on Sundays. They were for people like Mary and her husband and their child, with not much money but expectations of more; Garden Place was already put down, in the minds of people who understood addresses, as less luxurious than Pine Hills but more desirable than Wellington Park. The bathrooms were beautiful, with three-part mirrors, ceramic tile, and coloured plumbing. The cupboards in the kitchen were light birch or mahogany, and there were copper lighting fixtures there and in the dining ells. Brick planters, matching the fireplaces, separated the living rooms and halls. The rooms were all large and light and the basements dry, and all this soundness. and excellence seemed to be clearly, proudly indicated on the face of each house—those ingenuously similar houses that looked calmly out at each other, all the way down the street.

Today, since it was Saturday, all the men were out working around their houses. They were digging drainage ditches and making rockeries and clearing off and burning torn branches and brush. They worked with competitive violence and energy,

all this being new to them; they were not men who made their
livings by physical work. All day Saturday and Sunday they
worked like this, so that in a year or two there should be green
terraces, rock walls, shapely flower beds and ornamental
shrubs. The earth must be heavy to dig now; it had been
raining last night and this morning. But the day was brighten-
ing; the clouds had broken, revealing a long thin triangle of
sky, its blue still cold and delicate, a winter colour. Behind
the houses on one side of the road were pine trees, their
ponderous symmetry not much stirred by any wind. These
were to be cut down any day now, to make room for a shopping
centre, which had been promised when the houses were sold.

And under the structure of this new subdivision, there was
still something else to be seen; that was the old city, the old
wilderness city that had lain on the side of the mountain. It
had to be called a city because there were tramlines running
into the woods, the houses had numbers and there were all the
public buildings of a city, down by the water. But houses like
Mrs. Fullerton's had been separated from each other by uncut
forest and a jungle of wild blackberry and salmonberry bushes;
these surviving houses, with thick smoke coming out of their
chimneys, walls unpainted and patched and showing different
degrees of age and darkening, rough sheds and stacked wood
and compost heaps and grey board fences around them—these
appeared every so often among the large new houses of
Mimosa and Marigold and Heather Drive—dark, enclosed,
expressing something like savagery in their disorder and the
steep, unmatched angles of roofs and lean-tos; not possible on
these streets, but there.

"What are they saying," said Edith, putting on more coffee.
She was surrounded in her kitchen by the ruins of the birthday
party—cake and molded jellies and cookies with animal faces.
A balloon rolled underfoot. The children had been fed, had
posed for flash cameras and endured the birthday games; now

they were playing in the back bedrooms and the basement, while their parents had coffee. "What are they saying in there?" said Edith.

"I wasn't listening," Mary said, holding the empty cream pitcher in her hand. She went to the sink window. The rent in the clouds had been torn wide open and the sun was shining. The house seemed too hot.

"Mrs. Fullerton's house," said Edith, hurrying back to the living-room. Mary knew what they were talking about. Her neighbours' conversation, otherwise not troubling, might at any moment snag itself on this subject and eddy menacingly in familiar circles of complaint, causing her to look despairingly out of windows, or down into her lap, trying to find some wonderful explanatory word to bring it to a stop; she did not succeed. She had to go back; they were waiting for cream.

A dozen neighbourhood women sat around the living room, absently holding the balloons they had been given by their children. Because the children on the street were so young, and also because any gathering-together of the people who lived there was considered a healthy thing in itself, most birthday parties were attended by mothers as well as children. Women who saw each other every day met now in earrings, nylons and skirts, with their hair fixed and faces applied. Some of the men were there too—Steve, who was Edith's husband, and others he had invited in for beer; they were all in their work clothes. The subject just introduced was one of the few on which male and female interest came together.

"I tell you what I'd do if I was next door to it, "Steve said, beaming good-naturedly in expectation of laughter. "I'd send my kids over there to play with matches."

"Oh, funny," Edith said. "It's past joking. You joke, I try to do something. I even phoned the Municipal Hall."

"What did they say?" said Mary Lou Ross.

"Well *I* said couldn't they get her to paint it, at least, or pull down some of the shacks, and they said no they couldn't. I

said I thought there must be some kind of ordinance applied
to people like that and they said they knew how I *felt* and they
were very *sorry*—"

"But no?"

"But no."

"But what about the chickens, I thought—"

"Oh, they wouldn't let you or me keep chickens, but she has
some special dispensation about that too, I forgot how it goes."

"I'm going to stop buying them," Janie Inger said. "The
supermarket's cheaper and who cares that much about fresh?
And my God, the smell. I said to Carl I knew we were coming
to the sticks but I somehow didn't picture us next door to a
barnyard."

"Across the street is worse than next door. It makes me
wonder why we ever bothered with a picture window, whenever anybody comes to see us I want to draw the drapes so
they won't see what's across from us."

"Okay, okay," Steve said, cutting heavily through these
female voices. "What Carl and I started out to tell you was
that, if we can work this lane deal, she has got to go. It's
simple and it's legal. That's the beauty of it."

"What lane deal?"

"We are getting to that. Carl and I been cooking this for a
couple of weeks, but we didn't like to say anything in case it
didn't work out. Take it, Carl."

"Well she's on the lane allowance, that's all," Carl said. He
was a real estate salesman, stocky, earnest, successful. "I had
an idea it might be that way, so I went down to the Municipal
Hall and looked it up."

"What does that mean, dear?" said Janie, casual, wifely.

"This is it," Carl said. "There's an allowance for a lane,
there always has been, the idea being if the area ever got built
up they would put a lane through. But they never thought
that would happen, people just built where they liked. She's
got part of her house and half a dozen shacks sitting right where

the lane has to go through. So what we do now, we get the municipality to put through a lane. We need a lane anyway. Then she has to get out. It's the law."

"It's the law," said Steve, radiating admiration. "What a smart boy. These real estate operators are smart boys."

"Does she get anything?" said Mary Lou. "I'm sick of looking at it and all but I don't want to see anybody in the poorhouse."

"Oh, she'll get paid. More than it's worth. Look, it's to her advantage. She'll get paid for it, and she couldn't sell it, she couldn't give it away."

Mary set her coffee cup down before she spoke and hoped her voice would sound all right, not emotional or scared. "But remember she's been here a long time," she said. "She was here before most of us were born," She was trying desperately to think of other words, words more sound and reasonable than these; she could not expose to this positive tide any notion that they might think flimsy and romantic, or she would destroy her argument. But she had no argument. She could try all night and never find any words to stand up to their words, which came at her now invincibly from all sides: *shack, eyesore, filthy, property, value.*

"Do you honestly think that people who let their property get so rundown have that much claim to our consideration?" Janie said, feeling her husband's plan was being attacked.

"She's been here forty years, now we're here," Carl said. "So it goes. And whether you realize it or not, just standing there that house is bringing down the resale value of every house on this street. I'm in the business, I know."

And these were joined by other voices; it did not matter much what they said as long as they were full of self-assertion and anger. That was their strength, proof of their adulthood, of themselves and their seriousness. The spirit of anger rose among them, bearing up their young voices, sweeping them together as on a flood of intoxication, and they admired each

other in this new behaviour as property-owners as people
admire each other for being drunk.

"We might as well get everybody now," Steve said. "Save
going around to so many places."

It was supper time, getting dark out. Everybody was preparing to go home, mothers buttoning their children's coats,
children clutching, without much delight, their balloons and
whistles and paper baskets full of jelly beans. They had
stopped fighting, almost stopped noticing each other; the
party had disintegrated. The adults too had grown calmer
and felt tired.

"Edith! Edith, have you got a pen?"

Edith brought a pen and they spread the petition for the
lane, which Carl had drawn up, on the dining-room table,
clearing away the paper plates with smears of dried ice cream.
People began to sign mechanically as they said goodbye.
Steve was still scowling slightly; Carl stood with one hand on
the paper, businesslike, but proud. Mary knelt on the floor
and struggled with Danny's zipper. She got up and put on her
own coat, smoothed her hair, put on her gloves and took them
off again. When she could not think of anything else to do she
walked past the dining-room table on her way to the door.
Carl held out the pen.

"I can't sign that," she said. Her face flushed up, at once,
her voice was trembling. Steve touched her shoulder.

"What's the matter, honey?"

"I don't think we have the right. We haven't the right."

"Mary, don't you care how things look? You live here too."

"No, I—I don't care." Oh, wasn't it strange, how in your
imagination, when you stood up for something, your voice
rang, people started, abashed; but in real life they all smiled
in rather a special way and you saw that what you had really
done was serve yourself up as a conversational delight for the
next coffee party.

"Don't worry, Mary, she's got money in the bank," Janie said. "She must have. I asked her to baby-sit for me once and she practically spit in my face. She isn't exactly a charming old lady, you know."

"I know she isn't a charming old lady," Mary said.

Steve's hand still rested on her shoulder. "Hey what do you think we are, a bunch of ogres?"

"Nobody wants to turn her out just for the fun of it," Carl said. "Its unfortunate. We all know that. But we have to think of the community."

"Yes," said Mary. But she put her hands in the pockets of her coat and turned to say thank you to Edith, thank you for the birthday party. It occurred to her that they were right, for themselves, for whatever it was they had to be. And Mrs. Fullerton was old, she had dead eyes, nothing could touch her. Mary went out and walked with Danny up the street. She saw the curtains being drawn across living-room windows; cascades of flowers, of leaves, of geometrical designs, shut off these rooms from the night. Outside it was quite dark, the white houses were growing dim, the clouds breaking and breaking, and smoke blowing from Mrs. Fullerton's chimney. The pattern of Garden Place, so assertive in the daytime, seemed to shrink at night into the raw black mountainside.

The voices in the living room have blown away, Mary thought. If they would blow away and their plans be forgotten, if one thing could be left alone. But these are people who win, and they are good people; they want homes for their children, they help each other when there is trouble, they plan a community—saying that word as if they found a modern and well-proportioned magic in it, and no possibility anywhere of a mistake.

There is nothing you can do at present but put your hands in your pockets and keep a disaffected heart.

Images

Now that Mary McQuade had come, I pretended not to remember her. It seemed the wisest thing to do. She herself said, "If you don't remember me you don't remember much," but let the matter drop, just once adding, "I bet you never went to your Grandma's house last summer. I bet you don't remember that either."

It was called, even that summer, my grandma's house, though my grandfather was then still alive. He had withdrawn into one room, the largest front bedroom. It had wooden shutters on the inside of the windows, like the living room and dining room; the other bedrooms had only blinds. Also, the verandah kept out the light so that my grandfather lay in near-darkness all day, with his white hair, now washed and tended and soft as a baby's, and his white nightshirt and pillows, making an island in the room which people approached with diffidence, but resolutely. Mary McQuade in her uniform was the other island in the room, and she sat mostly not moving where the fan, as if it was tired, stirred the air like soup. It must have been too dark to read or knit, supposing she wanted to do those things, and so she merely waited and breathed, making a sound like the fan made, full of old indefinable complaint.

I was so young then I was put to sleep in a crib—not at

home but this was what was kept for me at my grandma's house—in a room across the hall. There was no fan there and the dazzle of outdoors—all the flat fields round the house turned, in the sun, to the brilliance of water—made lightning cracks in the drawn-down blinds. Who could sleep? My mother's my grandmother's my aunts' voices wove their ordinary repetitions, on the verandah in the kitchen in the dining room (where with a little brass-handled brush my mother cleaned the white cloth, and the lighting-fixture over the round table hung down unlit flowers of thick, butterscotch glass). All the meals in that house, the cooking, the visiting, the conversation, even someone playing on the piano (it was my youngest aunt, Edith, not married, singing and playing with one hand, *Nita, Juanita, softly falls the southern moon*); all this life going on. Yet the ceilings of the rooms were very high and under them was a great deal of dim wasted space, and when I lay in my crib too hot to sleep I could look up and see that emptiness, the stained corners, and feel, without knowing what it was, just what everybody else in the house must have felt—under the sweating heat the fact of death-contained, that little lump of magic ice. And Mary McQuade waiting in her starched white dress, big and gloomy as an iceberg herself, implacable, waiting and breathing. I held her responsible.

So I pretended not to remember her. She had not put on her white uniform, which did not really make her less dangerous but might mean, at least, that the time of her power had not yet come. Out in the daylight, and not dressed in white, she turned out to be freckled all over, everywhere you could see, as if she was sprinkled with oatmeal, and she had a crown of frizzy, glinting, naturally brass-coloured hair. Her voice was loud and hoarse and complaint was her everyday language. "Am I going to have to hang up this wash all by myself?" she shouted at me, in the yard, and I followed her to the clothesline platform where with a groan she let down the basket of wet clothes. "Hand me them clothespins. One at a time. Hand me them right side up. I shouldn't be out in this wind at all, I've got a bronchial condition." Head hung, like an animal chained to her side, I fed her clothespins. Outdoors, in the cold March air, she lost some of her bulk and her smell. In the house I could always smell her, even in the rooms she seldom entered. What was her smell like? It was like metal and like some dark spice (cloves—she did suffer from tooth-ache) and like the preparation rubbed on my chest when I had a cold. I mentioned it once to my mother, who said, "Don't be silly, *I* don't smell anything." So I never told about the taste, and there was a taste too. It was in all the food Mary McQuade prepared and perhaps in all food eaten in her presence—in my porridge at breakfast and my fried potatoes at noon and the slice of bread and butter and brown sugar she gave me to eat in the yard—something foreign, gritty, depressing. How could my parents not know about it? But for reasons of their own they would pretend. This was something I had not known a year ago.

After she had hung out the wash she had to soak her feet. Her legs came straight up, round as drainpipes, from the steaming basin. One hand on each knee, she bent into the steam and gave grunts of pain and satisfaction.

"Are you a nurse?" I said, greatly daring, though my mother had said she was.

"Yes I am and I wish I wasn't."

"Are you my aunt too?"

"If I was your Aunt you would call me Aunt Mary, wouldn't you? Well you don't, do you? I'm your cousin, I'm your father's cousin. That's why they get me instead of getting an ordinary nurse. I'm a practical nurse. And there is always somebody sick in this family and I got to go to them. I never get a rest."

I doubted this. I doubted that she was asked to come. She came, and cooked what she liked and rearranged things to suit herself, complaining about draughts, and let her power loose in the house. If she had never come my mother would never have taken to her bed.

My mother's bed was set up in the dining room, to spare Mary McQuade climbing the stairs. My mother's hair was done in two little thin dark braids, her cheeks were sallow, her neck warm and smelling of raisins as it always did, but the rest of her under the covers had changed into some large, fragile and mysterious object, difficult to move. She spoke of herself gloomily in the third person, saying, "Be careful, don't hurt Mother, don't sit on Mother's legs." Every time she said Mother I felt chilled, and a kind of wretchedness and shame spread through me as it did at the name of Jesus. This *Mother* that my own real, warm-necked, irascible and comforting human mother set up between us was an everlastingly wounded phantom, sorrowing like Him over all the wickedness I did not yet know I would commit.

My mother crocheted squares for an afghan, in all shades of purple. They fell among the bedclothes and she did not care. Once they were finished she forgot about them. She had forgotten all her stories which were about Princes in the Tower and a queen getting her head chopped off while a little dog was hiding under her dress and another queen sucking poison out of her husband's wound; and also about her own childhood, a time as legendary to me as any other. Given over to Mary's care she whimpered childishly, "Mary, I'm dying for you to rub my back." "Mary, could you make me a cup of tea? I feel if I drink any more tea I'm going to bob up to the ceiling, just like a big balloon, but you know it's all I want." Mary laughed shortly. "You," she said, "You're not going to bob up anywhere. Take a derrick to move *you*. Come on now, raise up, you'll be worse before you're better!" She shooed me off the bed and began to pull the sheets about with not very gentle jerks. "You been tiring your Momma out? What do you want to bother your Momma for on this nice a day?" "I think she's lonesome," my mother said, a weak and insincere defence.

"She can be lonesome in the yard just as well as here," said Mary, with her grand, vague, menacing air. "You put your things on, out you go!"

My father, too, had altered since her coming. When he came in for his meals she was always waiting for him, some joke swelling her up like a bullfrog, making her ferocious-looking and red in the face. She put uncooked white beans in his soup, hard as pebbles, and waited to see if good manners would make him eat them. She stuck something to the bottom of his water glass to look like a fly. She gave him a fork with a prong missing, pretending it was by accident. He threw it at her, and missed, but startled me considerably. My mother and father, eating supper, talked quietly and seriously. But in my father's family even grownups played tricks with rubber worms and beetles, fat aunts were always invited to sit on little rickety chairs and uncles broke wind in public and said, "Whoa, hold on there!" proud of themselves as if they had whistled a complicated tune. Nobody could ask your age without a rigmarole of teasing. So with Mary McQuade my father returned to family ways, just as he went back to eating heaps of fried potatoes and side meat and thick, floury pies, and drinking tea black and strong as medicine out of a tin pot, saying gratefully, "Mary, you know what it is a man ought to eat!" He followed that up with, "Don't you think it's time you got a man of your own to feed?" which earned him, not a fork thrown, but the dishrag.

His teasing of Mary was always about husbands. "I thought up one for you this morning!" he would say. "Now Mary I'm not fooling you, you give this some consideration." Her laughter would come out first in little angry puffs and explosions through her shut lips, while her face grew redder than you would have thought possible and her body twitched and rumbled threateningly in its chair. There was no doubt she enjoyed all this, all these preposterous imagined matings, though my mother would certainly have said it was cruel,

cruel and indecent, to tease an old maid about men. In my
father's family of course it was what she was always teased
about, what else was there? And the heavier and coarser and
more impossible she became, the more she would be teased. A
bad thing in that family was to have them say you were
sensitive, as they did of my mother. All the aunts and cousins
and uncles had grown tremendously hardened to any sort of
personal cruelty, reckless, even proud, it seemed, of a failure
or deformity that could make for general laughter.

At supper-time it was dark in the house, in spite of the
lengthening days. We did not yet have electricity. It came in
soon afterwards, maybe the next summer. But at present there
was a lamp on the table. In its light my father and Mary
McQuade threw gigantic shadows, whose heads wagged clumsily with their talk and laughing. I watched the shadows
instead of the people. They said, "What are you dreaming
about?" but I was not dreaming, I was trying to understand
the danger, to read the signs of invasion.

My father said, "Do you want to come with me and look at the
traps?" He had a trapline for muskrats along the river. When
he was younger he used to spend days, nights, weeks in the
bush, following creeks all up and down Wawanash County,
and he trapped not only muskrat then but red fox, wild mink,
marten, all animals whose coats are prime in the fall. Muskrat
is the only thing you can trap in the spring. Now that he was
married and settled down to farming he just kept the one line,
and that for only a few years. This may have been the last
year he had it.

We went across a field that had been plowed the previous
fall. There was a little snow lying in the furrows but it was not
real snow, it was a thin crust like frosted glass that I could
shatter with my heels. The field went downhill slowly, down
to the river flats. The fence was down in some places from the
weight of the snow, we could step over it.

My father's boots went ahead. His boots were to me as unique and familiar, as much an index to himself as his face was. When he had taken them off they stood in a corner of the kitchen, giving off a complicated smell of manure, machine oil, caked black mud, and the ripe and disintegrating material that lined their soles. They were a part of himself, temporarily discarded, waiting. They had an expression that was dogged and uncompromising, even brutal, and I thought of that as part of my father's look, the counterpart of his face, with its readiness for jokes and courtesies. Nor did that brutality surprise me; my father came back to us always, to my mother and me, from places where our judgment could not follow.

For instance, there was a muskrat in the trap. At first I saw it waving at the edge of the water, like something tropical, a dark fern. My father drew it up and the hairs ceased waving, clung together, the fern became a tail with the body of the rat attached to it, sleek and dripping. Its teeth were bared, its eyes wet on top, dead and dull beneath, glinted like washed pebbles. My father shook it and whirled it around, making a little rain of icy river water. "This is a good old rat," he said. "This is a big old king rat. Look at his tail!" Then perhaps thinking that I was worried, or perhaps only wanting to show me the charm of simple, perfect mechanical devices, he lifted the trap out of the water and explained to me how it worked, dragging the rat's head under at once and mercifully drowning him. I did not understand or care. I only wanted, but did not dare, to touch the stiff, soaked body, a fact of death.

My father baited the trap again using some pieces of yellow, winter-wrinkled apple. He put the rat's body in a dark sack which he carried slung over his shoulder, like a pedlar in a picture. When he cut the apple I had seen the skinning knife, its slim bright blade.

Then we went along the river, the Wawanash River, which was high, running full, silver in the middle where the sun hit it and where it arrowed in to its swiftest motion. That is the current, I thought, and I pictured the current as something separate from the water, just as the wind was separate from the air and had its own invading shape. The banks were steep and slippery and lined with willow bushes, still bare and bent over and looking weak as grass. The noise the river made was not loud but deep, and seemed to come from away down in the middle of it, some hidden place where the water issued with a roar from underground.

The river curved, I lost my sense of direction. In the traps we found more rats, released them, shook them and hid them in the sack, replaced the bait. My face, my hands, my feet grew cold, but I did not mention it. I could not, to my father. And he never told me to be careful, to stay away from the edge of the water, he took it for granted that I would have sense enough not to fall in. I never asked how far we were going, or if the trapline would ever end. After a while there was a bush behind us, the afternoon darkened. It did not occur to me, not till long afterwards, that this was the same bush you could see from our yard, a fan-shaped hill rising up in the middle of it with bare trees in wintertime that looked like bony little twigs against the sky.

Now the bank, instead of willows, grew thick bushes higher than my head. I stayed on the path, about halfway up the bank, while my father went down to the water. When he bent over the trap, I could no longer see him. I looked around slowly and saw something else. Further along, and higher up the bank, a man was making his way down. He made no noise coming through the bushes and moved easily, as if he followed a path I could not see. At first I could just see his head and the upper part of his body. He was dark, with a high bald forehead, hair long behind the ears, deep vertical creases in his cheeks. When the bushes thinned I could see the rest of him, his long clever legs, thinness, drab camouflaging clothes, and what he carried in his hand, gleaming where the sun caught it —a little axe, or hatchet.

I never moved to warn or call my father. The man crossed my path somewhere ahead, continuing down to the river. People say they have been paralyzed by fear, but I was transfixed, as if struck by lightning, and what hit me did not feel like fear so much as recognition. I was not surprised. This is the sight that does not surprise you, the thing you have always known was there that comes so naturally, moving delicately and contentedly and in no hurry, as if it was made, in the first place, from a wish of yours, a hope of something final, terrifying. All my life I had known there was a man like this and he was behind doors, around the corner at the dark end of a hall. So now I saw him and just waited, like a child in an old negative, electrified against the dark noon sky, with blazing hair and burned-out Orphan Annie eyes. The man slipped down through the bushes to my father. And I never thought, or even hoped for, anything but the worst.

My father did not know. When he straightened up, the man was not three feet away from him and hid him from me. I heard my father's voice come out, after a moment's delay, quiet and neighbourly.

"Hello, Joe. Well. Joe. I haven't seen you in a long time."

The man did not say a word, but edged around my father giving him a close look. "Joe, you know me," my father told him. "Ben Jordan. I been out looking at my traps. There's a lot of good rats in the river this year, Joe."

The man gave a quick not-trusting look at the trap my father had baited.

"You ought to set a line out yourself."

No answer. The man took his hatchet and chopped lightly at the air.

"Too late this year, though. The river is already started to go down."

"Ben Jordan," the man said with a great splurt, a costly effort, like somebody leaping over a stutter.

"I thought you'd recognize me, Joe."

"I never knew it was you, Ben. I thought it was one them Silases."

"Well I been telling you it was me."

"They's down here all the time choppin my trees and pullin down my fences. You know they burned me out, Ben. It was them done it."

"I heard about that," my father said.

"I didn't know it was you, Ben. I never knew it was you. I got this axe, I just take it along with me to give them a little scare. I wouldn't of if I'd known it was you. You come on up and see where I'm living now."

My father called me. "I got my young one out following me today."

"Well you and her both come up and get warm."

We followed this man, who still carried and carelessly swung his hatchet, up the slope and into the bush. The trees chilled the air, and underneath them was real snow, left over from winter, a foot, two feet deep. The tree trunks had rings around them, a curious dark space like the warmth you make with your breath.

We came out in a field of dead grass, and took a track across it to another, wider, field where there was something sticking out of the ground. It was a roof, slanting one way, not peaked, and out of the roof came a pipe with a cap on it, smoke blowing out. We went down the sort of steps that lead to a cellar, and that was what it was—a cellar with a roof on. My father said, "Looks like you fixed it up all right for yourself, Joe."

"It's warm. Being down in the ground the way it is, naturally it's warm. I thought what is the sense of building a house up again, they burned it down once, they'll burn it down again. What do I need a house for anyways? I got all the room I need here, I fixed it up comfortable." He opened the door at the bottom of the steps. "Mind your head here. I don't say everybody should live in a hole in the ground, Ben. Though animals do it, and what an animal does, by and large

it makes sense. But if you're married, that's another story."
He laughed. "Me, I don't plan on getting married."

It was not completely dark. There were the old cellar
windows, letting in a little grimy light. The man lit a coal-oil
lamp, though, and set it on the table.

"There, you can see where you're at."

It was all one room, an earth floor with boards not nailed
together, just laid down to make broad paths for walking, a
stove on a sort of platform, table, couch, chairs, even a kitchen
cupboard, several thick, very dirty blankets of the type used in
sleighs and to cover horses. Perhaps if it had not had such a
terrible smell—of coal oil, urine, earth and stale heavy air—I
would have recognized it as the sort of place I would like to
live in myself, like the houses I made under snow drifts, in
winter, with sticks of firewood for furniture, like another house
I had made long ago under the verandah, my floor the strange
powdery earth that never got sun or rain.

But I was wary, sitting on the dirty couch, pretending not
to look at anything. My father said, "You're snug here, Joe,
that's right." He sat by the table, and there the hatchet lay.

"You should of seen me before the snow started to melt.
Wasn't nothing showing but a smokestack."

"Nor you don't get lonesome?"

"Not me. I was never one for lonesome. And I got a cat,
Ben. Where is that cat? There he is, in behind the stove. He
don't relish company, maybe." He pulled it out, a huge, grey
tom with sullen eyes. "Show you what he can do." He took
a saucer from the table and a Mason jar from the cupboard
and poured something into the saucer. He set it in front of
the cat.

"Joe that cat don't drink whisky, does he?"

"You wait and see."

The cat rose and stretched himself stiffly, took one baleful
look around and lowered his head to drink.

"Straight whisky," my father said.

"I bet that's a sight you ain't seen before. And you ain't likely to see it again. That cat'd take whisky ahead of milk any day. A matter of fact he don't get no milk, he's forgot what it's like. You want a drink, Ben?"

"Not knowing where you got that. I don't have a stomach like your cat."

The cat, having finished, walked sideways from the saucer, waited a moment, gave a clawing leap and landed unsteadily, but did not fall. It swayed, pawed the air a few times, meowing despairingly, then shot forward and slid under the end of the couch.

"Joe, you keep that up, you're not going to have a cat."

"It don't hurt him, he enjoys it. Let's see, what've we got for the little girl to eat?" Nothing, I hoped, but he brought a tin of Christmas candies, which seemed to have melted then hardened then melted again, so the coloured stripes had run. They had a taste of nails.

"It's them Silases botherin me, Ben. They come by day and by night. People won't ever quit botherin me. I can hear them on the roof at night. Ben, you see them Silases you tell them what I got waitin for them." He picked up the hatchet and chopped down at the table, splitting the rotten oilcloth. "Got a shotgun too."

"Maybe they won't come and bother you no more, Joe."

The man groaned and shook his head. "They never will stop. No. They never will stop."

"Just try not paying any attention to them, they'll tire out and go away."

"They'll burn me in my bed. They tried to before."

My father said nothing, but tested the axe blade with his finger. Under the couch, the cat pawed and meowed in more and more feeble spasms of delusion. Overcome with tiredness, with warmth after cold, with bewilderment quite past bearing, I was falling asleep with my eyes open.

My father set me down. "You're woken up now. Stand up. See. I can't carry you and this sack full of rats both."

We had come to the top of a long hill and that is where I woke. It was getting dark. The whole basin of country drained by the Wawanash River lay in front of us—greenish brown smudge of bush with the leaves not out yet and evergreens, dark, shabby after winter, showing through, straw-brown fields and the others, darker from last year's plowing, with scales of snow faintly striping them (like the field we had walked across hours, hours earlier in the day) and the tiny fences and colonies of grey barns, and houses set apart, looking squat and small.

"Whose house is that?" my father said, pointing.

It was ours, I knew it after a minute. We had come around in a half-circle and there was the side of the house that nobody saw in winter, the front door that went unopened from November to April and was still stuffed with rags around its edges, to keep out the east wind.

"That's no more'n half a mile away and downhill. You can easy walk home. Soon we'll see the light in the dining room where your Momma is."

On the way I said, "Why did he have an axe?"

"Now listen," my father said. "Are you listening to me? He don't mean any harm with that axe. It's just his habit, carrying it around. But don't say anything about it at home. Don't mention it to your Momma or Mary, either one. Because they might be scared about it. You and me aren't, but they might be. And there is no use of that."

After a while he said, "What are you not going to mention about?" and I said, "The axe."

"You weren't scared, were you?"

"No," I said hopefully. "Who is going to burn him and his bed?"

"Nobody. Less he manages it himself like he did last time."

"Who is the Silases?"

"Nobody," my father said. "Just nobody."

"We found the one for you today, Mary. Oh, I wisht we could've brought him home."

"We thought you'd fell in the Wawanash River," said Mary McQuade furiously, ungently pulling off my boots and my wet socks.

"Old Joe Phippen that lives up in no man's land beyond the bush."

"Him!" said Mary like an explosion. "He's the one burned his house down, I know him!"

"That's right, and now he gets along fine without it. Lives in a hole in the ground. You'd be as cosy as a groundhog, Mary."

"I bet he lives in his own dirt, all right." She served my father his supper and he told her the story of Joe Phippen, the roofed cellar, the boards across the dirt floor. He left out the axe but not the whisky and the cat. For Mary, that was enough.

"A man that'd do a thing like that ought to be locked up."

"Maybe so," my father said. "Just the same I hope they don't get him for a while yet. Old Joe."

"Eat your supper," Mary said, bending over me. I did not for some time realize that I was no longer afraid of her. "Look at her," she said. "Her eyes dropping out of her head, all she's been and seen. Was he feeding the whisky to her too?"

"Not a drop," said my father, and looked steadily down the table at me. Like the children in fairy stories who have seen their parents make pacts with terrifying strangers, who have discovered that our fears are based on nothing but the truth, but who come back fresh from marvellous escapes and take up their knives and forks, with humility and good manners, prepared to live happily ever after—like them, dazed and powerful with secrets, I never said a word.

Thanks for the Ride

My cousin George and I were sitting in a restaurant called Pop's Cafe, in a little town close to the Lake. It was getting dark in there, and they had not turned the lights on, but you could still read the signs plastered against the mirror between the fly-speckled and slightly yellowed cutouts of strawberry sundaes and tomato sandwiches.

"Don't ask for information," George read. "If we knew anything we wouldn't be here" and "If you've got nothing to do, you picked a hell of a good place to do it in." George always read everything out loud—posters, billboards, Burma-Shave signs, "Mission Creek. Population 1700. Gateway to the Bruce. We love our children."

I was wondering whose sense of humour provided us with the signs. I thought it would be the man behind the cash register. Pop? Chewing on a match, looking out at the street, not watching for anything except for somebody to trip over a crack in the sidewalk or have a blowout or make a fool of himself in some way that Pop, rooted behind the cash register, huge and cynical and incurious, was never likely to do. Maybe not even that; maybe just by walking up and down, driving up and down, going places, the rest of the world proved its absurdity. You see that judgment on the faces of people looking out of windows, sitting on front steps in some little towns; so deeply,

deeply uncaring they are, as if they had sources of disillusion-
ment which they would keep, with some satisfaction, in the
dark.

There was only the one waitress, a pudgy girl who leaned
over the counter and scraped at the polish on her fingernails.
When she had flaked most of the polish off her thumbnail she
put the thumb against her teeth and rubbed the nail back and
forth absorbedly. We asked her what her name was and she
didn't answer. Two or three minutes later the thumb came out
of her mouth and she said, inspecting it: "That's for me to know
and you to find out."

"All right," George said. "Okay if I call you Mickey?"

"I don't care."

"Because you remind me of Mickey Rooney," George said.
"Hey, where's everybody go in this town? Where's everybody
go?" Mickey had turned her back and begun to drain out the
coffee. It looked as if she didn't mean to talk any more, so
George got a little jumpy, as he did when he was threatened
with having to be quiet or be by himself. "Hey, aren't there
any girls in this town?" he said almost plaintively. "Aren't
there any girls or dances or anything? We're strangers in
town," he said. "Don't you want to help us out?"

"Dance hall down on the beach closed up Labour Day,"
Mickey said coldly.

"There any other dance halls?"

"There's a dance tonight out at Wilson's *school*," Mickey
said.

"That old-time? No, no, I don't go for that old-time. *All-a-
man left* and that, used to have that down in the basement of
the church. Yeah, *ever'body swing*—I don't go for that. Inna
basement of the *church*," George said, obscurely angered.
"You don't remember that," he said to me. "Too young."

I was just out of high-school at this time, and George had
been working for three years in the Men's Shoes in a downtown
department store, so there was that difference. But we had

never bothered with each other back in the city. We were together now because we had met unexpectedly in a strange place and because I had a little money, while George was broke. Also I had my father's car, and George was in one of his periods between cars, which made him always a little touchy and dissatisfied. But he would have to rearrange these facts a bit, they made him uneasy. I could feel him manufacturing a sufficiency of good feeling, old-pal feeling, and dressing me up as Old Dick, good kid, real character—which did not matter one way or the other, though I did not think, looking at his tender blond piggish handsomeness, the nudity of his pink mouth, and the surprised, angry creases that frequent puzzlement was beginning to put into his forehead, that I would be able to work up an Old George.

I had driven up to the Lake to bring my mother home from a beach resort for women, a place where they had fruit juice and cottage cheese for reducing, and early-morning swims in the Lake, and some religion, apparently, for there was a little chapel attached. My aunt, George's mother, was staying there at the same time, and George arrived about an hour or so after I did, not to take his mother home, but to get some money out of her. He did not get along well with his father, and he did not make much money working in the shoe department, so he was very often broke. His mother said he could have a loan if he would stay over and go to church with her the next day. George said he would. Then George and I got away and drove half a mile along the lake to this little town neither of us had seen before, which George said would be full of bootleggers and girls.

It was a town of unpaved, wide, sandy streets and bare yards. Only the hardy things like red and yellow nasturtiums, or a lilac bush with brown curled leaves, grew out of that cracked earth. The houses were set wide apart, with their own pumps and sheds and privies out behind; most of them were built of wood and painted green or grey or yellow. The trees that grew there were big willows or poplars, their fine leaves greyed with the dust. There were no trees along the main street, but spaces of tall grass and dandelions and blowing thistles—open country between the store buildings. The town hall was surprisingly large, with a great bell in a tower, the red brick rather glaring in the midst of the town's walls of faded, pale-painted wood. The sign beside the door said that it was a memorial to the soldiers who had died in the First World War. We had a drink out of the fountain in front.

We drove up and down the main street for a while, with George saying: "What a dump! Jesus, what a dump!" and "Hey, look at that! Aw, not so good either." The people on the street went home to supper, the shadows of the store buildings lay solid across the street, and we went into Pop's.

"Hey," George said, "is there any other restaurant in this town? Did you see any other restaurant?"

"No," I said.

"Any other town I ever been," George said, "pigs hangin' out the windows, practically hangin' off the trees. Not here. Jesus! I guess it's late in the season," he said.

"You want to go to a show?"

The door opened. A girl came in, walked up and sat on a stool, with most of her skirt bunched up underneath her. She had a long somnolent face, no bust, frizzy hair; she was pale, almost ugly, but she had that inexplicable aura of sexuality. George brightened, though not a great deal. "Never mind," he said. "This'll do. This'll do in a pinch, eh? In a pinch."

He went to the end of the counter and sat down beside her and started to talk. In about five minutes they came back to me, the girl drinking a bottle of orange pop.

"This is Adelaide,' George said. 'Adelaide, Adeline—Sweet Adeline. I'm going to call her Sweet A, Sweet A."

Adelaide sucked at her straw, paying not much attention.

"She hasn't got a date," George said. "You haven't got a date have you, honey?"

Adelaide shook her head very slightly.

"Doesn't hear half what you say to her," George said. "Adelaide, Sweet A, have you got any friends? Have you got any nice, young little girl friend to go out with Dickie? You and me and her and Dickie?"

"Depends," said Adelaide. "Where do you want to go?"

"Anywhere you say. Go for a drive. Drive up to Owen Sound, maybe."

"You got a car?"

"Yeah, yeah, we got a car. C'mon, you must have some nice little friend for Dickie." He put his arm around this girl, spreading his fingers over her blouse. "C'mon out and I'll show you the car."

Adelaide said: "I know one girl might come. The guy she goes around with, he's engaged, and his girl came up and she's staying at his place up the beach, his mother and dad's place, and—"

"Well that is certainly int-er-esting," George said. "What's her name? Come on, let's go round and get her. You want to sit around drinking pop all night?"

"I'm finished," Adelaide said. "She might not come. I don't know."

"Why not? Her mother not let her out nights?"

"Oh, she can do what she likes," said Adelaide. "Only there's times she don't want to. I don't know."

We went out and got into the car, George and Adelaide in the back. On the main street about a block from the cafe we passed a thin, fair-haired girl in slacks and Adelaide cried: "Hey stop! That's her! That's Lois!"

I pulled in and George stuck his head out of the window, whistling. Adelaide yelled, and the girl came unhesitatingly, unhurriedly to the car. She smiled, rather coldly and politely, when Adelaide explained to her. All the time George kept saying: "Hurry up, come on, get in! We can talk in the car." The girl smiled, did not really look at any of us, and in a few moments, to my surprise, she opened the door and slid into the car.

"I don't have anything to do," she said. "My boy friend's away."

"That so?" said George, and I saw Adelaide, in the rear-vision mirror, make a cross warning face. Lois did not seem to have heard him.

"We better drive around to my house," she said. "I was just going down to get some Cokes, that's why I only have my slacks on. We better drive around to my house and I'll put on something else."

"Where are we going to go," she said, "so I know what to put on?"

I said: "Where do you want to go?"

"Okay, okay," George said. "First things first. We gotta get a bottle, then we'll decide. You know where to get one?" Adelaide and Lois both said yes, and then Lois said to me: "You can come in the house and wait while I change, if you want to." I glanced in the rear mirror and thought that there was probably some agreement she had with Adelaide.

Lois's house had an old couch on the porch and some rugs hanging down over the railing. She walked ahead of me across the yard. She had her long pale hair tied at the back of her neck; her skin was dustily freckled, but not tanned; even her eyes were light-coloured. She was cold and narrow and pale. There was derision, and also great gravity, about her mouth. I thought she was about my age or a little older.

She opened the front door and said in a clear, stilted voice: "I would like you to meet my family."

The little front room had linoleum on the floor and flowered paper curtains at the windows. There was a glossy chesterfield with a Niagara Falls and a To Mother cushion on it, and there was a little black stove with a screen around it for summer, and a big vase of paper apple blossoms. A tall, frail woman came into the room drying her hands on a dishtowel, which she flung into a chair. Her mouth was full of blue-white china teeth, the long cords trembled in her neck. I said how-do-you-do to her, embarrassed by Lois's announcement, so suddenly and purposefully conventional. I wondered if she had any misconceptions about this date, engineered by George for such specific purposes. I did not think so. Her face had no innocence in it that I could see; it was knowledgeable, calm, and hostile. She might have done it, then, to mock me, to make me into this caricature of The Date, the boy who grins and shuffles in the front hall and waits to be presented to the nice girl's family. But that was a little far-fetched. Why should she want to embarrass me when she had agreed to go out with me without even looking into my face? Why should she care enough?

Lois's mother and I sat down on the chesterfield. She began to make conversation, giving this the Date interpretation. I noticed the smell in the house, the smell of stale small rooms, bedclothes, frying, washing, and medicated ointments. And dirt, though it did not look dirty. Lois's mother said: "That's a nice car you got out front. Is that your car?"

"My father's."

"Isn't that lovely! Your father has such a nice car. I always think it's lovely for people to have things. I've got no time for these people that's just eaten up with malice 'n envy. I say it's lovely. I bet your mother, every time she wants anything, she just goes down to the store and buys it—new coat, bedspread, pots and pans. What does your father do? Is he a lawyer or doctor or something like that?"

"He's a chartered accountant."

"Oh. That's in an office, is it?"

"Yes."

"My brother, Lois's uncle, he's in the office of the CPR in London. He's quite high up there, I understand."

She began to tell me about how Lois's father had been killed in an accident at the mill. I noticed an old woman, the grandmother probably, standing in the doorway of the room. She was not thin like the others, but as soft and shapeless as a collapsed pudding, pale brown spots melting together on her face and arms, bristles of hairs in the moisture around her mouth. Some of the smell in the house seemed to come from her. It was a smell of hidden decay, such as there is when some obscure little animal has died under the verandah. The smell, the slovenly, confiding voice—something about this life I had not known, something about these people. I thought: my mother, George's mother, they are innocent. Even George, George is innocent. But these others are born sly and sad and knowing.

I did not hear much about Lois's father except that his head was cut off.

"Clean off, imagine, and rolled on the floor! Couldn't open the coffin. It was June, the hot weather. And everybody in town just stripped their gardens, stripped them for the funeral. Stripped their spirea bushes and peenies and climbin' clemantis. I guess it was the worst accident ever took place in this town.

"Lois had a nice boy friend this summer," she said. "Used to take her out and sometimes stay here overnight when his folks weren't up at the cottage and he didn't feel like passin' his time there all alone. He'd bring the kids candy and even me he'd bring presents. That china elephant up there, you can plant flowers in it, he brought me that. He fixed the radio for me and I never had to take it into the shop. Do your folks have a summer cottage up here?"

I said no, and Lois came in, wearing a dress of yellow-green stuff—stiff and shiny like Christmas wrappings—high-heeled shoes, rhinestones, and a lot of dark powder over her freckles. Her mother was excited.

"You like that dress?" she said. "She went all the way to London and bought that dress, didn't get it anywhere round here!"

We had to pass by the old woman as we went out. She

looked at us with sudden recognition, a steadying of her pale, jellied eyes. Her mouth trembled open, she stuck her face out at me.

"You can do what you like with my gran'daughter," she said in her old, strong voice, the rough voice of a country woman. "But you be careful. And you know what I mean!"

Lois's mother pushed the old woman behind her, smiling tightly, eyebrows lifted, skin straining over her temples. "Never mind," she mouthed at me, grimacing distractedly. "Never mind. Second childhood." The smile stayed on her face; the skin pulled back from it. She seemed to be listening all the time to a perpetual din and racket in her head. She grabbed my hand as I followed Lois out. "Lois is a nice girl," she whispered. "You have a nice time, don't let her mope!" There was a quick, grotesque, and, I suppose, originally flirtatious, flickering of brows and lids. "'Night!"

Lois walked stiffly ahead of me, rustling her papery skirt. I said: "Did you want to go to a dance or something?"

"No," she said. "I don't care."

"Well you got all dressed up—"

"I always get dressed up on Saturday night," Lois said, her voice floating back to me, low and scornful. Then she began to laugh, and I had a glimpse of her mother in her, that jaggedness and hysteria. "Oh, my God!" she whispered. I knew she meant what had happened in the house, and I laughed too, not knowing what else to do. So we went back to the car laughing as if we were friends, but we were not.

We drove out of town to a farmhouse where a woman sold us a whisky bottle full of muddy-looking homemade liquor, something George and I had never had before. Adelaide had said that his woman would probably let us use her front room, but it turned out that she would not, and that was because of Lois. When the woman peered up at me from under the man's cap she had on her head and said to Lois, "Change's as good as a rest, eh?" Lois did not answer, kept a cold face. Then later the woman said that if we were so stuck-up tonight her front room wouldn't be good enough for us and we better go back to the bush. All the way back down the lane Adelaide kept saying: "Some people can't take a joke, can they? Yeah, stuck-up is right—" until I passed her the bottle to keep her quiet. I saw George did not mind, thinking this had taken her mind off driving to Owen Sound.

We parked at the end of the lane and sat in the car drinking. George and Adelaide drank more than we did. They did not talk, just reached for the bottle and passed it back. This stuff was different from anything I had tasted before; it was heavy and sickening in my stomach. There was no other effect, and I began to have the depressing feeling that I was not going to get drunk. Each time Lois handed the bottle back to me she said "Thank you" in a mannerly and subtly contemptuous way. I put my arm around her, not much wanting to. I was wondering what was the matter. This girl lay against my arm, scornful, acquiescent, angry, inarticulate and out-of-reach. I wanted to talk to her then more than to touch her, and that was out of the question; talk was not so little a thing to her as touching. Meanwhile I was aware that I should be beyond this, beyond the first stage and well into the second (for I had a knowledge, though it was not very comprehensive, of the orderly progression of stages, the ritual of back- and front-seat seduction). Almost I wished I was with Adelaide.

"Do you want to go for a walk?" I said.

"That's the first bright idea you've had all night," George told me from the back seat. "Don't hurry," he said as we got out. He and Adelaide were muffled and laughing together. "Don't hurry back!"

Lois and I walked along a wagon track close to the bush. The fields were moonlit, chilly and blowing. Now I felt vengeful, and I said softly, "I had quite a talk with your mother."

"I can imagine," said Lois.

"She told me about that guy you went out with last summer."

"This summer."

"It's last summer now. He was engaged or something, wasn't he?"

"Yes."

I was not going to let her go. "Did he like you better?" I said. "Was that it? Did he like you better?"

"No, I wouldn't say he liked me," Lois said. I thought, by some thickening of the sarcasm in her voice, that she was beginning to be drunk. "He liked Momma and the kids okay but he didn't like me. *Like me*," she said. "What's that?"

"Well, he went out with you—"

"He just went around with me for the summer. That's what those guys from up the beach always do. They come down here to the dances and get a girl to go around with. For the summer. They always do.

"How I know he didn't *like* me," she said, "he said I was always bitching. You have to act grateful to those guys, you know, or they say you're bitching."

I was a little startled at having loosed all this. I said: "Did you like him?"

"Oh, sure! I should, shouldn't I? I should just get down on my knees and thank him. That's what my mother does. He brings her a cheap old spotted elephant—"

"Was this guy the first?" I said.

"The first steady. Is that what you mean?"

It wasn't. "How old are you?"

She considered. "I'm almost seventeen. I can pass for eighteen or nineteen. I can pass in a beer parlour. I did once."

"What grade are you in at school?"

She looked at me, rather amazed. "Did you think I still went to school? I quit that two years ago. I've got a job at the glove-works in town."

"That must have been against the law. When you quit."

"Oh, you can get a permit if your father's dead or something."

"What do you do at the glove-works?" I said.

"Oh, I run a machine. It's like a sewing machine. I'll be getting on piecework soon. You make more money."

"Do you like it?"

"Oh, I wouldn't say I loved it. It's a job—you ask a lot of questions," she said.

"Do you mind?"

"I don't have to answer you," she said, her voice flat and small again. "Only if I like." She picked up her skirt and spread it out in her hands. "I've got burrs on my skirt," she said. She bent over, pulling them one by one. "I've got burrs on my dress," she said. "It's my good dress. Will they leave a mark? If I pull them all—slowly—I won't pull any threads."

"You shouldn't have worn that dress," I said. "What'd you wear that dress for?"

She shook the skirt, tossing a burr loose. "I don't know," she said. She held it out, the stiff, shining stuff, with faintly drunken satisfaction. "I wanted to show you guys!" she said, with a sudden small explosion of viciousness. The drunken, nose-thumbing, toe-twirling satisfaction could not now be mistaken as she stood there foolishly, tauntingly, with her skirt spread out. "I've got an imitation cashmere sweater at home. It cost me twelve dollars," she said. "I've got a fur coat I'm paying on, paying on for next winter. I've got a fur coat—"

"That's nice," I said. "I think it's lovely for people to have things."

She dropped the skirt and struck the flat of her hand on my face. This was a relief to me, to both of us. We felt a fight had been building in us all along. We faced each other as warily as we could, considering we were both a little drunk, she tensing to slap me again and I to grab her or slap her back. We would have it out, what we had against each other. But the moment of this keenness passed. We let out our breath; we had not moved in time. And the next moment, not bothering to shake off our enmity, nor thinking how the one thing could give way to the other, we kissed. It was the first time, for me, that a kiss was accomplished without premeditation, or hesitancy, or over-haste, or the usual vague ensuing disappointment. And laughing shakily against me, she began to talk again, going back to the earlier part of our conversation as if nothing had come between.

"Isn't it funny?" she said. "You know, all winter all the girls do is talk about last summer, talk and talk about those guys, and I bet you those guys have forgotten even what their names were—"

But I did not want to talk any more, having discovered another force in her that lay side by side with her hostility, that was, in fact, just as enveloping and impersonal. After a while I whispered: "Isn't there some place we can go?"

And she answered: "There's a barn in the next field."

She knew the countryside; she had been there before.

We drove back into town after midnight. George and Adelaide were asleep in the back seat. I did not think Lois was asleep, though she kept her eyes closed and did not say anything. I had read somewhere about *Omne animal*, and I was going to tell her, but then I thought she would not know Latin words and would think I was being—oh, pretentious and superior. Afterwards I wished that I had told her. She would have known what it meant.

Afterwards the lassitude of the body, and the cold; the separation. To brush away the bits of hay and tidy ourselves with heavy unconnected movements, to come out of the barn and find the moon gone down, but the flat stubble fields still there, and the poplar trees, and the stars. To find our same selves, chilled and shaken, who had gone that headlong journey and

were here still. To go back to the car and find the others
sprawled asleep. That is what it is: *triste. Triste est.*

That headlong journey. Was it like that because it was the
first time, because I was a little, strangely drunk? No. It was
because of Lois. There are some people who can go only a
little way with the act of love, and some others who can go
very far, who can make a greater surrender, like the mystics.
And Lois, this mystic of love, sat now on the far side of the car-
seat, looking cold and rumpled, and utterly closed up in herself. All the things I wanted to say to her went clattering
emptily through my head. *Come and see you again—Remember—
Love*—I could not say any of these things. They would not
seem even half-true across the space that had come between us.
I thought: I will say something to her before the next tree, the
next telephone pole. But I did not. I only drove faster, too fast,
making the town come nearer.

The street lights bloomed out of the dark trees ahead; there
were stirrings in the back seat.

"What time is it?" George said.

"Twenty past twelve."

"We musta finished that bottle. I don't feel so good. Oh,
Christ, I don't feel so good. How do you feel?"

"Fine."

"Fine, eh? Feel like you finished your education tonight, eh?
That how you feel? Is yours asleep? Mine is."

"I am not," said Adelaide drowsily. "Where's my belt?
George—oh. Now where's my other shoe? It's early for Saturday night, isn't it? We could go and get something to eat."

"I don't feel like food," George said. "I gotta get some sleep.
Gotta get up early tomorrow and go to church with my
mother."

"Yeah, I know," said Adelaide, disbelieving, though not
too ill-humoured. "You could've anyways bought me a hamburger!"

I had driven around to Lois's house. Lois did not open her eyes until the car stopped.

She sat still a moment, and then pressed her hands down over the skirt of her dress, flattening it out. She did not look at me. I moved to kiss her, but she seemed to draw slightly away, and I felt that there had after all been something fraudulent and theatrical about this final gesture. She was not like that.

George said to Adelaide: "Where do you live? You live near here?"

"Yeah. Half a block down."

"Okay. How be you get out here too? We gotta get home sometime tonight."

He kissed her and both the girls got out.

I started the car. We began to pull away, George settling down on the back seat to sleep. And then we heard the female voice calling after us, the loud, crude, female voice, abusive and forlorn:

"Thanks for the ride!"

It was not Adelaide calling; it was Lois.

The Office

The solution to my life occurred to me one evening while I was ironing a shirt. It was simple but audacious. I went into the living room where my husband was watching television and I said, "I think I ought to have an office."

It sounded fantastic, even to me. What do I want an office for? I have a house; it is pleasant and roomy and has a view of the sea; it provides appropriate places for eating and sleeping, and having baths and conversations with one's friends. Also I have a garden; there is no lack of space.

No. But here comes the disclosure which is not easy for me: I am a writer. That does not sound right. Too presumptuous; phony, or at least unconvincing. Try again. I write. Is that better? I *try* to write. That makes it worse. Hypocritical humility. Well then?

It doesn't matter. However I put it, the words create their space of silence, the delicate moment of exposure. But people are kind, the silence is quickly absorbed by the solicitude of friendly voices, crying variously, how wonderful, and good for *you*, and well, that *is* intriguing. And what do you write, they inquire with spirit. Fiction, I reply, bearing my humiliation by this time with ease, even a suggestion of flippancy, which was not always mine, and again, again, the perceptible circles of dismay are smoothed out by such ready and tactful voices—

which have however exhausted their stock of consolatory phrases, and can say only, "*Ah!*"

So this is what I want an office for (I said to my husband): to write in. I was at once aware that it sounded like a finicky requirement, a piece of rare self-indulgence. To write, as everyone knows, you need a typewriter, or at least a pencil, some paper, a table and chair; I have all these things in a corner of my bedroom. But now I want an office as well.

And I was not even sure that I was going to write in it, if we come down to that. Maybe I would sit and stare at the wall; even that prospect was not unpleasant to me. It was really the sound of the word "office" that I liked, its sound of dignity and peace. And purposefulness and importance. But I did not care to mention this to my husband, so I launched instead into a high-flown explanation which went, as I remember, like this:

A house is all right for a man to work in. He brings his work into the house, a place is cleared for it; the house rearranges itself as best it can around him. Everybody recognizes that his work *exists*. He is not expected to answer the telephone, to find things that are lost, to see why the children are crying, or feed the cat. He can shut his door. Imagine (I said) a mother shutting her door, and the children knowing she is behind it; why, the very thought of it is outrageous to them. A woman who sits staring into space, into a country that is not her husband's or her children's is likewise known to be an offence against nature. So a house is not the same for a woman. She is not someone who walks into the house, to make use of it, and will walk out again. She *is* the house; there is no separation possible.

(And this is true, though as usual when arguing for something I am afraid I do not deserve, I put it in too emphatic and emotional terms. At certain times, perhaps on long spring evenings, still rainy and sad, with the cold bulbs in bloom and a light too mild for promise drifting over the sea, I have opened the windows and felt the house shrink back into wood and plaster and those humble elements of which is it made, and the life in it subside, leaving me exposed, empty-handed, but feeling a fierce and lawless quiver of freedom, of loneliness too harsh and perfect for me now to bear. Then I know how the rest of the time I am sheltered and encumbered, how insistently I am warmed and bound.)

"Go ahead, if you can find one cheap enough," is all my husband had to say to this. He is not like me, he does not really want explanations. That the heart of another person is a closed book, is something you will hear him say frequently, and without regret.

Even then I did not think it was something that could be accomplished. Perhaps at bottom it seemed to me too improper a wish to be granted. I could almost more easily have wished for a mink coat, for a diamond necklace; these are things women do obtain. The children, learning of my plans, greeted them with the most dashing skepticism and unconcern. Nevertheless I went down to the shopping centre which is two blocks from where I live; there I had noticed for several months, and without thinking how they could pertain to me, a couple of For Rent signs in the upstairs windows of a building that housed a drugstore and a beauty parlour. As I went up the stairs I had a feeling of complete unreality; surely renting was a complicated business, in the case of offices; you did not simply knock on the door of the vacant premises and wait to be admitted; it would have to be done through channels. Also, they would want too much money.

As it turned out, I did not even have to knock. A woman came out of one of the empty offices, dragging a vacuum cleaner, and pushing it with her foot, towards the open door across the hall, which evidently led to an apartment in the rear of the building. She and her husband lived in this apartment; their name was Malley; and it was indeed they who owned the building and rented out the offices. The rooms she had just been vacuuming were, she told me, fitted out for a dentist's office, and so would not interest me, but she would show me the other place. She invited me into her apartment while she put away the vacuum and got her key. Her husband, she said with a sigh I could not interpret, was not at home.

Mrs. Malley was a black-haired, delicate-looking woman, perhaps in her early forties, slatternly but still faintly appealing, with such arbitrary touches of femininity as the thin line of bright lipstick, the pink feather slippers on obviously tender and swollen feet. She had the swaying passivity, the air of exhaustion and muted apprehension, that speaks of a life spent in close attention on a man who is by turns vigorous, crotchety and dependent. How much of this I saw at first, how much decided on later is of course impossible to tell. But I did think that she would have no children, the stress of her life, whatever it was, did not allow it, and in this I was not mistaken.

The room where I waited was evidently a combination living room and office. The first things I noticed were models of ships—galleons, clippers, Queen Marys—sitting on the tables, the window sills, the television. Where there were no ships there were potted plants and a clutter of what are sometimes called "masculine" ornaments—china deer heads, bronze horses, huge ashtrays of heavy, veined, shiny material. On the walls were framed photographs and what might have been diplomas. One photo showed a poodle and a bulldog, dressed in masculine and feminine clothing, and assuming with dismal embarrassment a pose of affection. Written across it was "Old Friends." But the room was really dominated by a portrait, with its own light and a gilded frame; it was of a good-looking, fair-haired man in middle age, sitting behind a desk, wearing a business suit and looking pre-eminently prosperous, rosy and agreeable. Here again, it is probably hindsight on my part that points out that in the portrait there is evident also some uneasiness, some lack of faith the man has in this role, a tendency he has to spread himself too bountifully and insistently, which for all anyone knows may lead to disaster.

Never mind the Malleys. As soon as I saw that office, I wanted it. It was larger than I needed, being divided in such a way that it would be suitable for a doctor's office. (We had a chiropractor in here but he left, says Mrs. Malley in her regretful but uninformative way.) The walls were cold and bare, white with a little grey, to cut the glare for the eyes. Since there were no doctors in evidence, nor had been, as Mrs. Malley freely told me, for some time, I offered twenty-five dollars a month. She said she would have to speak to her husband.

The next time I came my offer was agreed upon, and I met Mr. Malley in the flesh. I explained, as I had already done to his wife, that I did not want to make use of my office during regular business hours, but during the weekends and some-times in the evening. He asked me what I would use it for, and I told him, not without wondering first whether I ought to say I did stenography.

He absorbed the information with good humour. "Ah, you're a writer."

"Well yes. I write."

"Then we'll do our best to see you're comfortable here," he said expansively. "I'm a great man for hobbies myself. All these ship-models, I do them in my spare time, they're a blessing for the nerves. People need an occupation for their nerves. I daresay you're the same."

"Something the same," I said, resolutely agreeable, even relieved that he saw my behaviour in this hazy and tolerant light. At least he did not ask me, as I half-expected, who was looking after the children, and did my husband approve? Ten years, maybe fifteen, had greatly softened, spread and defeated the man in the picture. His hips and thighs had now a startling accumulation of fat, causing him to move with a sigh, a cushiony settling of flesh, a ponderous matriarchal discomfort. His hair and eyes had faded, his features blurred, and the affable, predatory expression had collapsed into one of troubling humility and chronic mistrust. I did not look at him. I had not planned, in taking an office, to take on the responsibility of knowing any more human beings.

On the weekend I moved in, without the help of my family, who would have been kind. I brought my typewriter and a card table and chair, also a little wooden table on which I set a hot plate, a kettle, a jar of instant coffee, a spoon and a yellow mug. That was all. I brooded with satisfaction on the bareness of my walls, the cheap dignity of my essential furnishings, the remarkable lack of things to dust, wash or polish.

The sight was not so pleasing to Mr. Malley. He knocked on my door soon after I was settled and said that he wanted to explain a few things to me—about unscrewing the light in the outer room, which I would not need, about the radiator and how to work the awning outside the window. He looked around at everything with gloom and mystification and said it was an awfully uncomfortable place for a lady.

"Its perfectly all right for me," I said, not as discouragingly as I would have liked to, because I always have a tendency to placate people whom I dislike for no good reason, or simply do not want to know. I make elaborate offerings of courtesy sometimes, in the foolish hope that they will go away and leave me alone.

"What you want is a nice easy chair to sit in, while you're waiting for inspiration to hit. I've got a chair down in the basement, all kinds of stuff down there since my mother passed on last year. There's a bit of carpet rolled up in a corner down there, it isn't doing anybody any good. We could get this place fixed up so's it'd be a lot more homelike for you."

But really, I said, but really I like it as it is.

"If you wanted to run up some curtains, I'd pay you for the

material. Place needs a touch of colour, I'm afraid you'll get morbid sitting in here."

Oh, no, I said, and laughed, I'm sure I won't.

"It'd be a different story if you was a man. A woman wants things a bit cosier."

So I got up and went to the window and looked down into the empty Sunday street through the slats of the Venetian blind, to avoid the accusing vulnerability of his fat face and I tried out a cold voice that is to be heard frequently in my thoughts but has great difficulty getting out of my cowardly mouth. "Mr. Malley, please don't bother me about this any more. I said it suits me. I have everything I want. Thanks for showing me about the light."

The effect was devastating enough to shame me. "I certainly wouldn't dream of bothering you," he said, with precision of speech and aloof sadness. "I merely made these suggestions for your comfort. Had I realized I was in your way, I would of left some time ago." When he had gone I felt better, even a little exhilarated at my victory though still ashamed of how easy it had been. I told myself that he would have had to be discouraged sooner or later, it was better to have it over with at the beginning.

The following weekend he knocked on my door. His expression of humility was exaggerated; almost enough so to seem mocking, yet in another sense it was real and I felt unsure of myself.

"I won't take up a minute of your time," he said. "I never meant to be a nuisance. I just wanted to tell you I'm sorry I offended you last time and I apologize. Here's a little present if you will accept."

He was carrying a plant whose name I did not know; it had thick, glossy leaves and grew out of a pot wrapped lavishly in pink and silver foil.

"There," he said, arranging this plant in a corner of my room. "I don't want any bad feelings with you and me. I'll take the blame. And I thought, maybe she won't accept furnishings, but what's the matter with a nice little plant, that'll brighten things up for you."

It was not possible for me, at this moment, to tell him that I did not want a plant. I hate house plants. He told me how to take care of it, how often to water it and so on; I thanked him. There was nothing else I could do, and I had the unpleasant feeling that beneath his offering of apologies and gifts he was well aware of this and in some way gratified by it. He kept on talking, using the words *bad feelings, offended, apologize.* I tried once to interrupt, with the idea of explaining that I had made provision for an area in my life where good feelings, or bad, did not enter in, that between him and me, in fact, it was not necessary that there be any feelings at all; but this struck me as a hopeless task. How could I confront, in the open, this craving for intimacy? Besides, the plant in its shiny paper had confused me.

"How's the writing progressing?" he said, with an air of putting all our unfortunate differences behind him.

"Oh, about as usual."

"Well if you ever run out of things to write about, I got a barrelful." Pause. "But I guess I'm just eatin' into your time here," he said with a kind of painful buoyancy. This was a test, and I did not pass it. I smiled, my eyes held by that magnificent plant; I said it was all right.

"I was just thinking about the fellow was in here before you. Chiropractor. You could of wrote a book about him."

I assumed a listening position, my hands no longer hovering over the keys. If cowardice and insincerity are big vices of mine, curiosity is certainly another.

"He had a good practice built up here. The only trouble was, he gave more adjustments than was listed in the book of chiropractory. Oh, he was adjusting right and left. I came in here after he moved out, and what do you think I found? Soundproofing! This whole room was soundproofed, to enable him to make his adjustments without disturbing anybody. This very room you're sitting writing your stories in.

"First we knew of it was a lady knocked on my door one day, wanted me to provide her with a passkey to his office. He'd locked his door against her.

"I guess he just got tired of treating her particular case. I guess he figured he'd been knocking away at it long enough. Lady well on in years, you know, and him just a young man. He had a nice young wife too and a couple of the prettiest children you ever would want to see. Filthy some of the things that go on in this world."

It took me some time to realize that he told this story not simply as a piece of gossip, but as something a writer would be particularly interested to hear. Writing and lewdness had a vague delicious connection in his mind. Even this notion, however, seemed so wistful, so infantile, that it struck me as a waste of energy to attack it. I knew now I must avoid hurting him for my own sake, not for his. It had been a great mistake to think that a little roughness would settle things.

The next present was a teapot. I insisted that I drank only coffee and told him to give it to his wife. He said that tea was better for the nerves and that he had known right away I was a nervous person, like himself. The teapot was covered with gilt and roses and I knew that it was not cheap, in spite of its extreme hideousness. I kept it on my table. I also continued to care for the plant, which thrived obscenely in the corner of my room. I could not decide what else to do. He bought me a wastebasket, a fancy one with Chinese mandarins on all eight sides; he got a foam rubber cushion for my chair. I despised myself for submitting to this blackmail. I did not even really pity him; it was just that I could not turn away, I could not turn away from that obsequious hunger. And he knew himself my tolerance was bought; in a way he must have hated me for it.

When he lingered in my office now he told me stories of himself. It occurred to me that he was revealing his life to me in the hope that I would write it down. Of course he had probably revealed it to plenty of people for no particular reason, but in my case there seemed to be a special, even desperate necessity. His life was a series of calamities, as people's lives often are; he had been let down by people he had trusted, refused help by those he had depended on, betrayed by the very friends to whom he had given kindness and material help. Other people, mere strangers and passersby, had taken time to torment him gratuitously, in novel and inventive ways. On occasion, his very life had been threatened. Moreover his wife was a difficulty, her health being poor and her temperament unstable; what was he to do? You see how it is, he said, lifting his hands, but I live. He looked to me to say yes.

I took to coming up the stairs on tiptoe, trying to turn my key without making a noise; this was foolish of course because I could not muffle my typewriter. I actually considered writing in longhand, and wished repeatedly for the evil chiropractor's soundproofing. I told my husband my problem and he said it was not a problem at all. Tell him you're busy, he said. As a matter of fact I did tell him; every time he came to my door, always armed with a little gift or an errand, he asked me how I was and I said that today I was busy. Ah, then, he said, as he eased himself through the door, he would not keep me a minute. And all the time, as I have said, he knew what was going on in my mind, how I weakly longed to be rid of him. He knew but could not afford to care.

One evening after I had gone home I discovered that I had left at the office a letter I had intended to post, and so I went back to get it. I saw from the street that the light was on in the room where I worked. Then I saw him bending over the card table. Of course, he came in at night and read what I had written!

He heard me at the door, and when I came in he was picking up my wastebasket, saying he thought he would just tidy things up for me. He went out at once. I did not say anything, but found myself trembling with anger and gratification. To have found a just cause was a wonder, an unbearable relief.

Next time he came to my door I had locked it on the inside. I knew his step, his chummy cajoling knock. I continued typing loudly, but not uninterruptedly, so he would know I heard. He called my name, as if I was playing a trick; I bit my lips together not to answer. Unreasonably as ever, guilt assailed me but I typed on. That day I saw the earth was dry around the roots of the plant; I let it alone.

I was not prepared for what happened next. I found a note taped to my door, which said that Mr. Malley would be obliged if I would step into his office. I went at once to get it over with. He sat at his desk surrounded by obscure evidences of his authority; he looked at me from a distance, as one who was now compelled to see me in a new and sadly unfavourable light; the embarrassment which he showed seemed not for himself, but me. He started off by saying, with a rather stagey reluctance, that he had known of course when he took me in that I was a writer.

"I didn't let that worry me, though I have heard things about writers and artists and that type of person that didn't strike me as very encouraging. You know the sort of thing I mean."

This was something new; I could not think what it might lead to.

"Now you came to me and said, Mr. Malley, I want a place to write in. I believed you. I gave it to you. I didn't ask any questions. That's the kind of person I am. But you know the more I think about it, well, the more I am inclined to wonder."

"Wonder what?" I said.

"And your own attitude, that hasn't helped to put my mind at ease. Locking yourself in and refusing to answer your door.

That's not a normal way for a person to behave. Not if they
got nothing to hide. No more than it's normal for a young
woman, says she has a husband and kids, to spend her time
rattling away on a typewriter."

"But I don't think that—"

He lifted his hand, a forgiving gesture. "Now all I ask is,
that you be open and aboveboard with me, I think I deserve
that much, and if you are using that office for any other purpose, or at any other times than you let on, and having your
friends or whoever they are up to see you—"

"I don't know what you mean."

"And another thing, you claim to be a writer. Well I read
quite a bit of material, and I never have seen your name in
print. Now maybe you write under some other name?"

"No," I said.

"Well I don't doubt there are writers whose names I haven't
heard," he said genially. "We'll let that pass. Just you give
me your word of honour there won't be any more deceptions,
or any carryings-on, et cetera, in that office you occupy—"

My anger was delayed somehow, blocked off by a stupid
incredulity. I only knew enough to get up and walk down the
hall, his voice trailing after me, and lock the door. I thought—
I must go. But after I had sat down in my own room, my work
in front of me, I thought again how much I liked this room, how
well I worked in it, and I decided not to be forced out. After
all, I felt, the struggle between us had reached a deadlock. I
could refuse to open the door, refuse to look at his notes, refuse
to speak to him when we met. My rent was paid in advance
and if I left now it was unlikely that I would get any refund.
I resolved not to care. I had been taking my manuscript home
every night, to prevent his reading it, and now it seemed that
even this precaution was beneath me. What did it matter if
he read it, any more than if the mice scampered over it in the
dark?

Several times after this I found notes on my door. I intended not to read them, but I always did. His accusations grew more specific. He had heard voices in my room. My behaviour was disturbing his wife when she tried to take her afternoon nap. (I never came in the afternoons, except on weekends.) He had found a whisky bottle in the garbage.

I wondered a good deal about that chiropractor. It was not comfortable to see how the legends of Mr. Malley's life were built up.

As the notes grew more virulent our personal encounters ceased. Once or twice I saw his stooped, sweatered back disappearing as I came into the hall. Gradually our relationship passed into something that was entirely fantasy. He accused me now, by note, of being intimate with people from *Numero Cinq*. This was a coffee-house in the neighbourhood, which I imagine he invoked for symbolic purposes. I felt that nothing much more would happen now, the notes would go on, their contents becoming possibly more grotesque and so less likely to affect me.

He knocked on my door on a Sunday morning, about eleven o'clock. I had just come in and taken my coat off and put my kettle on the hot plate.

This time it was another face, remote and transfigured, that shone with the cold light of intense joy at discovering the proofs of sin.

"I wonder," he said with emotion, "if you would mind following me down the hall?"

I followed him. The light was on in the washroom. This washroom was mine and no one else used it, but he had not given me a key for it and it was always open. He stopped in front of it, pushed back the door and stood with his eyes cast down, expelling his breath discreetly.

"Now who done that?" he said, in a voice of pure sorrow.

The walls above the toilet and above the washbasin were

covered with drawings and comments of the sort you see sometimes in public washrooms on the beach, and in town hall
lavatories in the little decaying towns where I grew up. They
were done with a lipstick, as they usually are. Someone must
have got up here the night before, I thought, possibly some of
the gang who always loafed and cruised around the shopping
centre on Saturday nights.

"It should have been locked," I said, coolly and firmly as if
thus to remove myself from the scene. "It's quite a mess."

"It sure is. It's pretty filthy language, in my book. Maybe
it's just a joke to your friends, but it isn't to me. Not to
mention the art work. That's a nice thing to see when you
open a door on your own premises in the morning."

I said, "I believe lipstick will wash off."

"I'm just glad I didn't have my wife see a thing like this.
Upsets a woman that's had a nice bringing up. Now why don't
you ask your friends up here to have a party with their pails
and brushes? I'd like to have a look at the people with that
kind of a sense of humour."

I turned to walk away and he moved heavily in front of me.

"I don't think there's any question how these decorations
found their way onto my walls."

"If you're trying to say I had anything to do with it," I said,
quite flatly and wearily, "you must be crazy."

"How did they get there then? Whose lavatory is this? Eh.
whose?"

"There isn't any key to it. Anybody can come up here and
walk in. Maybe some kids off the street came up here and did
it last night after I went home, how do I know?"

"It's a shame the way the kids gets blamed for everything,
when it's the elders that corrupts them. That's a thing you
might do some thinking about, you know. There's laws.
Obscenity laws. Applies to this sort of thing and literature too
as I believe."

This is the first time I ever remember taking deep breaths, consciously, for purposes of self-control. I really wanted to murder him. I remember how soft and loathsome his face looked, with the eyes almost closed, nostrils extended to the soothing odour of righteousness, the odour of triumph. If this stupid thing had not happened, he would never have won. But he had. Perhaps he saw something in my face that unnerved him, even in this victorious moment, for he drew back to the wall, and began to say that actually, as a matter of fact, he had not really felt it was the sort of thing I personally would do, more the sort of thing that perhaps certain friends of mine— I got into my own room, shut the door.

The kettle was making a fearful noise, having almost boiled dry. I snatched it off the hot plate, pulled out the plug and stood for a moment choking on rage. This spasm passed and I did what I had to do. I put my typewriter and paper on the chair and folded the card table. I screwed the top tightly on the instant coffee and put it and the yellow mug and the teaspoon into the bag in which I had brought them; it was still lying folded on the shelf. I wished childishly to take some vengeance on the potted plant, which sat in the corner with the flowery teapot, the wastebasket, the cushion, and—I forgot— a little plastic pencil sharpener behind it.

When I was taking things down to the car Mrs. Malley came. I had seen little of her since that first day. She did not seem upset, but practical and resigned.

"He is lying down," she said. "He is not himself."

She carried the bag with the coffee and the mug in it. She was so still I felt my anger leave me, to be replaced by an absorbing depression.

I have not yet found another office. I think that I will try again some day, but not yet. I have to wait at least until that picture fades that I see so clearly in my mind, though I never saw it in reality—Mr. Malley with his rags and brushes and a pail of soapy water, scrubbing in his clumsy way, his deliberately clumsy way, at the toilet walls, stooping with difficulty, breathing sorrowfully, arranging in his mind the bizarre but somehow never quite satisfactory narrative of yet another betrayal of trust. While I arrange words, and think it is my right to be rid of him.

An Ounce of Cure

My parents didn't drink. They weren't rabid about it, and in fact I remember that when I signed the pledge in grade seven, with the rest of that superbly if impermanently indoctrinated class, my mother said, "It's just nonsense and fanaticism, children of that age." My father would drink a beer on a hot day, but my mother did not join him, and—whether accidentally or symbolically—this drink was always consumed *outside* the house. Most of the people we knew were the same way, in the small town where we lived. I ought not to say that it was this which got me into difficulties, because the difficulties I got into were a faithful expression of my own incommodious nature—the same nature that caused my mother to look at me, on any occasion which traditionally calls for feelings of pride and maternal accomplishment (my departure for my first formal dance, I mean, or my hellbent preparations for a descent on college) with an expression of brooding and fascinated despair, as if she could not possibly expect, did not ask, that it should go with me as it did with other girls; the dreamed-of spoils of daughters—orchids, nice boys, diamond rings—would be borne home in due course by the daughters of her friends, but not by me; all she could do was hope for a lesser rather than a greater disaster—an elopement, say, with a boy who could never earn his living, rather than an abduction into the White Slave trade.

But ignorance, my mother said, ignorance, or innocence if you like, is not always such a fine thing as people think and I am not sure it may not be dangerous for a girl like you; then she emphasized her point, as she had a habit of doing, with some quotation which had an innocent promposity and odour of mothballs. I didn't even wince at it, knowing full well how it must have worked wonders with Mr. Berryman.

The evening I baby-sat for the Berrymans must have been in April. I had been in love all year, or at least since the first week in September, when a boy named Martin Collingwood had given me a surprised, appreciative, and rather ominously complacent smile in the school assembly. I never knew what surprised him; I was not looking like anybody but me; I had an old blouse on and my home-permanent had turned out badly. A few weeks after that he took me out for the first time, and kissed me on the dark side of the porch—also, I ought to say, on the mouth; I am sure it was the first time anybody had ever kissed me effectively, and I know that I did not wash my face that night or the next morning, in order to keep the imprint of those kisses intact. (I showed the most painful banality in the conduct of this whole affair, as you will see.) Two months, and a few amatory stages later, he dropped me. He had fallen for the girl who played opposite him in the Christmas production of *Pride and Prejudice*.

I said I was not going to have anything to do with that play, and I got another girl to work on Makeup in my place, but of course I went to it after all, and sat down in front with my girl friend Joyce, who pressed my hand when I was overcome with pain and delight at the sight of Mr. Darcy in white breeches, silk waistcoast, and sideburns. It was surely seeing Martin as Darcy that did for me; every girl is in love with Darcy anyway, and the part gave Martin an arrogance and male splendour in my eyes which made it impossible to remember that he was simply a high-school senior, passably good-looking and of medium intelligence (and with a reputation slightly tainted, at that, by such preferences as the Drama Club and the Cadet *Band*) who happened to be the first boy, the first really presentable boy, to take an interest in me. In the last act they gave him a chance to embrace Elizabeth (Mary Bishop, with a sallow complexion and no figure, but big vivacious eyes) and during this realistic encounter I dug my nails bitterly into Joyce's sympathetic palm.

That night was the beginning of months of real, if more or less self-inflicted, misery for me. Why is it a temptation to refer to this sort of thing lightly, with irony, with amazement even, at finding oneself involved with such preposterous emotions in the unaccountable past? That is what we are apt to do, speaking of love; with adolescent love, of course, it's practically obligatory; you would think we sat around, dull afternoons, amusing ourselves with these tidbit recollections of pain. But it really doesn't make me feel very gay—worse still, it doesn't really surprise me—to remember all the stupid, sad, half-ashamed things I did, that people in love always do. I hung around the places where he might be seen, and then pretended not to see him; I made absurdly roundabout approaches, in conversation, to the bitter pleasure of casually mentioning his name. I daydreamed endlessly; in fact if you want to put it mathematically, I spent perhaps ten times as many hours thinking about Martin Collingwood—yes, pining and weeping for him—as I ever spent with him; the idea of him dominated my mind relentlessly and, after a while, against my will. For if at first I had dramatized my feelings, the time came when I would have been glad to escape them; my well-worn daydreams had become depressing and not even temporarily consoling. As I worked my math problems I would torture myself, quite mechanically and helplessly, with an exact recollection of Martin kissing my throat. I had an exact recollection of *everything*. One night I had an impulse to swallow all the aspirins in the bathroom cabinet, but stopped after I had taken six.

My mother noticed that something was wrong and got me some iron pills. She said, "Are you sure everything is going all right at school?" *School!* When I told her that Martin and I had broken up all she said was, "Well so much the better for that. I never saw a boy so stuck on himself." "Martin has enough conceit to sink a battleship," I said morosely and went upstairs and cried.

The night I went to the Berrymans was a Saturday night. I baby-sat for them quite often on Saturday nights because they liked to drive over to Baileyville, a much bigger, livelier town about twenty miles away, and perhaps have supper and go to a show. They had been living in our town only two or three years—Mr. Berryman had been brought in as plant manager of the new door-factory—and they remained, I suppose by choice, on the fringes of its society; most of their friends were youngish couples like themselves, born in other places, who lived in new ranch-style houses on a hill outside town where we used to go tobogganing. This Saturday night they had two other couples in for drinks before they all drove over to Baileyville for the opening of a new supper-club; they were all rather festive. I sat in the kitchen and pretended to do Latin. Last night had been the Spring Dance at the High School. I had not gone, since the only boy who had asked me was Millerd Crompton, who asked so many girls that he was suspected of working his way through the whole class alphabetically. But the dance was held in the Armouries, which was only half a block away from our house; I had been able to see the boys in dark suits, the girls in long pale formals under their coats, passing gravely under the street-lights, stepping around the last patches of snow. I could even hear the music and I have not forgotten to this day that they played "Ballerina," and—oh, song of my aching heart—"Slow Boat to China." Joyce had phoned me up this morning and told me in her hushed way (we might have been discussing an incurable disease I had) that yes, M.C. *had* been there with M.B., and she had on a formal that must have been made out of somebody's old lace tablecloth, it just *hung*.

When the Berrymans and their friends had gone I went into the living room and read a magazine. I was mortally depressed. The big softly lit room, with its green and leaf-brown colours, made an uncluttered setting for the development of the emotions, such as you would get on a stage. At home the life of the emotions went on all right, but it always seemed to get buried under the piles of mending to be done, the ironing, the children's jigsaw puzzles and rock collections. It was the sort of house where people were always colliding with one another on the stairs and listening to hockey games and Superman on the radio.

I got up and found the Berrymans' "Danse Macabre" and put it on the record player and turned out the living-room lights. The curtains were only partly drawn. A street light shone obliquely on the windowpane, making a rectangle of thin dusty gold, in which the shadows of bare branches moved, caught in the huge sweet winds of spring. It was a mild black night when the last snow was melting. A year ago all this— the music, the wind and darkness, the shadows of the branches —would have given me tremendous happiness; when they did not do so now, but only called up tediously familiar, somehow humiliatingly personal thoughts, I gave up my soul for dead and walked into the kitchen and decided to get drunk.

No, it was not like that. I walked into the kitchen to look for a coke or something in the refrigerator, and there on the front of the counter were three tall beautiful bottles, all about half full of gold. But even after I had looked at them and lifted them to feel their weight I had not decided to get drunk; I had decided to have a drink.

Now here is where my ignorance, my disastrous innocence,

comes in. It is true that I had seen the Berrymans and their friends drinking their highballs as casually as I would drink a coke, but I did not apply this attitude to myself. No; I thought of hard liquor as something to be taken in extremities, and relied upon for extravagant results, one way or another. My approach could not have been less casual if I had been the Little Mermaid drinking the witch's crystal potion. Gravely, with a glance at my set face in the black window above the sink, I poured a little whisky from each of the bottles (I think now there were two brands of rye and an expensive Scotch) until I had my glass full. For I had never in my life seen anyone pour a drink and I had no idea that people frequently diluted their liquor with water, soda, et cetera, and I had seen that the glasses the Berrymans' guests were holding when I came through the living room were nearly full.

I drank it off as quickly as possible. I set the glass down and stood looking at my face in the window, half expecting to see it altered. My throat was burning, but I felt nothing else. It was very disappointing, when I had worked myself up to it. But I was not going to let it go at that. I poured another full glass, then filled each of the bottles with water to approximately the level I had seen when I came in. I drank the second glass only a little more slowly than the first. I put the empty glass down on the counter with care, perhaps feeling in my head a rustle of things to come, and went and sat down on a chair in the living room. I reached up and turned on a floor lamp beside the chair, and the room jumped on me.

When I say that I was expecting extravagant results I do not mean that I was expecting this. I had thought of some sweeping emotional change, an upsurge of gaiety and irresponsibility, a feeling of lawlessness and escape, accompanied by a little dizziness and perhaps a tendency to giggle out loud. I did not have in mind the ceiling spinning like a great plate somebody had thrown at me, nor the pale green blobs of the chairs swelling, converging, disintegrating, playing with me a game full of enormous senseless inanimate malice. My head sank back; I closed my eyes. And at once opened them, opened them wide, threw myself out of the chair and down the hall and reached—thank God, thank God!—the Berrymans' bathroom, where I was sick everywhere, everywhere, and dropped like a stone.

From this point on I have no continuous picture of what happened; my memories of the next hour or two are split into vivid and improbable segments, with nothing but murk and uncertainty between. I do remember lying on the bathroom floor looking sideways at the little six-sided white tiles, which lay together in such an admirable and logical pattern, seeing them with the brief broken gratitude and sanity of one who has just been torn to pieces with vomiting. Then I remember sitting on the stool in front of the hall phone, asking weakly for Joyce's number. Joyce was not home. I was told by her mother (a rather rattlebrained woman, who didn't seem to notice a thing the matter—for which I felt weakly, mechanically grateful) that she was at Kay Stringer's house. I didn't know Kay's number so I just asked the operator; I felt I couldn't risk looking down at the telephone book.

Kay Stringer was not a friend of mine but a new friend of Joyce's. She had a vague reputation for wildness and a long switch of hair, very oddly, though naturally, coloured—from soap-yellow to caramel-brown. She knew a lot of boys more exciting than Martin Collingwood, boys who had quit school or been imported into town to play on the hockey team. She and Joyce rode around in these boys' cars, and sometimes went with them—having lied of course to their mothers—to the Gay-la dance hall on the highway north of town.

I got Joyce on the phone. She was very keyed-up, as she always was with boys around, and she hardly seemed to hear what I was saying.

"Oh, I can't tonight," she said. "Some kids are here. We're

going to play cards. You know Bill Kline? He's here. Ross Armour—"

"I'm *sick*," I said trying to speak distinctly; it came out an inhuman croak. "I'm *drunk*. Joyce!" Then I fell off the stool and the receiver dropped out of my hand and banged for a while dismally against the wall.

I had not told Joyce where I was, so after thinking about it for a moment she phoned my mother, and using the elaborate and unnecessary subterfuge that young girls delight in, she found out. She and Kay and the boys—there were three of them—told some story about where they were going to Kay's mother, and got into the car and drove out. They found me still lying on the broadloom carpet in the hall; I had been sick again, and this time I had not made it to the bathroom.

It turned out that Kay Stringer, who arrived on this scene only by accident, was exactly the person I needed. She loved a crisis, particularly one like this, which had a shady and scandalous aspect and which must be kept secret from the adult world. She became excited, aggressive, efficient; that energy which was termed wildness was simply the overflow of a great female instinct to manage, comfort and control. I could hear her voice coming at me from all directions, telling me not to worry, telling Joyce to find the biggest coffeepot they had and make it full of coffee (*strong* coffee, she said), telling the boys to pick me up and carry me to the sofa. Later, in the fog beyond my reach, she was calling for a scrub-brush.

Then I was lying on the sofa, covered with some kind of crocheted throw they had found in the bedroom. I didn't want to lift my head. The house was full of the smell of coffee. Joyce came in, looking very pale; she said that the Berryman kids had wakened up but she had given them a cookie and told them to go back to bed, it was all right; she hadn't let them out of their room and she didn't believe they'd remember. She said that she and Kay had cleaned up the bathroom and the hall though she was afraid there was still a spot on the rug.

The coffee was ready. I didn't understand anything very well. The boys had turned on the radio and were going through the Berrymans' record collection; they had it out on the floor. I felt there was something odd about this but I could not think what it was.

Kay brought me a huge breakfast mug full of coffee.

"I don't know if I can," I said. "Thanks."

"Sit up," she said briskly, as if dealing with drunks was an everyday business for her, I had no need to feel myself important. (I met, and recognized, that tone of voice years later, in the maternity ward.) "Now drink," she said. I drank, and at the same time realized that I was wearing only my slip. Joyce and Kay had taken off my blouse and skirt. They had brushed off the skirt and washed out the blouse, since it was nylon; it was hanging in the bathroom. I pulled the throw up under my arms and Kay laughed. She got everybody coffee. Joyce brought in the coffeepot and on Kay's instructions she kept filling my cup whenever I drank from it. Somebody said to me with interest. "You must have really wanted to tie one on."

"No," I said rather sulkily, obediently drinking my coffee. "I only had two drinks."

Kay laughed, "Well it certainly gets to you, I'll say that. What time do you expect *they*'ll be back?" she said.

"Late, After one I think."

"You should be all right by that time. Have some more coffee."

Kay and one of the boys began dancing to the radio. Kay danced very sexily, but her face had the gently superior and indulgent, rather cold look it had when she was lifting me up to drink the coffee. The boy was whispering to her and she was smiling, shaking her head. Joyce said she was hungry, and she went out to the kitchen to see what there was— potato chips or crackers, or something like that, that you could eat without making too noticeable a dint. Bill Kline came over and sat on the sofa beside me and patted my legs through the crocheted throw. He didn't say anything to me, just patted my legs and looked at me with what seemed to me a very stupid, half-sick, absurd and alarming expression. I felt very uncomfortable; I wondered how it had ever got around that Bill Kline was so good looking, with an expression like that. I moved my legs nervously and he gave me a look of contempt, not ceasing to pat me. Then I scrambled off the sofa, pulling the throw around me, with the idea of going to the bathroom to see if my blouse was dry. I lurched a little when I started to walk, and for some reason—probably to show Bill Kline that he had not panicked me—I immediately exaggerated this, and calling out, "Watch me walk a straight line!" I lurched and stumbled, to the accompaniment of everyone's laughter, towards the hall. I was standing in the archway between the hall and the living room when the knob of the front door turned with a small matter-of-fact click and everything became silent behind me except the radio of course and the crocheted throw inspired by some delicate malice of its own slithered down around my feet and there—oh, delicious moment in a well-organized farce!—there stood the Berrymans, Mr. and Mrs., with expressions on their faces as appropriate to the occasion as any old-fashioned director of farces could wish. They must have been preparing those expressions, of course; they could not have produced them in the first moment of shock; with the noise we were making, they had no doubt heard us as soon as they got out of the car; for the same reason, we had not heard them. I don't think I ever knew what brought them home so early—a headache, an argument—and I was not really in a position to ask.

Mr. Berryman drove me home. I don't remember how I got into that car, or how I found my clothes and put them on, or what kind of a good-night, if any, I said to Mrs. Berryman. I don't remember what happened to my friends, though I imagine they gathered up their coats and fled, covering up the ignominy of their departure with a mechanical roar of defiance. I remember Joyce with a box of crackers in her hand, saying that I had become terribly sick from eating—I think she said *sauerkraut*—for supper, and that I had called them for help. (When I asked her later what they made of this she said, "It wasn't any use. You *reeked*.") I remember also her saying, "Oh, no, Mr. Berryman I beg of you, my mother is a terribly nervous person I don't know what the shock might do to her. I will go down on my knees to you if you like but *you must not phone my mother*." I have no picture of her down on her knees—and she would have done it in a minute—so it seems this threat was not carried out.

Mr. Berryman said to me, "Well I guess you know your behaviour tonight is a pretty serious thing." He made it sound as if I might be charged with criminal negligence or something worse. "It would be very wrong of me to overlook it," he said. I suppose that besides being angry and disgusted with *me*, he was worried about taking me home in this condition to my strait-laced parents, who could always say I got the liquor in his house. Plenty of Temperance people would think that enough to hold him responsible, and the town was full of Temperance people. Good relations with the town were very important to him from a business point of view.

"I have an idea it wasn't the first time," he said. "If it was the first time, would a girl be smart enough to fill three bottles up with water? No. Well in this case, she *was* smart enough, but not smart enough to know I could spot it. What do you say to that?" I opened my mouth to answer and although I was feeling quite sober the only sound that came out was a loud, desolate-sounding giggle. He stopped in front of our house. "Light's on," he said. "Now go in and tell your parents the straight truth. And if you don't, remember I will." He did not mention paying me for my baby-sitting services of the evening and the subject did not occur to me either.

I went into the house and tried to go straight upstairs but my mother called to me. She came into the front hall, where I had not turned on the light, and she must have smelled me at once for she ran forward with a cry of pure amazement, as if she had seen somebody falling, and caught me by the shoulders as I did indeed fall down against the bannister, overwhelmed by my fantastic lucklessness, and I told her everything from the start, not omitting even the name of Martin Collingwood and my flirtation with the aspirin bottle, which was a mistake.

On Monday morning my mother took the bus over to Bailey-ville and found the liquor store and bought a bottle of Scotch whisky. Then she had to wait for a bus back, and she met some people she knew and she was not quite able to hide the bottle in her bag; she was furious with herself for not bringing a proper shopping-bag. As soon as she got back she walked out to the Berrymans'; she had not even had lunch. Mr. Berryman had not gone back to the factory. My mother went in and had a talk with both of them and made an excellent impression and then Mr. Berryman drove her home. She talked to them in the forthright and unemotional way she had, which was always agreeably surprising to people prepared to deal with a mother, and she told them that although I seemed to do well enough at school I was extremely backward—or perhaps eccentric—in my emotional development. I imagine that this analysis of my behaviour was especially effective with Mrs. Berryman, a great reader of Child Guidance books. Relations between them warmed to the point where my mother brought up a specific instance of my difficulties, and disarmingly related the whole story of Martin Collingwood.

Within a few days it was all over town and the school that I had tried to commit suicide over Martin Collingwood. But it was already all over school and the town that the Berrymans had come home on Saturday night to find me drunk, stagger-ing, wearing nothing but my slip, in a room with three boys, one of whom was Bill Kline. My mother had said that I was to pay for the bottle she had taken the Berrymans out of my baby-sitting earnings, but my clients melted away like the last April snow, and it would not be paid for yet if newcomers to town had not moved in across the street in July, and needed a baby sitter before they talked to any of their neighbours.

My mother also said that it had been a great mistake to let me go out with boys and that I would not be going out again until well after my sixteenth birthday, if then. This did not prove to be a concrete hardship at all, because it was at least that long before anybody asked me. If you think that news of the Berrymans adventure would put me in demand for whatever gambols and orgies were going on in and around that town, you could not be more mistaken. The extraordinary publicity which attended my first debauch may have made me seemed marked for a special kind of ill luck, like the girl whose illegitimate baby turns out to be triplets: nobody wants to have anything to do with her. At any rate I had at the same time one of the most silent telephones and positively the most sinful reputation in the whole High School. I had to put up with this until the next fall, when a fat blonde girl in Grade Ten ran away with a married man and was picked up two months later, living in sin—though not with the same man—in the city of Sault Ste. Marie. Then everybody forgot about me.

But there was a positive, a splendidly unexpected, result of this affair: I got completely over Martin Collingwood. It was not only that he at once said, publicly, that he had always thought I was a nut; where he was concerned I had no pride, and my tender fancy could have found a way around that, a month, a week, before. What was it that brought me back into the world again? It was the terrible and fascinating reality of my disaster; it was *the way things happened*. Not that I enjoyed it; I was a self-conscious girl and I suffered a good deal from all this exposure. But the development of events on that Saturday night—that fascinated me; I felt that I had had a glimpse of the shameless, marvellous, shattering absurdity with which the plots of life, though not of fiction, are improvised. I could not take my eyes off it.

And of course Martin Collingwood wrote his Senior Matric that June, and went away to the city to take a course at a school for Morticians, as I think it is called, and when he came back he went into his uncle's undertaking business. We lived in the same town and we would hear most things that happened to each other but I do not think we met face to face or saw one another, except at a distance, for years. I went to a shower for the girl he married, but then everybody went to everybody else's showers. No, I do not think I really saw him again until I came home after I had been married several years, to attend a relative's funeral. Then I saw him; not quite Mr. Darcy but still very nice-looking in those black clothes. And I saw him looking over at me with an expression as close to a reminiscent smile as the occasion would permit, and I knew that he had been surprised by a memory either of my devotion or my little buried catastrophe. I gave him a gentle uncomprehending look in return. I am a grown-up woman now; let him unbury his own catastrophes.

The Time of Death

Afterwards the mother, Leona Parry, lay on the couch, with a quilt around her, and the women kept putting more wood on the fire although the kitchen was very hot, and no one turned the light on. Leona drank some tea and refused to eat, and talked, beginning like this, in a voice that was ragged and insistent but not yet hysterical: I wasn't hardly out of the house, I wasn't out of the house twenty minutes—

(Three-quarters of an hour at the least, Allie McGee thought, but she did not say so, not at the time. But she remembered, because there were three serials on the radio she was trying to listen to, she listened to every day, and she couldn't get half of them; Leona was there in her kitchen going on about Patricia. Leona was sewing this cowgirl outfit for Patricia on Allie's machine; she raced the machine and she pulled the thread straight out to break it instead of pulling it back though Allie had told her don't do that please it's liable to break the needle. Patricia was supposed to have the outfit for that night when she sang at a concert up the valley; she was singing Western pieces. Patricia sang with the Maitland Valley Entertainers, who went all over the country playing at concerts and dances. Patricia was introduced as the Little Sweetheart of Maitland Valley, the Baby Blonde, the Pint-Size Kiddie with the Great Big Voice. She did have a big voice, almost alarming in so frail a child.

Leona had started her singing in public when she was three years old.

Never was ascared once, Leona said, leaning forward with a jerky pressure on the pedal, it just comes natural to her to perform. Her kimona fallen open revealed her lean chest, her wilted breasts with their large blue veins sloping into the grey-pink nightgown. She don't care, it could be the King of England watching her, she'd get up and sing, and when she was through singing she'd sit down, that's just the way she is. She's even got a good name for a singer, Patricia Parry, doesn't that sound like you just heard it announced over the air? Another thing is natural blonde hair. I have to do it up in rags every night of her life, but that real natural blonde is a lot scarcer than natural curly. It don't get dark, either, there's that strain of natural blondes in my family that don't get dark. My cousin I told you about, that won the Miss St. Catharines of 1936, she was one, and my aunt that died—)

Allie McGee did not say, and Leona caught her breath and plunged on: Twenty minutes. And that last thing I said to her as I went out the door was, you keep an eye on the kids! She's nine years old, isn't she? I'm just going to run acrost the road to sew up this outfit, you keep an eye on the kids. And I went out the door and down the steps and down to the end of the garden and just as I took the hook off the gate something stopped me, I thought, *something's wrong!* What's wrong, I said to myself. I stood there and I looked back at the garden and all I could see was the cornstalks standing and the cabbages there frozen, we never got them in this year, and I looked up and down the road and all I could see was Mundy's old hound laying out in front of their place, no cars comin' one way or the other and the yards all empty, it was cold I guess and no kids playin' out—And I thought, My Lord, maybe I got my days mixed up and this isn't Saturday morning, it's some special day I forgot about— Then I thought all it was was the snow coming I could feel in the air, and you know how cold it was,

the puddles in the road was all turned to ice and splintered up
—but it didn't snow, did it, it hasn't snowed yet—And I run
acrost the road then over to McGee's and up the front steps
and Allie says, Leona, what's the matter with you, you look so
white, she says—

Allie McGee heard this too and said nothing, because it was
not a time for any sort of accuracy. Leona's voice had gone
higher and higher as she talked and any time now she might
break off and begin to scream: Don't let that kid come near me,
don't let me see her, just don't let her come near me.

And the women in the kitchen would crowd around the
couch, their big bodies indistinct in the half-light, their faces
looming pale and heavy, hung with the ritual masks of mourn-
ing and compassion. Now lay down, they would say, in the
stately tones of ritual soothing. Lay down, Leona, she ain't
here, it's all right.

And the girl from the Salvation Army would say, in her
gentle unchanging voice, You must forgive her, Mrs. Parry,
she is only a child. Sometimes the Salvation Army girl would
say: It is God's will, we do not understand. The other woman
from the Salvation Army, who was older, with an oily, sallow
face and an almost masculine voice, said: In the garden of
heaven the children bloom like flowers. God needed another
flower and he took your child. Sister, you should thank him
and be glad.

The other women listened uneasily while these spoke; their
faces at such words took on a look of embarrassed childish
solemnity. They made tea and set out on the table the pies
and fruitcake and scones that people had sent, and they themselves had made. Nobody ate anything because Leona would
not eat. Many of the women cried, but not the two from the
Army. Allie McGee cried. She was stout, placid-faced, big-
breasted; she had no children. Leona drew up her knees under
the quilt and rocked herself back and forth as she wept, and
threw her head down and then back (showing, as some of them

noticed with a feeling of shame, the dirty lines on her neck). Then she grew quiet and said with something like surprise: I nursed him till he was ten months old. He was so good, too, you never would of known you had him in the house. I always said, that's the best one I ever had.

In the dark overheated kitchen the woman felt the dignity of this sorrow in their maternal flesh, they were humble before this unwashed, unliked and desolate Leona. When the men came in—the father, a cousin, a neighbour, bringing a load of wood or asking shamefacedly for something to eat—they were at once aware of something that shut them out, that reproved them. They went out and said to the other men, Yeah, they're still at it. And the father who was getting a little drunk, and belligerent, because he felt that something was expected of him and he was not equal to it, it was not fair, said, Yeah, that won't do Benny any good, they can bawl their eyes out.

George and Irene had been playing their cut-out game, cutting things out of the catalogue. They had this family they had cut out of the catalogue, the mother and father and the kids, and they cut out clothes for them. Patricia watched them cutting and she said, Look at the way you kids cut out! Lookit all the white around the edges! How are you going to make those clothes stay on, she said, you didn't even cut any fold-over things. She took the scissors and she cut very neatly, not leaving any white around the edges; her pale shrewd little face was bent to one side; her lips bitten together. She did things the way a grown-up does; she did not pretend things. She did not play at being a singer, though she was going to be a singer when she grew up, maybe in the movies or maybe on the radio. She liked to look at movie magazines and magazines with pictures of clothes and rooms in them; she liked to look in the windows of some of the houses uptown.

Benny was trying to climb up on the couch. He grabbed at the catalogue and Irene hit his hand. He began to whimper.

Patricia picked him up competently and carried him to the window. She stood him on a chair looking out, saying to him, Bow-wow, Benny, see bow-wow— It was Mundy's dog, getting up and shaking himself and going off down the road.

Bow-wow, said Benny interrogatively, putting his hands flat and leaning against the window to see where the dog went. Benny was eighteen months old and the only words he knew how to say were Bow-wow and Bram. Bram was for the scissors-man who came along the road sometimes; Brandon was his name. Benny remembered him, and ran out to meet him when he came. Other little kids only thirteen, fourteen months old knew more words than Benny, and could do more things, like waving bye-bye and clapping hands, and most of them were cuter to look at. Benny was long and thin and bony and his face was like his father's—pale, mute, unexpectant; all it needed was a soiled peaked cap. But he was good; he would stand for hours just looking out a window saying Bow-wow, bow-wow, now in a low questioning tone, now crooningly, stroking his hands down the window-pane. He liked you to pick him up and hold him, long as he was, just like a little baby; he would lie looking up and smiling, with a little timidity or misgiving. Patricia knew he was stupid; she hated stupid things. He was the only stupid thing she did not hate. She would go and wipe his nose, expertly and impersonally, she would try to get him to talk, repeating words after her, she would put her face down to his, saying anxiously, Hi, Benny, *Hi*, and he would look at her and smile in his slow dubious way. That gave her this feeling, a kind of sad tired feeling, and she would go away and leave him, she would go and look at a movie magazine.

She had had a cup of tea and part of a sugar-bun for breakfast; now she was hungry. She rummaged around among the dirty dishes and puddles of milk and porridge on the kitchen table; she picked up a bun, but it was sopping with milk and she threw it down again.

This place stinks, she said. Irene and George paid no attention. She kicked at a crust of porridge that had dried on the linoleum. Lookit that, she said. Lookit *that!* What's it always a mess around here for? She walked around kicking at things perfunctorily. Then she got the scrub-pail from under the sink and a dipper, and she began to dip water from the reservoir of the stove.

I'm going to clean this place up, she said. It never gets cleaned up like other places. The first thing I'm going to do I'm going to scrub the floor and you kids have to help me—

She put the pail on the stove.

That water is hot to start with, Irene said.

It's not hot enough. It's got to be good and boiling hot. I seen Mrs. McGee scrub *her* floor.

They stayed at Mrs. McGee's all night. They had been over there since the ambulance came. They saw Leona and Mrs. McGee and the other neighbours start to pull off Benny's clothes and it looked like parts of his skin were coming away too, and Benny was making a noise not like crying, but more a noise like they had heard a dog making after its hind parts were run over, but worse, and louder— But Mrs. McGee saw them; she cried, Go away, go away from here! Go over to my place, she cried. After that the ambulance had come and taken Benny away to the hospital, and Mrs. McGee came over and told them that Benny was going to the hospital for a while and they were going to stay at her place. She gave them bread and peanut butter and bread and strawberry jam.

The bed they slept in had a feather tick and smooth ironed sheets; the blankets were pale and fluffy and smelled faintly of mothballs. On top of everything else was a Star-of-Bethlehem quilt; they knew it was called that because when they were getting ready for bed Patricia said, My, what a beautiful quilt! and Mrs. McGee looking surprised and rather distracted said, Oh, yes, that's a Star-of-Bethlehem.

Patricia was very polite in Mrs. McGee's house. It was not as nice as some of the houses uptown but it was covered on the outside with imitation brick and inside it had an imitation fireplace, as well as a fern in a basket; it was not like the other houses along the highway. Mr. McGee did not work in the mill like the other men, but in a store.

George and Irene were so shy and alarmed in this house that they could not answer when they were spoken to.

They all woke up very early; they lay on their backs, uneasy between the fresh sheets, and they watched the room getting light. This room had mauve silk curtains and Venetian blinds and mauve and yellow roses on the wallpaper; it was the guest room. Patricia said, We slept in the guest room.

I have to go, George said.

I'll show you where the bathroom is, Patricia said. It's down the hall.

But George wouldn't go down there to the bathroom. He didn't like it. Patricia tried to make him but he wouldn't.

See if there is a pot under the bed, Irene said.

They got a bathroom here they haven't got any pots, Patricia said angrily. What would they have a stinking old pot for?

George said stolidly that he wouldn't go down there.

Patricia got up and tip-toed to the dresser and got a big vase. When George had gone she opened the window very carefully with hardly any noise and emptied the vase and dried it out with Irene's underpants.

Now, she said, you kids shut up and lay still. Don't talk out loud just whisper.

George whispered, Is Benny still in the hospital?

Yes he is, said Patricia shortly.

Is he going to die?

I told you a hundred times, no.

Is he?

No! Just his skin got burnt, he didn't get burnt inside. He

isn't going to die of a little bit of burnt skin is he? Don't talk so loud.

Irene began to twist her head into the pillow.

What's the matter with you? Patricia said.

He cried awful, Irene said, her face in the pillow.

Well it hurt, that's why he cried. When they got him to the hospital they gave him some stuff that made it stop hurting.

How do you know? George said.

I know.

They were quiet for a while and then Patricia said, I never in my life heard of anybody that died of a burnt skin. Your whole skin could be burnt off it wouldn't matter you could just grow another. Irene stop crying or I'll hit you.

Patricia lay still, looking up at the ceiling, her sharp profile white against the mauve silk curtains of Mrs. McGee's guestroom.

For breakfast they had grapefruit, which they did not remember having tasted before, and cornflakes and toast and jam. Patricia watched George and Irene and snapped at them, Say please! Say thank-you! She said to Mr. and Mrs. McGee, What a cold day, I wouldn't be surprised if it snowed today would you?

But they did not answer. Mrs. McGee's face was swollen. After breakfast she said, Don't get up, children, listen to me. Your little brother—

Irene began to cry and that started George crying too; he said sobbingly, triumphantly to Patricia. He did so die, he did so! Patricia did not answer. *It's her fault*, George sobbed, and Mrs. McGee said, Oh, no, oh, no! But Patricia sat still, with her face wary and polite. She did not say anything until the crying had died down a bit and Mrs. McGee got up sighing and began to clear the table. Then Patricia offered to help with the dishes.

Mrs. McGee took them downtown to buy them all new shoes for the funeral. Patricia was not going to the funeral because

Leona said she never wanted to see her again as long as she lived, but she was to get new shoes too; it would have been unkind to leave her out. Mrs. McGee took them into the store and sat them down and explained the situation to the man who owned it; they stood together nodding and whispering gravely. The man told them to take off their shoes and socks. George and Irene took theirs off and stuck out their feet, with the black dirt-caked toenails. Patricia whispered to Mrs. McGee that she had to go to the bathroom and Mrs. McGee told her where it was, at the back of the store, and she went out there and took off her shoes and her socks. She got her feet as clean as she could with cold water and paper towels. When she came back she heard Mrs. McGee was saying softly to the store-man, You should of seen the bedsheets I had them on. Patricia walked past them not letting on she heard.

Irene and George got oxfords and Patricia got a pair she chose herself, with a strap across. She looked at them in the low mirror. She walked back and forth looking at them until Mrs. McGee said, Patricia never mind about shoes now! Would you believe it? she said in that same soft voice to the store-man as they walked out of the store.

After the funeral was over they went home. The women had cleaned up the house and put Benny's things away. Their father had got sick from so much beer in the back shed after the funeral and he stayed away from the house. Their mother had been put to bed. She stayed there for three days and their father's sister looked after the house.

Leona said they were not to let Patricia come near her room. Don't let her come up here, she cried, I don't want to see her, I haven't forgot my baby boy. But Patricia did not try to go upstairs. She paid no attention to any of this; she looked at movie magazines and did her hair up in rags. If someone cried she did not notice; with her it was as if nothing had happened.

The man who was the manager of the Maitland Valley Entertainers came to see Leona. He told her they were doing

the program for a big concert and barn-dance over at Rockland, and he wanted Patricia to sing in it, if it wasn't too soon
after what happened and all. Leona said she would have to
think about it. She got out of bed and went downstairs.
Patricia was sitting on the couch with one of her magazines.
She kept her head down.

That's a fine head of hair you got there, Leona said. I see
you been doing it up your ownself. Get me the brush and
comb!

To her sister-in-law she said, What's life? You gotta go on.

She went downtown and bought some sheet music, two
songs: May the Circle Be Unbroken, and It Is No Secret, What
God Can Do. She had Patricia learn them, and Patricia sang
these two songs at the concert in Rockland. People in the
audience started whispering, because they had heard about
Benny, it had been in the paper. They pointed out Leona, who
was dressed up and sitting on the platform, and she had her
head down, she was crying. Some people in the audience cried
too. Patricia did not cry.

In the first week of November (and the snow had not come,
the snow had not come yet) the scissors-man with his cart came
walking along beside the highway. The children were playing
out in the yards and they heard him coming; when he was still
far down the road they heard his unintelligible chant, mournful
and shrill, and so strange that you would think, if you did not
know it was the scissors-man, that there was a madman loose
in the world. He wore the same stained brown overcoat, with
the hem hanging ragged, and the same crownless felt hat; he
came up the road, calling like this and the children ran into the
houses to get knives and scissors, or they ran out in the road
calling excitedly, Old Brandon, old Brandon (for that was his
name).

Then in the Parry's yard Patricia began to scream: I hate
that old scissors-man! I hate him! she screamed. I hate that

old scissors-man, I hate him! She screamed, standing stock-still in the yard with her face looking so wizened and white. The shrill shaking cries brought Leona running out, and the neighbours; they pulled her into the house, still screaming. They could not get her to say what was the matter; they thought she must be having some kind of fit. Her eyes were screwed up tight and her mouth wide open; her tiny pointed teeth were almost transparent, and faintly rotten at the edges; they made her look like a ferret, a wretched little animal insane with rage or fear. They tried shaking her, slapping her, throwing cold water on her face; at last they got her to swallow a big dose of soothing-syrup with a lot of whisky in it, and they put her to bed.

That is a prize kid of Leona's, the neighbours said to each other as they went home. That *singer*, they said, because now things were back to normal and they disliked Leona as much as before. They laughed gloomily and said, Yeah, that future movie-star. Out in the yard yelling, you'd think she'd gone off her head.

There was this house, and the other wooden houses that had never been painted, with their steep patched roofs and their narrow, slanting porches, the wood-smoke coming out of their chimneys and dim children's faces pressed against their windows. Behind them there was the strip of earth, plowed in some places, run to grass in others, full of stones, and behind this the pine trees, not very tall. In front were the yards, the dead gardens, the grey highway running out from town. The snow came, falling slowly, evenly, between the highway and the houses and the pine trees, falling in big flakes at first and then in smaller and smaller flakes that did not melt on the hard furrows, the rock of the earth.

Day of the Butterfly

I do not remember when Myra Sayla came to town, though she must have been in our class at school for two or three years. I start remembering her in the last year, when her little brother Jimmy Sayla was in Grade One. Jimmy Sayla was not used to going to the bathroom by himself and he would have to come to the Grade Six door and ask for Myra and she would take him downstairs. Quite often he would not get to Myra in time and there would be a big dark stain on his little button-on cotton pants. Then Myra had to come and ask the teacher: "Please may I take my brother home, he has wet himself?"

That was what she said the first time and everybody in the front seats heard her—though Myra's voice was the lightest singsong—and there was a muted giggling which alerted the rest of the class. Our teacher, a cold gentle girl who wore glasses with thin gold rims and in the stiff solicitude of certain poses resembled a giraffe, wrote something on a piece of paper and showed it to Myra. And Myra recited uncertainly: "My brother has had an accident, please, teacher."

Everybody knew of Jimmy Sayla's shame and at recess (if he was not being kept in, as he often was, for doing something he shouldn't in school) he did not dare go out on the school grounds, where the other little boys, and some bigger ones, were waiting to chase him and corner him against the back fence and thrash him with tree branches. He had to stay with Myra. But at our school there were the two sides, the Boys' Side and the Girls' Side, and it was believed that if you so much as stepped on the side that was not your own you might easily get the strap. Jimmy could not go out on the Girls' Side and Myra could not go out on the Boys' Side, and no one was allowed to stay in the school unless it was raining or snowing. So Myra and Jimmy spent every recess standing in the little back porch between the two sides. Perhaps they watched the baseball games, the tag and skipping and building of leaf houses in the fall and snow forts in the winter; perhaps they did not watch at all. Whenever you happened to look at them their heads were slightly bent, their narrow bodies hunched in, quite still. They had long smooth oval faces, melancholy and discreet—dark, oily, shining hair. The little boy's was long, clipped at home, and Myra's was worn in heavy braids coiled on top of her head so that she looked, from a distance, as if she was wearing a turban too big for her. Over their dark eyes the lids were never fully raised; they had a weary look. But it was more than that. They were like children in a medieval painting, they were like small figures carved of wood, for worship or magic, with faces smooth and aged, and meekly, cryptically uncommunicative.

Most of the teachers at our school had been teaching for a long time and at recess they would disappear into the teachers' room and not bother us. But our own teacher, the young woman of the fragile gold-rimmed glasses, was apt to watch us from a window and sometimes come out, looking brisk and uncomfortable, to stop a fight among the little girls or start a running game among the big ones, who had been huddled together playing Truth or Secrets. One day she came out and called, "Girls in Grade Six, I want to talk to you!" She smiled persuasively, earnestly, and with dreadful unease, showing fine gold rims around her teeth. She said, "There is a girl in Grade Six called Myra Sayla. She *is* in your grade, isn't she?"

We mumbled. But there was a coo from Gladys Healey. "Yes, Miss Darling!"

"Well, why is she never playing with the rest of you? Every day I see her standing in the back porch, never playing. Do you think she looks very happy standing back there? Do you think you would be very happy, if *you* were left back there?"

Nobody answered; we faced Miss Darling, all respectful, self-possessed, and bored with the unreality of her question. Then Gladys said, "Myra can't come out with us, Miss Darling. Myra has to look after her little brother!"

"Oh," said Miss Darling dubiously. "Well you ought to try to be nicer to her anyway. Don't you think so? Don't you? You will try to be nicer, won't you? I *know* you will." Poor Miss Darling! Her campaigns were soon confused, her persuasions turned to bleating and uncertain pleas.

When she had gone Gladys Healey said softly, "You will try to be nicer, won't you? I *know* you will!" and then drawing her lip back over her big teeth she yelled exuberantly, "I don't care if it rains or freezes." She went through the whole verse and ended it with a spectacular twirl of her Royal Stuart tartan skirt. Mr. Healey ran a Dry Goods and Ladies' Wear, and his daughter's leadership in our class was partly due to her flashing plaid skirts and organdie blouses and velvet jackets with brass buttons, but also to her early-maturing bust and the fine brutal force of her personality. Now we all began to imitate Miss Darling.

We had not paid much attention to Myra before this. But now a game was developed; it started with saying, "Let's be nice to Myra!" Then we would walk up to her in formal groups of three or four and at a signal, say together, "Hel-lo Myra, Hello *My*-ra!" and follow up with something like, "What do you wash your hair in, Myra, it's so nice and shiny,

My-ra." "Oh she washes it in cod-liver oil, don't you, Myra, she washes it in cod-liver oil, can't you smell it?"

And to tell the truth there was a smell about Myra, but it was a rotten-sweetish smell as of bad fruit. That was what the Saylas did, kept a little fruit store. Her father sat all day on a stool by the window, with his shirt open over his swelling stomach and tufts of black hair showing around his belly button; he chewed garlic. But if you went into the store it was Mrs. Sayla who came to wait on you, appearing silently between the limp print curtains hung across the back of the store. Her hair was crimped in black waves and she smiled with her full lips held together, stretched as far as they would go; she told you the price in a little rapping voice, daring you to challenge her and, when you did not, handed you the bag of fruit with open mockery in her eyes.

One morning in the winter I was walking up the school hill very early; a neighbour had given me a ride into town. I lived about half a mile out of town, on a farm, and I should not have been going to the town school at all, but to a country school nearby where there were half a dozen pupils and a teacher a little demented since her change of life. But my mother, who was an ambitious woman, had prevailed on the town trustees to accept me and my father to pay the extra tuition, and I went to school in town. I was the only one in the class who carried a lunch pail and ate peanut-butter sandwiches in the high, bare, mustard-coloured cloakroom, the only one who had to wear rubber boots in the spring, when the roads were heavy with mud. I felt a little danger, on account of this; but I could not tell exactly what it was.

I saw Myra and Jimmy ahead of me on the hill; they always went to school very early—sometimes so early that they had to stand outside waiting for the janitor to open the door. They were walking slowly, and now and then Myra half turned around. I had often loitered in that way, wanting to walk with some important girl who was behind me, and not quite

daring to stop and wait. Now it occurred to me that Myra
might be doing this with me. I did not know what to do. I
could not afford to be seen walking with her, and I did not
even want to—but, on the other hand, the flattery of those
humble, hopeful turnings was not lost on me. A role was
shaping for me that I could not resist playing. I felt a great
pleasurable rush of self-conscious benevolence; before I thought
what I was doing I called, "Myra! Hey, Myra, wait up, I
got some Cracker Jack!" and I quickened my pace as she
stopped.

Myra waited, but she did not look at me; she waited in the
withdrawn and rigid attitude with which she always met us.
Perhaps she thought I was playing a trick on her, perhaps she
expected me to run past and throw an empty Cracker Jack
box in her face. And I opened the box and held it out to her.
She took a little. Jimmy ducked behind her coat and would not
take any when I offered the box to him.

"He's shy," I said reassuringly. "A lot of little kids are shy
like that. He'll probably grow out of it."

"Yes," said Myra.

"I have a brother four," I said. "He's awfully shy." He
wasn't. "Have some more Cracker Jack," I said. "I used to
eat Cracker Jack all the time but I don't any more. I think it's
bad for your complexion."

There was a silence.

"Do you like Art?" said Myra faintly.

"No. I like Social Studies and Spelling and Health."

"I like Art and Arithmetic." Myra could add and multiply
in her head faster than anyone else in the class.

"I wish I was as good as you. In Arithmetic," I said, and
felt magnanimous.

"But I am no good at Spelling," said Myra. "I make the
most mistakes, I'll fail maybe." She did not sound unhappy
about this, but pleased to have such a thing to say. She kept
her head turned away from me staring at the dirty snowbanks

along Victoria Street, and as she talked she made a sound as if she was wetting her lips with her tongue.

"You won't fail," I said. "You are too good in Arithmetic. What are you going to be when you grow up?"

She looked bewildered. "I will help my mother," she said. "And work in the store."

"Well I am going to be an airplane hostess," I said. "But don't mention it to anybody. I haven't told many people."

"No, I won't," said Myra. "Do you read Steve Canyon in the paper?"

"Yes." It was queer to think that Myra, too, read the comics, or that she did anything at all, apart from her role at the school. "Do you read Rip Kirby?"

"Do you read Orphan Annie?"

"Do you read Betsy and the Boys?"

"You haven't had hardly any Cracker Jack," I said. "Have some. Take a whole handful."

Myra looked into the box. "There's a prize in there," she said. She pulled it out. It was a brooch, a little tin butterfly, painted gold with bits of coloured glass stuck onto it to look like jewels. She held it in her brown hand, smiling slightly.

I said, "Do you like that?"

Myra said, "I like them blue stones. Blue stones are sapphires."

"I know. My birthstone is sapphire. What is your birthstone?"

"I don't know."

"When is your birthday?"

"July."

"Then yours is ruby."

"I like sapphire better," said Myra. "I like yours." She handed me the brooch.

"You keep it," I said. "Finders keepers."

Myra kept holding it out, as if she did not know what I meant. "Finders keepers," I said.

"It was your Cracker Jack," said Myra, scared and solemn. "You bought it."

"Well you found it."

"No—" said Myra.

"Go on!" I said. "Here, I'll *give* it to you." I took the brooch from her and pushed it back into her hand.

We were both surprised. We looked at each other; I flushed but Myra did not. I realized the pledge as our fingers touched; I was panicky, but *all right*. I thought, I can come early and walk with her other mornings. I can go and talk to her at recess. Why not? *Why not?*

Myra put the brooch in her pocket. She said, "I can wear it on my good dress. My good dress is blue."

I knew it would be. Myra wore out her good dresses at school. Even in midwinter among the plaid wool skirts and serge tunics, she glimmered sadly in sky-blue taffeta, in dusty turquoise crepe, a grown woman's dress made over, weighted by a big bow at the v of the neck and folding empty over Myra's narrow chest.

And I was glad she had not put it on. If someone asked her where she got it, and she told them, what would I say?

It was the day after this, or the week after, that Myra did not come to school. Often she was kept at home to help. But this time she did not come back. For a week, then two weeks, her desk was empty. Then we had a moving day at school and Myra's books were taken out of her desk and put on a shelf in the closet. Miss Darling said, "We'll find a seat when she comes back." And she stopped calling Myra's name when she took attendance.

Jimmy Sayla did not come to school either, having no one to take him to the bathroom.

In the fourth week or the fifth, that Myra had been away, Gladys Healey came to school and said, "Do you know what— Myra Sayla is sick in the hospital."

It was true. Gladys Healey had an aunt who was a nurse. Gladys put up her hand in the middle of Spelling and told Miss Darling. "I thought you might like to know," she said. "Oh yes," said Miss Darling. "I do know."

"What has she got?" we said to Gladys.

And Gladys said, "Akemia, or something. And she has blood transfusions." She said to Miss Darling, "My aunt is a nurse."

So Miss Darling had the whole class write Myra a letter, in which everybody said, "Dear Myra, We are all writing you a letter. We hope you will soon be better and be back to school, Yours truly . . . ." And Miss Darling said, "I've thought of something. Who would like to go up to the hospital and visit Myra on the twentieth of March, for a birthday party?"

I said, "Her birthday's in July."

"I know," said Miss Darling. "It's the twentieth of July. So this year she could have it on the twentieth of March, because she's sick."

"But her *birthday* is in July."

"Because she's sick," said Miss Darling, with a warning shrillness. "The cook at the hospital would make a cake and you could all give a little present, twenty-five cents or so. It would have to be between two and four, because that's visiting hours. And we couldn't all go, it'd be too many. So who wants to go and who wants to stay here and do supplementary reading?"

We all put up our hands. Miss Darling got out the spelling records and picked out the first fifteen, twelve girls and three boys. Then the three boys did not want to go so she picked out the next three girls. And I do not know when it was, but I think it was probably at this moment that the birthday party of Myra Sayla became fashionable.

Perhaps it was because Gladys Healey had an aunt who was a nurse, perhaps it was the excitement of sickness and hospitals, or simply the fact that Myra was so entirely, impressively set free of all the rules and conditions of our lives. We began to talk of her as if she were something we owned, and her party became a cause; with womanly heaviness we discussed it at recess, and decided that twenty-five cents was too low.

We all went up to the hospital on a sunny afternoon when the snow was melting, carrying our presents, and a nurse led us upstairs, single file, and down a hall past half-closed doors and dim conversations. She and Miss Darling kept saying, "Sh-sh," but we were going on tiptoe anyway; our hospital demeanor was perfect.

At this small country hospital there was no children's ward, and Myra was not really a child; they had put her in with two grey old women. A nurse was putting screens around them as we came in.

Myra was sitting up in bed, in a bulky stiff hospital gown. Her hair was down, the long braids falling over her shoulders and down the coverlet. But her face was the same, always the same.

She had been told something about the party, Miss Darling said, so the surprise would not upset her; but it seemed she had not believed, or had not understood what it was. She watched us as she used to watch in the school grounds when we played.

"Well, here we are!" said Miss Darling. "Here we are!"

And we said, "Happy birthday, Myra! Hello, Myra, happy birthday!" Myra said, "My birthday is in July." Her voice was lighter than ever, drifting, expressionless.

"Never mind when it is, really," said Miss Darling. "Pretend it's now! How old are you, Myra?"

"Eleven," Myra said. "In July."

Then we all took off our coats and emerged in our party dresses, and laid our presents, in their pale flowery wrappings on Myra's bed. Some of our mothers had made immense, complicated bows of fine satin ribbon, some of them had even taped on little bouquets of imitation roses and lilies of the valley. "Here Myra," we said, "here Myra, happy birthday." Myra did not look at us, but at the ribbons, pink and blue and speckled with silver, and the miniature bouquets; they pleased her, as the butterfly had done. An innocent look came into her face, a partial, private smile.

"Open them, Myra," said Miss Darling. "They're for you!"

Myra gathered the presents around her, fingering them, with this smile, and a cautious realization, an unexpected pride. She said, "Saturday I'm going to London to St. Joseph's Hospital."

"That's where my mother was at," somebody said. "We went and saw her. They've got all nuns there."

"My father's sister is a nun," said Myra calmly.

She began to unwrap the presents, with an air that not even Gladys could have bettered, folding the tissue paper and the ribbons, and drawing out books and puzzles and cutouts as if they were all prizes she had won. Miss Darling said that maybe she should say thank you, and the person's name with every gift she opened, to make sure she knew whom it was from, and so Myra said, "Thank you, Mary Louise, thank you, Carol," and when she came to mine she said, "Thank you, Helen." Everyone explained their presents to her and there was talking and excitement and a little gaiety, which Myra presided over, though she was not gay. A cake was brought in with *Happy Birthday Myra* written on it, pink on white, and eleven candles. Miss Darling lit the candles and we all sang Happy Birthday to You, and cried, "Make a wish, Myra, make a wish—" and Myra blew them out. Then we all had cake and strawberry ice cream.

At four o'clock a buzzer sounded and the nurse took out what was left of the cake, and the dirty dishes, and we put on our coats to go home. Everybody said, "Goodbye, Myra," and Myra sat in the bed watching us go, her back straight, not supported by any pillow, her hands resting on the gifts. But at the door I heard her call; she called, "Helen!" Only a couple of the others heard; Miss Darling did not hear, she had gone out ahead. I went back to the bed.

Myra said, "I got too many things. You take something."

"What?" I said. "It's for your birthday. You always get a lot at a birthday."

"Well you take something," Myra said. She picked up a leatherette case with a mirror in it, a comb and a nail file and a natural lipstick and a small handkerchief edged with gold thread. I had noticed it before. "You take that," she said.

"Don't you want it?"

"You take it." She put it into my hand. Our fingers touched again.

"When I come back from London," Myra said, "you can come and play at my place after school."

"Okay," I said. Outside the hospital window there was a clear carrying sound of somebody playing in the street, maybe chasing with the last snowballs of the year. This sound made Myra, her triumph and her bounty, and most of all her future in which she had found this place for me, turn shadowy, turn dark. All the presents on the bed, the folded paper and ribbons, those guilt-tinged offerings, had passed into this shadow, they were no longer innocent objects to be touched, exchanged, accepted without danger. I didn't want to take the case now but I could not think how to get out of it, what lie to tell. I'll give it away, I thought, I won't ever play with it. I would let my little brother pull it apart.

The nurse came back, carrying a glass of chocolate milk.

"What's the matter, didn't you hear the buzzer?"

So I was released, set free by the barriers which now closed about Myra, her unknown, exalted, ether-smelling hospital world, and by the treachery of my own heart. "Well thank you," I said. "Thank you for the thing. Goodbye."

Did Myra ever say goodbye? Not likely. She sat in her high bed, her delicate brown neck, rising out of a hospital gown too big for her, her brown carved face immune to treachery, her offering perhaps already forgotten, prepared to be set apart for legendary uses, as she was even in the back porch at school.

Boys and Girls

My father was a fox farmer. That is, he raised silver foxes, in pens; and in the fall and early winter, when their fur was prime, he killed them and skinned them and sold their pelts to the Hudson's Bay Company or the Montreal Fur Traders. These companies supplied us with heroic calendars to hang, one on each side of the kitchen door. Against a background of cold blue sky and black pine forests and treacherous northern rivers, plumed adventurers planted the flags of England or of France; magnificent savages bent their backs to the portage.

For several weeks before Christmas, my father worked after supper in the cellar of our house. The cellar was white-washed, and lit by a hundred-watt bulb over the worktable. My brother Laird and I sat on the top step and watched. My father removed the pelt inside-out from the body of the fox, which looked surprisingly small, mean and rat-like, deprived of its arrogant weight of fur. The naked, slippery bodies were collected in a sack and buried at the dump. One time the hired man, Henry Bailey, had taken a swipe at me with this sack, saying, "Christmas present!" My mother thought that was not funny. In fact she disliked the whole pelting operation —that was what the killing, skinning, and preparation of the furs was called—and wished it did not have to take place in the house. There was the smell. After the pelt had been

stretched inside-out on a long board my father scraped away
delicately, removing the little clotted webs of blood vessels,
the bubbles of fat; the smell of blood and animal fat, with the
strong primitive odour of the fox itself, penetrated all parts of
the house. I found it reassuringly seasonal, like the smell of
oranges and pine needles.

Henry Bailey suffered from bronchial troubles. He would
cough and cough until his narrow face turned scarlet, and his
light blue, derisive eyes filled up with tears; then he took the
lid off the stove, and, standing well back, shot out a great clot
of phlegm—hsss—straight into the heart of the flames. We
admired him for this performance and for his ability to make
his stomach growl at will, and for his laughter, which was full
of high whistlings and gurglings and involved the whole faulty
machinery of his chest. It was sometimes hard to tell what he
was laughing at, and always possible that it might be us.

After we had been sent to bed we could still smell fox and
still hear Henry's laugh, but these things, reminders of the
warm, safe, brightly lit downstairs world, seemed lost and
diminished, floating on the stale cold air upstairs. We were
afraid at night in the winter. We were not afraid of *outside*
though this was the time of year when snowdrifts curled around
our house like sleeping whales and the wind harassed us all
night, coming up from the buried fields, the frozen swamp,
with its old bugbear chorus of threats and misery. We were
afraid of *inside*, the room where we slept. At this time the
upstairs of our house was not finished. A brick chimney went
up one wall. In the middle of the floor was a square hole, with
a wooden railing around it; that was where the stairs came up.
On the other side of the stairwell were the things that nobody
had any use for any more—a soldiery roll of linoleum, standing
on end, a wicker baby carriage, a fern basket, china jugs and
basins with cracks in them, a picture of the Battle of Balaclava,
very sad to look at. I had told Laird, as soon as he was old
enough to understand such things, that bats and skeletons lived

over there; whenever a man escaped from the county jail, twenty miles away, I imagined that he had somehow let himself in the window and was hiding behind the linoleum. But we had rules to keep us safe. When the light was on, we were safe as long as we did not step off the square of worn carpet which defined our bedroom-space; when the light was off no place was safe but the beds themselves. I had to turn out the light kneeling on the end of my bed, and stretching as far as I could to reach the cord.

In the dark we lay on our beds, our narrow life rafts, and fixed our eyes on the faint light coming up the stairwell, and sang songs. Laird sang "Jingle Bells," which he would sing any time, whether it was Christmas or not, and I sang "Danny Boy." I loved the sound of my own voice, frail and supplicating, rising in the dark. We could make out the tall frosted shapes of the windows now, gloomy and white. When I came to the part, *When I am dead, as dead I well may be*—a fit of shivering caused not by the cold sheets but by pleasurable emotion almost silenced me. *You'll kneel and say, an Ave there above me*— What was an Ave? Every day I forgot to find out.

Laird went straight from singing to sleep. I could hear his long, satisfied, bubbly breaths. Now for the time that remained to me, the most perfectly private and perhaps the best time of the whole day, I arranged myself tightly under the covers and went on with one of the stories I was telling myself from night to night. These stories were about myself, when I had grown a little older; they took place in a world that was recognizably mine, yet one that presented opportunities for courage, boldness and self-sacrifice, as mine never did. I rescued people from a bombed building (it discouraged me that the real war had gone on so far away from Jubilee). I shot two rabid wolves who were menacing the schoolyard (the teachers cowered terrified at my back). I rode a fine horse spiritedly down the main street of Jubilee, acknowledging the townspeople's gratitude for some yet-to-be-worked-out piece of heroism (nobody ever rode a horse there, except King Billy in the Orangemen's Day parade). There was always riding and shooting in these stories, though I had only been on a horse twice—bareback because we did not own a saddle—and the second time I had slid right around and dropped under the horse's feet; it had stepped placidly over me. I really was learning to shoot, but I could not hit anything yet, not even tin cans on fence posts.

Alive, the foxes inhabited a world my father made for them. It was surrounded by a high guard fence, like a medieval town, with a gate that was padlocked at night. Along the streets of this town were ranged large, sturdy pens. Each of them had a real door that a man could go through, a wooden ramp along the wire, for the foxes to run up and down on, and a kennel—something like a clothes chest with airholes—where they slept and stayed in winter and had their young. There were feeding and watering dishes attached to the wire in such a way that they could be emptied and cleaned from the outside. The dishes were made of old tin cans, and the ramps and kennels of odds and ends of old lumber. Everything was tidy and ingenious; my father was tirelessly inventive and his favourite book in the world was Robinson Crusoe. He had fitted a tin drum on a wheelbarrow, for bringing water down to the pens. This was my job in summer, when the foxes had to have water twice a day. Between nine and ten o'clock in the morning, and again after supper, I filled the drum at the pump and trundled it down through the barnyard to the pens, where I parked it, and filled my watering can and went along the streets. Laird came too, with his little cream and green gardening can, filled too full and knocking against his legs and slopping water on his canvas shoes. I had the real watering can, my father's, though I could only carry it three-quarters full.

The foxes all had names, which were printed on a tin plate and hung beside their doors. They were not named when they were born, but when they survived the first year's pelting and were added to the breeding stock. Those my father had named were called names like Prince, Bob, Wally and Betty. Those I had named were called Star or Turk, or Maureen or Diana. Laird named one Maud after a hired girl we had when he was little, one Harold after a boy at school, and one Mexico, he did not say why.

Naming them did not make pets out of them, or anything like it. Nobody but my father ever went into the pens, and he had twice had blood-poisoning from bites. When I was bringing them their water they prowled up and down on the paths they had made inside their pens, barking seldom—they saved that for nighttime, when they might get up a chorus of community frenzy—but always watching me, their eyes burning, clear gold, in their pointed, malevolent faces. They were beautiful for their delicate legs and heavy, aristocratic tails and the bright fur sprinkled on dark down their backs—which gave them their name—but especially for their faces, drawn exquisitely sharp in pure hostility, and their golden eyes.

Besides carrying water I helped my father when he cut the long grass, and the lamb's quarter and flowering money-musk, that grew between the pens. He cut with the scythe and I raked into piles. Then he took a pitchfork and threw fresh-cut grass all over the top of the pens, to keep the foxes cooler and shade their coats, which were browned by too much sun. My father did not talk to me unless it was about the job we were doing. In this he was quite different from my mother, who, if she was feeling cheerful, would tell me all sorts of things—the name of a dog she had had when she was a little girl, the names of boys she had gone out with later on when she was grown up, and what certain dresses of hers had looked like—she could not imagine now what had become of them. Whatever thoughts and stories my father had were private, and I was shy of him and would never ask him questions. Nevertheless I worked willingly under his eyes, and with a feeling of pride. One time a feed salesman came down into the pens to talk to him and my father said, "Like to have you meet my new hired man." I turned away and raked furiously, red in the face with pleasure.

"Could of fooled me," said the salesman. "I thought it was only a girl."

After the grass was cut, it seemed suddenly much later in the year. I walked on stubble in the earlier evening, aware of the reddening skies, the entering silences, of fall. When I wheeled the tank out of the gate and put the padlock on, it was almost dark. One night at this time I saw my mother and father standing talking on the little rise of ground we called the gangway, in front of the barn. My father had just come from the meathouse; he had his stiff bloody apron on, and a pail of cut-up meat in his hand.

It was an odd thing to see my mother down at the barn. She did not often come out of the house unless it was to do something—hang out the wash or dig potatoes in the garden. She looked out of place, with her bare lumpy legs, not touched by the sun, her apron still on and damp across the stomach from the supper dishes. Her hair was tied up in a kerchief, wisps of it falling out. She would tie her hair up like this in the morning, saying she did not have time to do it properly, and it would stay tied up all day. It was true, too; she really did not have time. These days our back porch was piled with baskets of peaches and grapes and pears, bought in town, and onions and tomatoes and cucumbers grown at home, all waiting to be made into jelly and jam and preserves, pickles and chili sauce. In the kitchen there was a fire in the stove all day, jars clinked in boiling water, sometimes a cheesecloth bag was strung on a pole between two chairs, straining blue-black grape pulp for jelly. I was given jobs to do and I would sit at the table peeling peaches that had been soaked in the hot water, or cutting up onions, my eyes smarting and streaming. As soon as I was done I ran out of the house, trying to get out of earshot before my mother thought of what she wanted me to do next. I hated the hot dark kitchen in summer, the green blinds and the flypapers, the same old oilcloth table and wavy mirror and bumpy linoleum. My mother was too tired and preoccupied to talk to me, she had no heart to tell about the Normal School Graduation Dance; sweat trickled over her face and she was always counting under her breath, pointing at jars, dumping cups of sugar. It seemed to me that work in the house was endless, dreary and peculiarly depressing; work done out of doors, and in my father's service, was ritualistically important.

I wheeled the tank up to the barn, where it was kept, and I heard my mother saying, "Wait till Laird gets a little bigger, then you'll have a real help."

What my father said I did not hear. I was pleased by the way he stood listening, politely as he would to a salesman or a stranger, but with an air of wanting to get on with his real work. I felt my mother had no business down here and I wanted him to feel the same way. What did she mean about Laird? He was no help to anybody. Where was he now? Swinging himself sick on the swing, going around in circles, or trying to catch caterpillars. He never once stayed with me till I was finished.

"And then I can use her more in the house," I heard my mother say. She had a dead-quiet, regretful way of talking about me that always made me uneasy. "I just get my back turned and she runs off. It's not like I had a girl in the family at all."

I went and sat on a feed bag in the corner of the barn, not wanting to appear when this conversation was going on. My mother, I felt, was not to be trusted. She was kinder than my father and more easily fooled, but you could not depend on her, and the real reasons for the things she said and did were not to be known. She loved me, and she sat up late at night making a dress of the difficult style I wanted, for me to wear when school started, but she was also my enemy. She was always plotting. She was plotting now to get me to stay in the house more, although she knew I hated it (*because* she knew I hated it) and keep me from working for my father. It seemed to me she would do this simply out of perversity, and to try her power. It did not occur to me that she could be lonely, or jealous. No grown-up could be; they were too fortunate. I sat and kicked my heels monotonously against a feedbag, raising dust, and did not come out till she was gone.

At any rate, I did not expect my father to pay any attention to what she said. Who could imagine Laird doing my work— Laird remembering the padlock and cleaning out the watering-dishes with a leaf on the end of a stick, or even wheeling the tank without it tumbling over? It showed how little my mother knew about the way things really were.

I have forgotten to say what the foxes were fed. My father's bloody apron reminded me. They were fed horsemeat. At this time most farmers still kept horses, and when a horse got too old to work, or broke a leg or got down and would not get up, as they sometimes did, the owner would call my father, and he and Henry went out to the farm in the truck. Usually they shot and butchered the horse there, paying the farmer from five to twelve dollars. If they had already too much meat on hand, they would bring the horse back alive, and keep it for a few days or weeks in our stable, until the meat was needed. After the war the farmers were buying tractors and gradually getting rid of horses altogether, so it sometimes happened that we got a good healthy horse, that there was just no use for any more. If this happened in the winter we might keep the horse in our stable till spring, for we had plenty of hay and if there was a lot of snow—and the plow did not always get our road cleared—it was convenient to be able to go to town with a horse and cutter.

The winter I was eleven years old we had two horses in the stable. We did not know what names they had had before, so

we called them Mack and Flora. Mack was an old black
workhorse, sooty and indifferent. Flora was a sorrel mare, a
driver. We took them both out in the cutter. Mack was slow
and easy to handle. Flora was given to fits of violent alarm,
veering at cars and even at other horses, but we loved her speed
and high-stepping, her general air of gallantry and abandon.
On Saturdays we went down to the stable and as soon as we
opened the door on its cosy, animal-smelling darkness Flora
threw up her head, rolled her eyes, whinnied despairingly and
pulled herself through a crisis of nerves on the spot. It was
not safe to go into her stall; she would kick.

This winter also I began to hear a great deal more on the
theme my mother had sounded when she had been talking in
front of the barn. I no longer felt safe. It seemed that in the
minds of the people around me there was a steady under-
current of thought, not to be deflected, on this one subject.
The word *girl* had formerly seemed to me innocent and unbur-
dened, like the word *child;* now it appeared that it was no such
thing. A girl was not, as I had supposed, simply what I was;
it was what I had to become. It was a definition, always
touched with emphasis, with reproach and disappointment.
Also it was a joke on me. Once Laird and I were fighting, and
for the first time ever I had to use all my strength against him;
even so, he caught and pinned my arm for a moment, really
hurting me. Henry saw this, and laughed, saying, "Oh, that
there Laird's gonna show you, one of these days!" Laird was
getting a lot bigger. But I was getting bigger too.

My grandmother came to stay with us for a few weeks and
I heard other things. "Girls don't slam doors like that."
"Girls keep their knees together when they sit down." And
worse still, when I asked some questions, "That's none of girls'
business." I continued to slam the doors and sit as awkwardly
as possible, thinking that by such measures I kept myself free.

When spring came, the horses were let out in the barnyard.
Mack stood against the barn wall trying to scratch his neck

and haunches, but Flora trotted up and down and reared at the fences, clattering her hooves against the rails. Snow drifts dwindled quickly, revealing the hard grey and brown earth, the familiar rise and fall of the ground, plain and bare after the fantastic landscape of winter. There was a great feeling of opening-out, of release. We just wore rubbers now, over our shoes; our feet felt ridiculously light. One Saturday we went out to the stable and found all the doors open, letting in the unaccustomed sunlight and fresh air. Henry was there, just idling around looking at his collection of calendars which were tacked up behind the stalls in a part of the stable my mother had probably never seen.

"Come to say goodbye to your old friend Mack?" Henry said. "Here, you give him a taste of oats." He poured some oats into Laird's cupped hands and Laird went to feed Mack. Mack's teeth were in bad shape. He ate very slowly, patiently shifting the oats around in his mouth, trying to find a stump of a molar to grind it on. "Poor old Mack," said Henry mournfully. "When a horse's teeth's gone, he's gone. That's about the way."

"Are you going to shoot him today?" I said. Mack and Flora had been in the stable so long I had almost forgotten they were going to be shot.

Henry didn't answer me. Instead he started to sing in a high, trembly, mocking-sorrowful voice, *Oh, there's no more work, for poor Uncle Ned, he's gone where the good darkies go*. Mack's thick, blackish tongue worked diligently at Laird's hand. I went out before the song was ended and sat down on the gangway.

I had never seen them shoot a horse, but I knew where it was done. Last summer Laird and I had come upon a horse's entrails before they were buried. We had thought it was a big black snake, coiled up in the sun. That was around in the field that ran up beside the barn. I thought that if we went inside the barn, and found a wide crack or a knothole to look through,

we would be able to see them do it. It was not something I
wanted to see; just the same, if a thing really happened, it was
better to see it, and know.

My father came down from the house, carrying the gun.

"What are you doing here?" he said.

"Nothing."

"Go on up and play around the house."

He sent Laird out of the stable. I said to Laird, "Do you
want to see them shoot Mack?" and without waiting for an
answer led him around to the front door of the barn, opened it
carefully, and went in. "Be quiet or they'll hear us," I said.
We could hear Henry and my father talking in the stable, then
the heavy, shuffling steps of Mack being backed out of his stall.

In the loft it was cold and dark. Thin, crisscrossed beams of
sunlight fell through the cracks. The hay was low. It was a
rolling country, hills and hollows, slipping under our feet.
About four feet up was a beam going around the walls. We
piled hay up in one corner and I boosted Laird up and hoisted
myself. The beam was not very wide; we crept along it with
our hands flat on the barn walls. There were plenty of knot-
holes, and I found one that gave me the view I wanted—a
corner of the barnyard, the gate, part of the field. Laird did
not have a knothole and began to complain.

I showed him a widened crack between two boards. "Be
quiet and wait. If they hear you you'll get us in trouble."

My father came in sight carrying the gun. Henry was lead-
ing Mack by the halter. He dropped it and took out his cigarette papers and tobacco; he rolled cigarettes for my father and
himself. While this was going on Mack nosed around in the
old, dead grass along the fence. Then my father opened the
gate and they took Mack through. Henry led Mack way from
the path to a patch of ground and they talked together, not
loud enough for us to hear. Mack again began searching for a
mouthful of fresh grass, which was not to be found. My father
walked away in a straight line, and stopped short at a distance

which seemed to suit him. Henry was walking away from
Mack too, but sideways, still negligently holding on to the
halter. My father raised the gun and Mack looked up as if he
had noticed something and my father shot him.

Mack did not collapse at once but swayed, lurched sideways
and fell, first on his side; then he rolled over on his back and,
amazingly, kicked his legs for a few seconds in the air. At this
Henry laughed, as if Mack had done a trick for him. Laird,
who had drawn a long, groaning breath of surprise when the
shot was fired, said out loud, "He's not dead." And it seemed
to me it might be true. But his legs stopped, he rolled on his
side again, his muscles quivered and sank. The two men walked over and looked at him in a businesslike way; they bent
down and examined his forehead where the bullet had gone in,
and now I saw his blood on the brown grass.

"Now they just skin him and cut him up," I said. "Let's
go." My legs were a little shaky and I jumped gratefully down
into the hay. "Now you've seen how they shoot a horse," I
said in a congratulatory way, as if I had seen it many times
before. "Let's see if any barn cat's had kittens in the hay."
Laird jumped. He seemed young and obedient again. Suddenly I remembered how, when he was little, I had brought
him into the barn and told him to climb the ladder to the top
beam. That was in the spring, too, when the hay was low. I
had done it out of a need for excitement, a desire for something
to happen so that I could tell about it. He was wearing a little
bulky brown and white checked coat, made down from one of
mine. He went all the way up, just as I told him, and sat down
on the top beam with the hay far below him on one side, and the
barn floor and some old machinery on the other. Then I ran
screaming to my father, "Laird's up on the top beam!" My
father came, my mother came, my father went up the ladder
talking very quietly and brought Laird down under his arm, at
which my mother leaned against the ladder and began to cry.
They said to me, "Why weren't you watching him?" but no-

body ever knew the truth. Laird did not know enough to tell. But whenever I saw the brown and white checked coat hanging in the closet, or at the bottom of the rag bag, which was where it ended up, I felt a weight in my stomach, the sadness of un-exorcized guilt.

I looked at Laird who did not even remember this, and I did not like the look on this thin, winter-pale face. His expression was not frightened or upset, but remote, concentrating. "Listen," I said, in an unusually bright and friendly voice, "you aren't going to tell, are you?"

"No," he said absently.

"Promise."

"Promise," he said. I grabbed the hand behind his back to make sure he was not crossing his fingers. Even so, he might have a nightmare; it might come out that way. I decided I had better work hard to get all thoughts of what he had seen out of his mind—which, it seemed to me, could not hold very many things at a time. I got some money I had saved and that after-noon we went into Jubilee and saw a show, with Judy Canova, at which we both laughed a great deal. After that I thought it would be all right.

Two weeks later I knew they were going to shoot Flora. I knew from the night before, when I heard my mother ask if the hay was holding out all right, and my father said, "Well, after to-morrow there'll just be the cow, and we should be able to put her out to grass in another week." So I knew it was Flora's turn in the morning.

This time I didn't think of watching it. That was something to see just one time. I had not thought about it very often since, but sometimes when I was busy, working at school, or standing in front of the mirror combing my hair and wondering if I would be pretty when I grew up, the whole scene would flash into my mind: I would see the easy, practised way my father raised the gun, and hear Henry laughing when Mack kicked his legs in the air. I did not have any great feeling of horror and opposition, such as a city child might have had; I was too used to seeing the death of animals as a necessity by which we lived. Yet I felt a little ashamed, and there was a new wariness, a sense of holding-off, in my attitude to my father and his work.

It was a fine day, and we were going around the yard picking up tree branches that had been torn off in winter storms. This was something we had been told to do, and also we wanted to use them to make a teepee. We heard Flora whinny, and then my father's voice and Henry's shouting, and we ran down to the barnyard to see what was going on.

The stable door was open. Henry had just brought Flora out, and she had broken away from him. She was running free in the barnyard, from one end to the other. We climbed up on the fence. It was exciting to see her running, whinnying, going up on her hind legs, prancing and threatening like a horse in a Western movie, an unbroken ranch horse, though she was just an old driver, an old sorrel mare. My father and Henry ran after her and tried to grab the dangling halter. They tried to work her into a corner, and they had almost succeeded when she made a run between them, wild-eyed, and disappeared around the corner of the barn. We heard the rails clatter down as she got over the fence, and Henry yelled, "She's into the field now!"

That meant she was in the long L-shaped field that ran up by the house. If she got around the center, heading towards the lane, the gate was open; the truck had been driven into the field this morning. My father shouted to me, because I was on the other side of the fence, nearest the lane, "Go shut the gate!"

I could run very fast. I ran across the garden, past the tree where our swing was hung, and jumped across a ditch into the lane. There was the open gate. She had not got out, I could not see her up on the road; she must have run to the other end of the field. The gate was heavy. I lifted it out of the gravel and carried it across the roadway. I had it half-way across

when she came in sight, galloping straight towards me. There
was just time to get the chain on. Laird came scrambling
through the ditch to help me.

Instead of shutting the gate, I opened it as wide as I could.
I did not make any decision to do this, it was just what I did.
Flora never slowed down; she galloped straight past me, and
Laird jumped up and down, yelling, "Shut it, shut it!" even
after it was too late. My father and Henry appeared in the field
a moment too late to see what I had done. They only saw Flora
heading for the township road. They would think I had not
got there in time.

They did not waste any time asking about it. They went
back to the barn and got the gun and the knives they used, and
put these in the truck; then they turned the truck around and
came bouncing up the field toward us. Laird called to them,
"Let me go too, let me go too!" and Henry stopped the truck
and they took him in. I shut the gate after they were all gone.

I supposed Laird would tell. I wondered what would happen
to me. I had never disobeyed my father before, and I could
not understand why I had done it. Flora would not really get
away. They would catch up with her in the truck. Or if they
did not catch her this morning somebody would see her and
telephone us this afternoon or tomorrow. There was no wild
country here for her to run to, only farms. What was more,
my father had paid for her, we needed the meat to feed the
foxes, we needed the foxes to make our living. All I had done
was make more work for my father who worked hard enough
already. And when my father found out about it he was not
going to trust me any more; he would know that I was not
entirely on his side. I was on Flora's side, and that made me
no use to anybody, not even to her. Just the same, I did not
regret it; when she came running at me and I held the gate
open, that was the only thing I could do.

I went back to the house, and my mother said, "What's all
the commotion?" I told her that Flora had kicked down the

fence and got away. "Your poor father," she said, "now he'll have to go chasing over the countryside. Well, there isn't any use planning dinner before one." She put up the ironing board. I wanted to tell her, but thought better of it and went upstairs and sat on my bed.

Lately I had been trying to make my part of the room fancy, spreading the bed with old lace curtains, and fixing myself a dressing-table with some leftovers of cretonne for a skirt. I planned to put up some kind of barricade between my bed and Laird's, to keep my section separate from his. In the sunlight, the lace curtains were just dusty rags. We did not sing at night any more. One night when I was singing Laird said, "You sound silly," and I went right on but the next night I did not start. There was not so much need to anyway, we were no longer afraid. We knew it was just old furniture over there, old jumble and confusion. We did not keep to the rules. I still stayed awake after Laird was asleep and told myself stories, but even in these stories something different was happening, mysterious alterations took place. A story might start off in the old way, with a spectacular danger, a fire or wild animals, and for a while I might rescue people; then things would change around, and instead, somebody would be rescuing me. It might be a boy from our class at school, or even Mr. Campbell, our teacher, who tickled girls under the arms. And at this point the story concerned itself at great length with what I looked like—how long my hair was, and what kind of dress I had on; by the time I had these details worked out the real excitement of the story was lost.

It was later than one o'clock when the truck came back. The tarpaulin was over the back, which meant there was meat in it. My mother had to heat dinner up all over again. Henry and my father had changed from their bloody overalls into ordinary working overalls in the barn, and they washed their arms and necks and faces at the sink, and splashed water on their hair and combed it. Laird lifted his arm to show off a streak of blood. "We shot old Flora," he said, "and cut her up in fifty pieces."

"Well I don't want to hear about it," my mother said. "And don't come to my table like that."

My father made him go and wash the blood off.

We sat down and my father said grace and Henry pasted his chewing-gum on the end of his fork, the way he always did; when he took it off he would have us admire the pattern. We began to pass the bowls of steaming, overcooked vegetables. Laird looked across the table at me and said proudly, distinctly, "Anyway it was her fault Flora got away."

"What?" my father said.

"She could of shut the gate and she didn't. She just open' it up and Flora run out."

"Is that right?" my father said.

Everybody at the table was looking at me. I nodded, swallowing food with great difficulty. To my shame, tears flooded my eyes.

My father made a curt sound of disgust. "What did you do that for?"

I did not answer. I put down my fork and waited to be sent from the table, still not looking up.

But this did not happen. For some time nobody said anything, then Laird said matter-of-factly, "She's crying."

"Never mind," my father said. He spoke with resignation, even good humour, the words which absolved and dismissed me for good. "She's only a girl," he said.

I didn't protest that, even in my heart. Maybe it was true.

Postcard

Yesterday afternoon, yesterday, I was going along the street to the Post Office, thinking how sick I was of snow, sore throats, the whole dragged-out tail-end of winter, and I wished I could pack off to Florida, like Clare. It was Wednesday afternoon, my half-day. I work in King's Department Store, which is nothing but a ready-to-wear and dry goods, in spite of the name. They used to have groceries, but I can just barely recall that. Momma used to take me in and set me on the high stool and old Mr. King would give me a handful of raisins and say, I only give them to the pretty girls. They took the groceries out when he died, old Mr. King, and it isn't even King's Department Store any more, it belongs to somebody named Kruberg. They never come near it themselves, just send Mr. Hawes in for manager. I run the upstairs, Children's Wear, and put in the Toyland at Christmas. I've been there fourteen years and Hawes doesn't pick on me, knowing I wouldn't take it if he did.

It being Wednesday the wickets in the Post Office were closed, but I had my key. I unlocked our box and took out the Jubilee paper, in Momma's name, the phone bill and a postcard I very nearly missed. I looked at the picture on it first and it showed me palm trees, a hot blue sky, the front of a motel with a sign out front in the shape of a big husky blonde creature, lit up

with neon I suppose at night. She was saying *Sleep at my place*—
that is, a balloon with those words in it came out of her mouth.
I turned it over and read, *I didn't sleep at her place though it was too
expensive. Weather could not be better. Mid-seventies. How is the
winter treating you in Jubilee? Not bad I hope. Be a good girl. Clare.*
The date was ten days back. Well, sometimes postcards are
slow, but I bet what happened was he carried this around in
his pocket a few days before he remembered to mail it. It was
my only card since he left for Florida three weeks ago, and here
I was expecting him back in person Friday or Saturday. He
made this trip every winter with his sister Porky and her husband, Harold, who lived in Windsor. I had the feeling they
didn't like me, but Clare said it was my imagination. Whenever I had to talk to Porky I would make some mistake like
saying something was irrevelant to me when I know the word is
irrelevant, and she never let on but I thought about it afterwards and burned. Though I know it serves me right for trying
to talk the way I never would normally talk in Jubilee. Trying
to impress her because she's a MacQuarrie, after all my lecturing Momma that *we*'re as good as *them*.

I used to say to Clare, write me a *letter* while you're away,
and he would say, what do you want me to write about? So I
told him to describe the scenery and the people he met, anything would be a pleasure for me to hear about, since I had
never been further away from home than Buffalo, for pleasure
(I won't count that train trip when I took Momma to Winnipeg
to see relatives). But Clare said, I can tell you just as well when
I get back. He never did, though. When I saw him again I
would say, well, tell me all about your trip and he would say,
what do you want me to tell? That just aggravated me, because
how would *I* know?

I saw Momma waiting for me, watching through the little
window in the front door. She opened the door when I turned
in our walk and called out, "Watch yourself, its slippery. The
milkman nearly took a header this morning."

"There's days when I think I wouldn't mind breaking a leg," I said, and she said, "Don't *say* things like that, its just asking for punishment."

"Clare sent you a postcard," I said.

"Oh, he did not!" She turned it over and said, "Addressed to you, just as I thought." But she was smiling away. "I don't care for the picture he picked but maybe you don't get much choice down there."

Clare was probably a favourite with old ladies from the time he could walk. To them he was still a nice fat boy, so mannerly, not stuck-up in spite of being a MacQuarrie, and with a way of teasing that perked them up and turned them pink. They had a dozen games going, Momma and Clare, that I could never keep up with. One was him knocking at the door and saying something like, "Good-evening, ma'am, I just wondered if I could interest you in a course in body development I'm selling to put myself through college." And Momma would swallow and put on a stern face and say, "Look here, young man do I look like I need a course in body development?" Or he would look doleful and say, "Ma'am, I'm here because I'm concerned about your soul." Momma would roar laughing. "You be concerned about your own," she said, and fed him chicken dumplings and lemon meringue pie, all his favourites. He told her jokes at the table I never thought she'd listen to. "Did you hear about this old gentleman married a young wife and he went to the doctor? Doctor he says I'm having a bit of trouble—" "Stop it," Momma said—but she waited till he was through— "you are just embarrassing Helen Louise." I have got rid of the Louise on the end of my name everywhere but at home. Clare picked it up from Momma and I told him I didn't care for it but he went right on. Sometimes I felt like their child, sitting between him and Momma with both of them joking and enjoying their food and telling me I smoked too much and if I didn't straighten up I'd get permanent round shoulders. Clare

was—is—twelve years older than I am and I don't ever remember him except as a grown-up man.

I used to see him on the street and he seemed old to me then, at
least old the way almost everybody grown-up did. He is one of
those people who look older than they are when they're young
and younger than they are when they're old. He was always
around the Queen's Hotel. Being a MacQuarrie he never had
to work too hard and he had a little office and did some work
as a notary public and a bit of insurance and real estate. He
still has the same place, and the front window is always bleary
and dusty and there's a light burning in the back, winter and
summer, where a lady about eighty years old, Miss Maitland,
does his typing or whatever he gives her to do. If he's not in the
Queen's Hotel he has one or two of his friends sitting around
the space heater doing a little card playing, a little quiet drinking, mostly just talking. There's a certain kind of men in
Jubilee and I guess every small town that you might call public
men. I don't mean public *figures*, important enough to run
for Parliament or even for mayor (though Clare could do that
if he wanted to be serious), just men who are always around on
the main street and you get to know their faces. Clare and
those friends of his are like that.

"He down there with his sister?" Momma said, as if I hadn't
told her. A lot of my conversations with Momma are replays.
"What is that name they call her?"

"Porky," I said.

"Yes, I remember thinking, that's some name for a grown
woman. And I remember her being baptized and her name
was Isabelle. Way back before I was married, I was still singing in the choir. They had one of these long, fangle-dangle
christening robes on her, you know them." Momma had a
soft spot for Clare but not for the MacQuarrie family. She
thought they were being stuck-up when they just breathed.
I remember a year or two ago, us going past their place, and

she said something about being careful not to step on the grass of the *Mansion*, and I told her, "Momma, in a few years' time I am going to be living here, this is going to be *my house*, so you better stop calling it the Mansion in that tone of voice." She and I both looked up at the house with all its dark green awnings decorated with big, white, old-English Ms, and all the verandahs and the stained-glass window set in the side wall, like in a church. No sign of life, but upstairs old Mrs. Mac-Quarrie was lying, and is still, paralyzed down one side and not able to speak, Willa Montgomery tending her by day and Clare by night. Strange voices in the house upset her, and every time Clare took me in we could only whisper so she wouldn't hear me and throw some kind of paralytic fit. After her long look Momma said, "It's a funny thing but I can't imagine your name MacQuarrie."

"I thought you were so fond of Clare."

"Well I am, but I just think of him coming to get you Saturday night, him coming to dinner Sunday night, I don't think of you and him married."

"You wait and see what happens when the old lady passes on."

"Is that what he told you?"

"It's understood."

"Well imagine," Momma said.

"You don't need to act like he's doing me a favour because I can tell you there are plenty of people would consider it the other way round."

"Can't I open my mouth without you taking offense?" said Momma mildly.

Clare and I used to slip in the side door on Saturday nights and make coffee and something to eat in the high, old-fashioned kitchen, being as quiet and sneaky about it as two kids after school. Then we'd tiptoe up the back stairs to Clare's room and turn on the television so she'd think he was by himself, watching that. If she called him I'd lie alone in the big bed watching the programme or looking at the old pictures on the wall—him on the high-school hockey team playing goalie, Porky in her graduation outfit, him and Porky and friends I didn't know on holidays. If she kept him a long time and I got bored I would get downstairs under cover of the television and have more coffee. (I never drank anything stronger, left that to Clare.) With just the kitchen light to see by I'd go into the dining room and pull out the drawers and look at her linen and open the china cabinet and the silver chest and feel like a thief. But I'd think, why shouldn't I have the enjoyment of this and the name MacQuarrie since I wouldn't have to do anything I'm not doing anyway? Clare said, "Marry me," soon after we started going out together and I said, "Don't bother me, I don't want to think about getting married," and he quit. When I brought it up myself, these years later, he seemed pleased. He said, "Well, there's not many old buffaloes like me hear a pretty girl like you say she wants to marry them." I thought, wait till I get married and go into King's Department Store and send Hawes scurrying around waiting on me, the old horse's neck. Wouldn't I like to give him a bad time, but I'd restrain myself, out of good taste.

"I'm going to take that postcard now and put it in my box," I said to Momma. "And I can't think of a better way for us to spend this afternoon than for us both to take naps." I went upstairs and put on my dressing gown (Chinese-embroidered, and Clare's present). I creamed my face and got out the box I keep postcards and letters and other mementoes in, and I put it with the Florida postcards from other years and some from Banff and Jasper and the Grand Canyon and Yellowstone Park. Then just idling away the time I looked at my school pictures and report cards and the programme for *H.M.S. Pinafore*, put on by the high school, in which I was the heroine, what's-her-name, the captain's daughter. I remember Clare meeting me on the street and congratulating me on my singing and how pretty I looked and me flirting with him a bit just because he seemed so old and safe and I would as soon flirt as turn around, I was so pleased with myself. Wouldn't I have been surprised if I had seen all of what was going to happen? I hadn't even met Ted Forgie, then.

I knew his letter just from looking at the outside, and I never read it anymore, but just out of curiosity I opened it up and started off. *I usually hate to write a typewritten letter because it lacks the personal touch but I am so worn out tonight with all the unfamiliar pressures here that I hope you will forgive me.* Typewritten or not it used to be that just looking at that letter I would get a feeling of love, if that is what you want to call it, strong enough to pretty near crumple me up and knock me over. Ted Forgie was an announcer at the Jubilee radio station for six months, around the time I was finishing high school. Momma said he was too old for me—she never said that about Clare—but all he was was twenty-four. He had spent two years in a San with T.B. and that had made him old for his years. We used to go up on Sullivan's Hill and he talked about how he had lived with death staring him in the face and he knew the value of being close to one human being, but all he had found was loneliness. He said he wanted to put his head down in my lap and weep, but all the time what he *was* doing was something else. When he went away I just turned into a sleepwalker. I only woke up in the afternoons when I went to the post office and opened the box with my knees going hollow, to see if I had a letter. And I never did, after that one. Places bothered me. Sullivan's Hill, the radio station, the coffee shop of the Queen's Hotel. I don't know how many hours I spent in that coffee shop, reciting in my head every conversation we ever had and visualizing every look on his face, not really comprehending yet that wishing wasn't going to drag him through that door again. I got friendly with Clare in there. He said I looked like I needed cheering up and he told me some of his stories. I never let on to him what my trouble was but when we started going out I explained to him that friendship was all I could offer. He said he appreciated that and he would bide his time. And he did.

I read the letter all the way through and I thought, not for the first time, well reading this letter any fool can see there is not going to be another. *I want you to know how grateful I am for all your sweetness and understanding. Sweetness* was the only word stuck in my mind then, to give me hope. I thought, when Clare and I get married I am just going to throw this letter away. So why not do it now? I tore it across and across and it was easy like tearing up notes when school is over. Then because I didn't want Momma commenting on what was in my wastepaper basket I wadded it up and put it in my purse. That being over I lay down on my bed and thought about several things. For instance, if I hadn't been in a stupor over Ted Forgie, would I have taken a different view of Clare? Not likely. If I hadn't been in that stupor I might have never bothered with Clare at all, I'd have gone off and done something different; but no use thinking about that now. The fuss he made at first made me sorry for him. I used to look down at his round balding head and listen to all his groaning and commotion and think, what can I do now except be polite? He didn't expect anything more of me, never expected anything, but just to lie there and let him, and I got used to that. I looked back and thought am I a heartless person, just to lie there and let him grab me and love me and moan around my neck and say the things he did, and never say one loving word back to him? I never wanted to be a heartless person and I was never mean to Clare, and I did let him, didn't I, nine times out of ten?

I heard Momma get up from her nap and go and put the kettle on so she could have a cup of tea and read her paper. Then some little time later she gave a yell and I thought somebody had died so I jumped off the bed and ran into the hall, but she was there underneath saying, "Go on back to your nap, I'm sorry I scared you. I made a mistake." I did go back and I heard her using the phone, probably calling one of her old cronies about some news in the paper, and then I guess I fell asleep.

What woke me was a car stopping, somebody getting out and coming up the front walk. I thought, is it Clare back early? And then, confused and half-asleep, I thought, I already tore up the letter, that's good. But it wasn't his step. Momma opened the door before the bell got a chance to ring and I heard Alma Stonehouse, who teaches at the Jubilee Public School and is my best friend. I went out in the hall and leaned over and called down, "Hey Alma are you eating here *again*?" She boards at Bailey's where the food has its ups and downs and when she smells their Shepherd's Pie she sometimes heads over to our place without an invitation.

Alma started upstairs without taking her coat off, her thin dark face just blazing with excitement so I knew something had happened. I thought it must have to do with her husband, because they are separated and he writes her terrible letters. She said, "Helen, hi, how are you feeling? Did you just wake up?"

"I heard your car," I said. "I thought for a minute maybe it was Clare but I'm not expecting him for another couple of days."

"Helen. Can you sit down? Come in your room where you can sit down. Are you prepared to get a shock? I wish I wasn't the one had to tell you. Hold yourself steady."

I saw Momma right behind her and I said, "Momma, is this some joke?"

Alma said, "Clare MacQuarrie has gotten married."

"What are you two up to?" I said. "Clare MacQuarrie is in Florida and I just today got a postcard from him as Momma well knows."

"He got married in Florida. Helen, be calm."

"How could he get married in Florida, he's on his holidays?"

"They're on their way to Jubilee right now and they're going to live here."

"Alma, wherever you heard that its a lot of garbage. I just had a postcard from him. Momma—"

Then I saw that Momma was looking at me like I was eight years old and had the measles and a temperature of a hundred and five degrees. She was holding the paper and she spread it out for me to read. "It's in there," she said, probably not realizing she was whispering. "It's written up in the *Bugle-Herald*."

"I don't believe it any more than fly," I said, and I started to read and read all the way through as if the names were ones I'd never heard of before, and some of them were. A quiet ceremony in Coral Gables, Florida, uniting in marriage Clare Alexander MacQuarrie, of Jubilee, son of Mrs. James MacQuarrie of this town and the late Mr. James MacQuarrie, prominent local businessman and long-time Member of Parliament, and Mrs. Margaret Thora Leeson, daughter of the late Mrs. and Mrs. Clive Tibbutt of Lincoln, Nebraska. Mr. and Mrs. Harold Johnson, sister and brother-in-law of the bridegroom, were the only attendants. The bride wore a sage green dressmaker suit with dark brown accessories and a corsage of bronze orchids. Mrs. Johnson wore a beige suit with black accessories and green orchids. The couple were at present travelling by automobile to their future home in Jubilee.

"Do you still think its garbage?" Alma said severely.

I said I didn't know.

"Are you feeling all right?"

All right.

Momma said we would all feel better if we went downstairs and had a cup of tea and something to eat, instead of staying cooped up in this little bedroom. It was about supper time, anyway. So we all trooped down, me still in my dressing gown, and Momma and Alma together prepared the sort of meal you might eat to keep your strength up when there is sickness in the house and you can't really bother too much about food. Cold meat sandwiches and little dishes of different pickles and sliced cheese and date squares. "Smoke a cigarette if you want to," Momma said to me—the first time she ever said *that* in her life. So I did, and Alma did, and Alma said, "I brought some tranquillizers along in my purse, they're not very strong and you're welcome to one or two." I said no thanks, not yet, anyway. I said I couldn't seem to take it in yet.

"He goes to Florida every year, right?"

I said yes.

"Well what I think is this, that he's met this woman before— widow or divorcee or whatever she is—and they have been corresponding and planning this all along."

Momma said it was awfully hard to think that of Clare.

"I'm only saying how it looks to me. And she's his sister's friend, I'll bet. The sister engineered it. They were the attendants, the sister and her husband. She wasn't any friend of yours, Helen, I remember you telling me."

"I didn't hardly know her."

"Helen Louise you told me you and him were just waiting for the old lady to pass on," Momma said. "Isn't that what he said to you? Clare?"

"Using her for an excuse," Alma said briskly.

"Oh, he wouldn't," Momma said. "Oh, its so hard to understand it—*Clare*!"

"Men are always out for what they can get," Alma said. There was a pause, both of them looking at me. I couldn't tell them anything. I couldn't tell them what I was thinking, which was about the last Saturday night up at his place, before he went away, him naked as a baby pulling my hair across his face and through his teeth and pretending he was going to bite it off. I didn't relish anybody's saliva in my hair but I let him, just warning him that if he did bite it off he would have to pay for me going to the hairdresser's to get it evened. He didn't act that night like anybody that is going off to be *married*.

Momma and Alma went on talking and speculating and I got sleepier and sleepier. I heard Alma say, "Worse things could happen. I had four years of living hell." And Momma say, "He was always the soul of kindness and he doted on that girl." I wondered how I could possibly be so sleepy, this early in the evening and after having a nap in the afternoon. Alma said, "Its very good you're sleepy, its nature's way. Nature's way, just like an anaesthetic." They both got me upstairs and into bed and I never heard them go down.

I didn't wake up early, either. I got up when I usually did and got my own breakfast. I could hear Momma stirring but I yelled to her to stay put, like any other morning. She called down, "Are you sure you want to go to work? I could phone Mr. Hawes you're sick." I said, "Why should I give any of them the satisfaction?" I did my makeup at the hall mirror without a light and went out and walked the two and a half blocks to King's, not noticing what kind of a morning it was, beyond the fact that it hadn't turned into spring overnight. Inside the store they were waiting, oh, how nice, good morning Helen, good morning Helen, such quiet kind hopeful voices waiting to see if I'm going to fall flat on the floor and start having hysterics. Mrs. McCool, Beryl Allen with her engagement ring, Mrs. Kress that got jilted herself twenty-five years ago and then took up with somebody else—Kress—and *he* vanished. What's she looking at me for? Old Hawes chewing his tongue when he smiles. I said good morning perfectly cheerfully and went on upstairs thanking God I have my own washroom and thinking, I bet this will be a big day for Children's Wear. It was, too. I never had a morning with so many mothers in to buy a hair ribbon or a little pair of socks, willing to climb that stairs for it.

I phoned Momma I wouldn't be home at noon. I thought I'd just go over to the Queen's Hotel and have a hamburger, with all the radio people I hardly know. But at a quarter to twelve in comes Alma. "I wouldn't let you eat by yourself *this* day!" So we have to go to the Queen's Hotel together. She was going to make me eat an egg sandwich, not a hamburger, and a glass of milk not coke, because she said my digestion was probably in a state, but I vetoed that. She waited till we got our food and were settled down to eating before she said, "Well, they're back."

It took a minute for me to know who. "When?" I said.

"Last night around supper time. Just when I was driving over to your place to break you the news. I might've run into them."

"Who told you?"

"Well Beechers live next to MacQuarries, don't they?" Mrs. Beecher teaches Grade Four, Alma Grade Three. "Grace saw them. She had already read the paper so she knew who it was."

"What is she like?" I said in spite of myself.

"She's no juvenile, Grace said. His age, anyway. What did I tell you it was his sister's friend? And she won't win any prizes in the looks department. Mind you she's all *right*."

"Is she big or little?" I couldn't stop now. "Dark or fair?"

"She had a hat on so Grace couldn't see the colour of her hair but she thought dark. She's a big woman. Grace said she had a rear end on her like a grand piano. Maybe she has money."

"Did Grace say that too?"

"No. I said it. Just speculating."

"Clare doesn't need to marry anybody with money. *He* has money."

"That's by our standards, maybe but not by his."

I kept thinking through the afternoon that Clare would come round, or at least phone me. Then I could start asking him

what did he think he had done. I made up in my mind some
crazy explanations he might give me, like this poor woman
had cancer and only six months to live and she had always been
deadly poor (a scrub-woman in his motel) and he wanted to
give her a little time of ease. Or that she was blackmailing his
brother-in-law about a crooked transaction and he married
her to shut her up. But I didn't have time to think up many
stories because of the steady stream of customers. Old ladies
puffing up the stairs with some story about birthday presents
for their grandchildren. Every grandchild in Jubilee must
have a birthday in March. They ought to be grateful to me,
I thought, haven't I given their day a bit of excitement? Even
Alma, she was looking better than she has all winter. I'm not
blaming her, I thought, but it's the truth. And who knows,
maybe I'd be the same if Don Stonehouse showed up like he
threatens to and raped her and left her a mass of purple
bruises—his words not mine—from head to foot. I'd be as
sorry as could be, and anything I could do to help her, I'd do,
but I might think well, awful as it is its something happening
and its been a long winter.

There was no use even thinking about not going home for
supper, that would finish Momma. There she was waiting with
a salmon loaf, cabbage and carrot salad with raisins in it, that
I like, and Brown Betty. But halfway through this the tears
started sliding down over her rouge. "It seems to me like I'm
the one ought to do the crying if anybody has to do it," I said.
"What's so terrible happened to you?"

"Well I was just so fond of him," she said. "I was that fond
of him. At my age there's not too many people that you look
forward to them coming all week."

"Well I'm sorry," I said.

"But once a man loses his respect for a girl, he is apt to get
tired of her."

"What do you mean by that, Momma?"

"If you don't know am I supposed to tell you?"

"You ought to be ashamed," I said, starting to cry too. "Talking like that to your own daughter." There! And I always thought she didn't know. Never blame Clare, of course, blame me.

"No, I'm not the one that ought to be ashamed," she continued, weeping. "I am an old woman but I know. If a man loses respect for a girl he don't marry her."

"If that was true there wouldn't be hardly one marriage in this town."

"You destroyed your own chances."

"You never said a word of this to me as long as he was coming here and I am not listening to it now," I said, and went upstairs. She didn't come after me. I sat and smoked, hour after hour. I didn't get undressed. I heard her come upstairs, go to bed. Then I went down and watched television for a while, news of car accidents. I put on my coat and went out.

I have a little car Clare gave me a year ago Christmas, a little Morris. I don't use it for work because driving two and a half blocks looks to me silly, and like showing off, though I know people who do it. I went around to the garage and backed it out. This was the first time I had driven it since the Sunday I took Momma to Tuppertown to see Auntie Kay in the nursing-home. I use it more in summer.

I looked at my watch and the time surprised me. Twenty after twelve. I felt shaky and weak from sitting so long. I wished now I had one of Alma's pills. I had an idea of just taking off, driving, but I didn't know which direction to go in. I drove around the streets of Jubilee and didn't see another car out but mine. All the houses in darkness, the streets black, the yards pale with the last snow. It seemed to me that in every one of those houses lived people who knew something I didn't. Who understood what had happened and perhaps had known it was going to happen and I was the only one who didn't know.

I drove out Grove Street and on to Minnie Street and saw his house from the back. No lights on there either. I drove around to see it from the front. Did they have to sneak up the stairs and keep the television on? I wondered. No woman with a rear end like a grand piano would settle for that. I bet he took her right up and into the old lady's room and said, "This is the new Mrs. MacQuarrie," and that was that.

I parked the car and rolled down the window. Then without thinking what I was going to do I leaned on the horn and sounded it as long and hard as I could stand.

The sound released me, so I could yell. And I did. "Hey Clare MacQuarrie, I want to talk to you!"

No answer anywhere. "Clare MacQuarrie!" I shouted up at his dark house. "Clare come on out!" I sounded the horn again, two, three, I don't know how many times. In between I yelled. I felt as if I was watching myself, way down here, so little, pounding my fist and yelling and leaning on the horn. Carrying on a commotion, doing whatever came into my head. It was enjoyable, in a way. I almost forgot what I was doing it for. I started honking the horn rhythmically and yelling at the same time. "Clare aren't you ever coming out? Clare MacQuarrie for nuts-in-May, if he don't come we'll pull-him-away—" I was crying as well as yelling, right out in the street, and it didn't bother me one bit.

"Helen you want to wake everybody up in this whole town?" said Buddy Shields, sticking his head in at the window. He is the night constable and I used to teach him in Sunday school.

"I'm just conducting a shivaree for the newly-married couple," I said. "What is the matter with that?"

"I got to tell you to stop that noise."

"I don't feel like stopping."

"Oh yes you do, Helen, you're just a little upset."

"I called and called him and he won't come out," I said. "All I want is him to come out."

"Well you got to be a good girl and stop honking that horn."

"I want him to come out."

"Stop it. Don't honk that horn one more time."

"Will you make him come out?"

"Helen I can't make a man come out of his own house if he don't want to come."

"I thought you were the Law, Buddy Shields."

"I am but there is a limit to what the Law can do. If you want to see him why don't you come back in the daytime and knock on his door nice the way any lady would do?"

"He is married in case you didn't know."

"Well Helen he is married just as much at night as in the daytime."

"Is that supposed to be funny?"

"No it's not, it's supposed to be true. Now why don't you move over and let me drive you home? Lookit the lights on up and down this street. There's Grace Beecher watching us and I can see the Holmses got their windows up. You don't want to give them anything more to talk about, do you?"

"They got nothing to do but talk anyway, they may as well talk about me."

Then Buddy Shields straightened up and moved a little away from the car window and I saw somebody in dark clothes coming across the MacQuarries' lawn and it was Clare. He was not wearing a dressing gown or anything, he was all dressed, in shirt and jacket and trousers. He came right up to the car while I sat there waiting to hear what I would say to him. He had not changed. He was a fat, comfortable, sleepy-faced man. But just his look, his everyday easygoing look, stopped me wanting to cry or yell. I could cry and yell till I was blue in the face and it would not change that look or make him get out of bed and across his yard one little bit faster.

"Helen, go on home," he said, like we had been watching television and so on all evening and now was time to go home and go to bed properly. "Give my love to your Momma," he said. "Go on home."

That was all he meant to say. He looked at Buddy and said, "You going to drive her?" and Buddy said yes. I was looking at Clare MacQuarrie and thinking, he is a man that goes his own way. It didn't bother him too much how I was feeling when he did what he did on top of me, and it didn't bother him too much what kind of ruckus I made in the street when he got married. And he was a man who didn't give out explanations, maybe didn't have any. If there was anything he couldn't explain, well, he would just forget about it. Here were all his neighbours watching us, but tomorrow, if he met them on the street, he would tell them a funny story. And what about me? Maybe if he met me on the street one of these days he would just say, "How are you doing, Helen?" and tell me a joke. And if I had really thought about what he was like, Clare MacQuarrie, if I had paid attention, I would have started out a lot differently with him and maybe felt differently too, though heaven knows if that would have mattered, in the end.

"Now aren't you sorry you made all this big fuss?" Buddy said, and I slid over on the seat and watched Clare going back to his house, thinking, yes, that's what I should have done, paid attention. Buddy said, "You're not going to bother him and his wife any more now, are you Helen?"

"What?" I said.

"You're not going to bother Clare and his wife any more? Because now he's married, that's over and done with. And you wake up tomorrow morning, you're going to feel pretty bad over what you done tonight, you won't see how you can go on and face people. But let me tell you things happen all the time, only thing to do is just go along, and remember you're not the only one." It never seemed to occur to him that it was funny for him to be lecturing me, that used to hear his Bible verses and caught him reading Leviticus on the sly.

"Like last week I'll tell you," he said, easing down Grove Street, in no hurry to get me home and have the lecture ended,

"last week we got a call and we had to go out to Dunnock
Swamp and there's a car stuck in there. This old farmer was
waving a loaded gun and talking about shooting this pair for
trespassing if they didn't get off of his property. They'd just
been following a wagon track after dark, where any idiot
would know you'd get stuck this time of year. You would
know both of them if I said their names and you'd know they
had no business being in that car together. One is a married
lady. And worst is, by this time her husband is wondering
why she don't come home from choir practice—both these
parties sings in the choir, I won't tell you which one—and he
has reported her missing. So we got to get a tractor to haul
out the car, and leave *him* there sweating, and quieten down
this old farmer, and then take her home separate in broad
daylight, crying all the way. That's what I mean by things
happening. I saw that man and wife downstreet buying their
groceries yesterday, and they didn't look too happy but there
they were. So just be a good girl Helen and go along like the
rest of us and pretty soon we'll see spring."

Oh, Buddy Shields, you can just go on talking, and Clare
will tell jokes, and Momma will cry, till she gets over it, but
what I'll never understand is why, right now, seeing Clare
MacQuarrie as an unexplaining man, I felt for the first time
that I wanted to reach out my hands and *touch* him.

Red Dress—1946

My mother was making me a dress. All through the month
of November I would come from school and find her in the
kitchen, surrounded by cut-up red velvet and scraps of tissue-
paper pattern. She worked at an old treadle machine pushed
up against the window to get the light, and also to let her look
out, past the stubble fields and bare vegetable garden, to see
who went by on the road. There was seldom anybody to see.

The red velvet material was hard to work with, it pulled,
and the style my mother had chosen was not easy either. She
was not really a good sewer. She liked to make things; that is
different. Whenever she could she tried to skip basting and
pressing and she took no pride in the fine points of tailoring,
the finishing of buttonholes and the overcasting of seams as,
for instance, my aunt and my grandmother did. Unlike them
she started off with an inspiration, a brave and dazzling idea;
from that moment on, her pleasure ran downhill. In the first
place she could never find a pattern to suit her. It was no
wonder; there were no patterns made to match the ideas that
blossomed in her head. She had made me, at various times
when I was younger, a flowered organdie dress with a high
Victorian neckline edged in scratchy lace, with a poke bonnet
to match; a Scottish plaid outfit with a velvet jacket and tam;
an embroidered peasant blouse worn with a full red skirt and

black laced bodice. I had worn these clothes with docility, even pleasure, in the days when I was unaware of the world's opinion. Now, grown wiser, I wished for dresses like those my friend Lonnie had, bought at Beale's store.

I had to try it on. Sometimes Lonnie came home from school with me and she would sit on the couch watching. I was embarrassed by the way my mother crept around me, her knees creaking, her breath coming heavily. She muttered to herself. Around the house she wore no corset or stockings, she wore wedge-heeled shoes and ankle socks; her legs were marked with lumps of blue-green veins. I thought her squatting position shameless, even obscene; I tried to keep talking to Lonnie so that her attention would be taken away from my mother as much as possible. Lonnie wore the composed, polite, appreciative expression that was her disguise in the presence of grownups. She laughed at them and was a ferocious mimic, and they never knew.

My mother pulled me about, and pricked me with pins. She made me turn around, she made me walk away, she made me stand still. "What do you think of it, Lonnie?" she said around the pins in her mouth.

"It's beautiful," said Lonnie, in her mild, sincere way. Lonnie's own mother was dead. She lived with her father who never noticed her, and this, in my eyes, made her seem both vulnerable and privileged.

"It *will* be, if I can ever manage the fit," my mother said. "Ah, well," she said theatrically, getting to her feet with a woeful creaking and sighing, "I doubt if she appreciates it." She enraged me, talking like this to Lonnie, as if Lonnie were grown up and I were still a child. "Stand still," she said, hauling the pinned and basted dress over my head. My head was muffled in velvet, my body exposed, in an old cotton school slip. I felt like a great raw lump, clumsy and goose-pimpled. I wished I was like Lonnie, light-boned, pale and thin; she had been a Blue Baby.

"Well nobody ever made me a dress when I was going to high school," my mother said, "I made my own, or I did without." I was afraid she was going to start again on the story of her walking seven miles to town and finding a job waiting on tables in a boarding-house, so that she could go to high school. All the stories of my mother's life which had once interested me had begun to seem melodramatic, irrelevant, and tiresome.

"One time I had a dress given to me," she said. "It was a cream-coloured cashmere wool with royal blue piping down the front and lovely mother-of-pearl buttons, I wonder what ever became of it?"

When we got free Lonnie and I went upstairs to my room. It was cold, but we stayed there. We talked about the boys in our class, going up and down the rows and saying, "Do you like him? Well, do you half-like him? Do you *hate* him? Would you go out with him if he asked you?" Nobody had asked us. We were thirteen, and we had been going to high school for two months. We did questionnaires in magazines, to find out whether we had personality and whether we would be popular. We read articles on how to make up our faces to accentuate our good points and how to carry on a conversation on the first date and what to do when a boy tried to go too far. Also we read articles on frigidity of the menopause, abortion and why husbands seek satisfaction away from home. When we were not doing school work, we were occupied most of the time with the garnering, passing on and discussing of sexual information. We had made a pact to tell each other everything. But one thing I did not tell was about this dance, the high school Christmas Dance for which my mother was making me a dress. It was that I did not want to go.

At high school I was never comfortable for a minute. I did not know about Lonnie. Before an exam, she got icy hands and palpitations, but I was close to despair at all times. When I was

asked a question in class, any simple little question at all, my voice
was apt to come out squeaky, or else hoarse and trembling. When
I had to go to the blackboard I was sure—even at a time of the
month when this could not be true—that I had blood on my skirt.
My hands became slippery with sweat when they were required
to work the blackboard compass. I could not hit the ball in
volleyball; being called upon to perform an action in front of
others made all my reflexes come undone. I hated Business
Practice because you had to rule pages for an account book,
using a straight pen, and when the teacher looked over my
shoulder all the delicate lines wobbled and ran together. I
hated Science; we perched on stools under harsh lights behind
tables of unfamiliar, fragile equipment, and were taught by
the principal of the school, a man with a cold, self-relishing
voice—he read the Scriptures every morning—and a great
talent for inflicting humiliation. I hated English because the
boys played bingo at the back of the room while the teacher,
a stout, gentle girl, slightly cross-eyed, read Wordsworth at the
front. She threatened them, she begged them, her face red
and her voice as unreliable as mine. They offered burlesqued
apologies and when she started to read again they took up
rapt postures, made swooning faces, crossed their eyes, flung
their hands over their hearts. Sometimes she would burst
into tears, there was no help for it, she had to run out into the
hall. Then the boys made loud mooing noises; our hungry
laughter—oh, mine too—pursued her. There was a carnival
atmosphere of brutality in the room at such times, scaring
weak and suspect people like me.

But what was really going on in the school was not Business
Practice and Science and English, there was something else
that gave life its urgency and brightness. That old building,
with its rock-walled clammy basements and black cloakrooms
and pictures of dead royalties and lost explorers, was full of
the tension and excitement of sexual competition, and in this,
in spite of daydreams of vast successes, I had premonitions of

total defeat. Something had to happen, to keep me from that dance.

With December came snow, and I had an idea. Formerly I had considered falling off my bicycle and spraining my ankle and I had tried to manage this, as I rode home along the hard-frozen, deeply rutted country roads. But it was too difficult. However, my throat and bronchial tubes were supposed to be weak; why not expose them? I started getting out of bed at night and opening my window a little. I knelt down and let the wind, sometimes stinging with snow, rush in around my bared throat. I took off my pajama top. I said to myself the words "blue with cold" and as I knelt there, my eyes shut, I pictured my chest and throat turning blue, the cold, greyed blue of veins under the skin. I stayed until I could not stand it any more, and then I took a handful of snow from the windowsill and smeared it all over my chest, before I buttoned my pajamas. It would melt against the flannelette and I would be sleeping in wet clothes, which was supposed to be the worst thing of all. In the morning, the moment I woke up, I cleared my throat, testing for soreness, coughed experimentally, hopefully, touched my forehead to see if I had fever. It was no good. Every morning, including the day of the dance, I rose defeated, and in perfect health.

The day of the dance I did my hair up in steel curlers. I had never done this before, because my hair was naturally curly, but today I wanted the protection of all possible female rituals. I lay on the couch in the kitchen, reading *The Last Days of Pompeii*, and wishing I was there. My mother, never satisfied, was sewing a white lace collar on the dress; she had decided it was too grown-up looking. I watched the hours. It was one of the shortest days of the year. Above the couch, on the wallpaper, were old games of Xs and Os, old drawings and scribblings my brother and I had done when we were sick with bronchitis. I looked at them and longed to be back safe behind the boundaries of childhood.

When I took out the curlers my hair, both naturally and artificially stimulated, sprang out in an exuberant glossy bush. I wet it, I combed it, beat it with the brush and tugged it down along my cheeks. I applied face powder, which stood out chalkily on my hot face. My mother got out her Ashes of Roses Cologne, which she never used, and let me splash it over my arms. Then she zipped up the dress and turned me around to the mirror. The dress was princess style, very tight in the midriff. I saw how my breasts, in their new stiff brassiere, jutted out surprisingly, with mature authority, under the childish frills of the collar.

"Well I wish I could take a picture," my mother said. "I am really, genuinely proud of that fit. And you might say thank you for it."

"Thank you," I said.

The first thing Lonnie said when I opened the door to her was, "Jesus, what did you do to your hair?"

"I did it up."

"You look like a Zulu. Oh, don't worry. Get me a comb and I'll do the front in a roll. It'll look all right. It'll even make you look older."

I sat in front of the mirror and Lonnie stood behind me, fixing my hair. My mother seemed unable to leave us. I wished she would. She watched the roll take shape and said, "You're a wonder, Lonnie. You should take up hairdressing."

"That's a thought," Lonnie said. She had on a pale blue crepe dress, with a peplum and bow; it was much more grown-up than mine even without the collar. Her hair had come out as sleek as the girl's on the bobby-pin card. I had always thought secretly that Lonnie could not be pretty because she had crooked teeth, but now I saw that crooked teeth or not, her stylish dress and smooth hair made me look a little like a golliwog, stuffed into red velvet, wide-eyed, wild-haired, with a suggestion of delirium.

My mother followed us to the door and called out into the

dark, "Au reservoir!" This was a traditional farewell of Lonnie's and mine; it sounded foolish and desolate coming from her, and I was so angry with her for using it that I did not reply. It was only Lonnie who called back cheerfully, encouragingly, "Good night!"

The gymnasium smelled of pine and cedar. Red and green bells of fluted paper hung from the basketball hoops; the high, barred windows were hidden by green boughs. Everybody in the upper grades seemed to have come in couples. Some of the Grade Twelve and Thirteen girls had brought boy friends who had already graduated, who were young businessmen around the town. These young men smoked in the gymnasium, nobody could stop them, they were free. The girls stood beside them, resting their hands casually on male sleeves, their faces bored, aloof and beautiful. I longed to be like that. They behaved as if only they—the older ones—were really at the dance, as if the rest of us, whom they moved among and peered around, were, if not invisible, inanimate; when the first dance was announced—a Paul Jones—they moved out languidly, smiling at each other as if they had been asked to take part in some half-forgotten childish game. Holding hands and shivering, crowding up together, Lonnie and I and the other Grade Nine girls followed.

I didn't dare look at the outer circle as it passed me, for fear I should see some unmannerly hurrying-up. When the music stopped I stayed where I was, and half-raising my eyes I saw a boy named Mason Williams coming reluctantly towards me. Barely touching my waist and my fingers, he began to dance with me. My legs were hollow, my arm trembled from the shoulder, I could not have spoken. This Mason Williams was one of the heroes of the school; he played basketball and hockey and walked the halls with an air of royal sullenness and barbaric contempt. To have to dance with a nonentity like me was as offensive to him as having to memorize Shakespeare. I felt this as keenly as he did, and imagined that he was exchanging looks of dismay with his friends. He steered me, stumbling, to the edge of the floor. He took his hand from my waist and dropped my arm.

"See you," he said. He walked away.

It took me a minute or two to realize what had happened and that he was not coming back. I went and stood by the wall alone. The Physical Education teacher, dancing past energetically in the arms of a Grade Ten boy, gave me an inquisitive look. She was the only teacher in the school who made use of the words social adjustment, and I was afraid that if she had seen, or if she found out, she might make some horribly public attempt to make Mason finish out the dance with me. I myself was not angry or surprised at Mason; I accepted his position, and mine, in the world of school and I saw that what he had done was the realistic thing to do. He was a Natural Hero, not a Student Council type of hero bound for success beyond the school; one of those would have danced with me courteously and patronizingly and left me feeling no better off. Still, I hoped not many people had seen. I hated people seeing. I began to bite the skin on my thumb.

When the music stopped I joined the surge of girls to the end of the gymnasium. Pretend it didn't happen, I said to myself. Pretend this is the beginning, now.

The band began to play again. There was movement in the dense crowd at our end of the floor, it thinned rapidly. Boys came over, girls went out to dance. Lonnie went. The girl on the other side of me went. Nobody asked me. I remembered a magazine article Lonnie and I had read, which said *Be gay! Let the boys see your eyes sparkle, let them hear laughter in your voice! Simple, obvious, but how many girls forget!* It was true, I had forgotten. My eyebrows were drawn together with tension, I must look scared and ugly. I took a deep breath and tried to loosen my face. I smiled. But I felt absurd, smiling at no one. And I observed that girls on the dance floor, popular girls, were not smiling; many of them had sleepy, sulky faces and never smiled at all.

Girls were still going out to the floor. Some, despairing, went with each other. But most went with boys. Fat girls, girls with pimples, a poor girl who didn't own a good dress and had to wear a skirt and sweater to the dance; they were claimed, they danced away. Why take them and not me? Why everybody else and not me? I have a red velvet dress, I did my hair in curlers, I used a deodorant and put on cologne. *Pray*, I thought. I couldn't close my eyes but I said over and over again in my mind, *Please, me, please*, and I locked my fingers behind my back in a sign more potent than crossing, the same secret sign Lonnie and I used not to be sent to the blackboard in Math.

It did not work. What I had been afraid of was true. I was going to be left. There was something mysterious the matter with me, something that could not be put right like bad breath or overlooked like pimples, and everybody knew it, and I knew it; I had known it all along. But I had not known it for sure, I had hoped to be mistaken. Certainty rose inside me like sickness. I hurried past one or two girls who were also left and went into the girls' washroom. I hid myself in a cubicle.

That was where I stayed. Between dances girls came in and went out quickly. There were plenty of cubicles; nobody noticed that I was not a temporary occupant. During the dances, I listened to the music which I liked but had no part of any more. For I was not going to try any more. I only wanted to hide in here, get out without seeing anybody, get home.

One time after the music started somebody stayed behind. She was taking a long time running the water, washing her hands, combing her hair. She was going to think it funny that I stayed in so long. I had better go out and wash my hands, and maybe while I was washing them she would leave.

It was Mary Fortune. I knew her by name, because she was an officer of the Girls' Athletic Society and she was on the

Honour Roll and she was always organizing things. She had something to do with organizing this dance; she had been around to all the classrooms asking for volunteers to do the decorations. She was in Grade Eleven or Twelve.

"Nice and cool in here," she said. "I came in to get cooled off. I get so hot."

She was still combing her hair when I finished my hands. "Do you like the band?" she said.

"Its all right." I didn't really know what to say. I was surprised at her, an older girl, taking this time to talk to me.

"I don't. I can't stand it. I hate dancing when I don't like the band. Listen. They're so choppy. I'd just as soon not dance as dance to that."

I combed my hair. She leaned against a basin, watching me.

"I don't want to dance and don't particularly want to stay in here. Let's go and have a cigarette."

"Where?"

"Come on, I'll show you."

At the end of the washroom there was a door. It was unlocked and led into a dark closet full of mops and pails. She had me hold the door open, to get the washroom light, until she found the knob of another door. This door opened into darkness.

"I can't turn on the light or somebody might see," she said. "It's the janitor's room." I reflected that athletes always seemed to know more than the rest of us about the school as a building; they knew where things were kept and they were always coming out of unauthorized doors with a bold, preoccupied air. "Watch out where you're going," she said. "Over at the far end there's some stairs. They go up to a closet on the second floor. The door's locked at the top, but there's like a partition between the stairs and the room. So if we sit on the steps, even if by chance someone did come in here, they wouldn't see us."

"Wouldn't they smell smoke?" I said.

"Oh, well. Live dangerously."

There was a high window over the stairs which gave us a
little light. Mary Fortune had cigarettes and matches in her
purse. I had not smoked before except the cigarettes Lonnie
and I made ourselves, using papers and tobacco stolen from her
father; they came apart in the middle. These were much
better.

"The only reason I even came to-night," Mary Fortune said,
"is because I am responsible for the decorations and I wanted
to see, you know, how it looked once people got in there and
everything. Otherwise why bother? I'm not boy-crazy."

In the light from the high window I could see her narrow,
scornful face, her dark skin pitted with acne, her teeth pushed
together at the front, making her look adult and commanding.

"Most girls are. Haven't you noticed that? The greatest
collection of boy-crazy girls you could imagine is right here in
this school."

I was grateful for her attention, her company and her cigarette. I said I thought so too.

"Like this afternoon. This afternoon I was trying to get
them to hang the bells and junk. They just get up on the
ladders and fool around with boys. They don't care if it ever
gets decorated. It's just an excuse. That's the only aim they
have in life, fooling around with boys. As far as I'm concerned,
they're idiots."

We talked about teachers, and things at school. She said she
wanted to be a physical education teacher and she would have
to go to college for that, but her parents did not have enough
money. She said she planned to work her own way through,
she wanted to be independent anyway, she would work in the
cafeteria and in the summer she would do farm work, like picking tobacco. Listening to her, I felt the acute phase of my
unhappiness passing. Here was someone who had suffered the
same defeat as I had—I saw that—but she was full of energy and

self respect. She had thought of other things to do. She would pick tobacco.

We stayed there talking and smoking during the long pause in the music, when, outside, they were having doughnuts and coffee. When the music started again Mary said, "Look, do we have to hang around here any longer? Let's get our coats and go. We can go down to Lee's and have a hot chocolate and talk in comfort, why not?"

We felt our way across the janitor's room, carrying ashes and cigarette butts in our hands. In the closet, we stopped and listened to make sure there was nobody in the washroom. We came back into the light and threw the ashes into the toilet. We had to go out and cut across the dance-floor to the cloak-room, which was beside the outside door.

A dance was just beginning. "Go round the edge of the floor," Mary said. "Nobody'll notice us."

I followed her. I didn't look at anybody. I didn't look for Lonnie. Lonnie was probably not going to be my friend any more, not as much as before anyway. She was what Mary would call boy-crazy.

I found that I was not so frightened, now that I had made up my mind to leave the dance behind. I was not waiting for anybody to choose me. I had my own plans. I did not have to smile or make signs for luck. It did not matter to me. I was on my way to have a hot chocolate, with my friend.

A boy said something to me. He was in my way. I thought he must be telling me that I had dropped something or that I couldn't go that way or that the cloakroom was locked. I didn't understand that he was asking me to dance until he said it over again. It was Raymond Bolting from our class, whom I had never talked to in my life. He thought I meant yes. He put his hand on my waist and almost without meaning to, I began to dance.

We moved to the middle of the floor. I was dancing. My

legs had forgotten to tremble and my hands to sweat. I was dancing with a boy who had asked me. Nobody told him to, he didn't have to, he just asked me. Was it possible, could I believe it, was there nothing the matter with me after all?

I thought that I ought to tell him there was a mistake, that I was just leaving, I was going to have a hot chocolate with my girl friend. But I did not say anything. My face was making certain delicate adjustments, achieving with no effort at all the grave absent-minded look of these who were chosen, those who danced. This was the face that Mary Fortune saw, when she looked out of the cloakroom door, her scarf already around her head. I made a weak waving motion with the hand that lay on the boy's shoulder, indicating that I apologized, that I didn't know what had happened and also that it was no use waiting for me. Then I turned my head away, and when I looked again she was gone.

Raymond Bolting took me home and Harold Simons took Lonnie home. We all walked together as far as Lonnie's corner. The boys were having an argument about a hockey game, which Lonnie and I could not follow. Then we separated into couples and Raymond continued with me the conversation he had been having with Harold. He did not seem to notice that he was now talking to me instead. Once or twice I said, "Well I don't know I didn't see that game," but after a while I decided just to say "H'm hmm," and that seemed to be all that was necessary.

One other thing he said was, "I didn't realize you lived such a long ways out." And he sniffled. The cold was making my nose run a little too, and I worked my fingers through the candy wrappers in my coat pocket until I found a shabby Kleenex. I didn't know whether I ought to offer it to him or not, but he sniffled so loudly that I finally said, "I just have this one Kleenex, it probably isn't even clean, it probably has ink on it. But if I was to tear it in half we'd each have something."

"Thanks," he said. "I sure could use it."

It was a good thing, I thought, that I had done that, for at my gate, when I said, "Well, good night," and after he said, "Oh, yeah. Good night," he leaned towards me and kissed me, briefly, with the air of one who knew his job when he saw it, on the corner of my mouth. Then he turned back to town, never knowing he had been my rescuer, that he had brought me from Mary Fortune's territory into the ordinary world.

I went around the house to the back door, thinking, I have been to a dance and a boy has walked me home and kissed me. It was all true. My life was possible. I went past the kitchen window and I saw my mother. She was sitting with her feet on the open oven door, drinking tea out of a cup without a saucer. She was just sitting and waiting for me to come home and tell her everything that had happened. And I would not do it, I never would. But when I saw the waiting kitchen, and my mother in her faded, fuzzy Paisley kimono, with her sleepy but doggedly expectant face, I understood what a mysterious and oppressive obligation I had, to be happy, and how I had almost failed it, and would be likely to fail it, every time, and she would not know.

Sunday Afternoon

Mrs. Gannett came into the kitchen walking delicately to a melody played in her head, flashing the polished cotton skirts of a flowered sundress. Alva was there, washing glasses. It was half-past two; people had started coming in for drinks about half-past twelve. They were the usual people; Alva had seen most of them a couple of times before, in the three weeks she had been working for the Gannetts. There was Mrs. Gannett's brother, and his wife, and the Vances and the Fredericks; Mrs. Gannett's parents came in for a little while, after service at St. Martin's bringing with them a young nephew, or cousin, who stayed when they went home. Mrs. Gannett's side of the family was the right side; she had three sisters, all fair, forthright and unreflective women, rather more athletic than she, and these magnificently outspoken and handsome parents, both of them with pure white hair. It was Mrs. Gannett's father who owned the island in Georgian Bay, where he had built summer homes for each of his daughters, the island that in a week's time Alva was to see. Mr. Gannett's mother, on the other hand, lived in half of the red brick house in a treeless street of exactly similar red brick houses, almost downtown. Once a week Mrs. Gannett picked her up and took her for a drive and home to supper, and nobody drank anything but grape juice until she had been taken home. Once when Mr.

and Mrs. Gannett had to go out immediately after supper she came into the kitchen and put away the dishes for Alva; she was rather cranky and aloof, as the women in Alva's own family would have been with a maid, and Alva minded this less than the practised, considerate affability of Mrs. Gannett's sisters.

Mrs. Gannett opened the refrigerator and stood there, holding the door. Finally she said, with something like a giggle, "Alva, I think we could have lunch—"

"All right," Alva said. Mrs. Gannett looked at her. Alva never said anything wrong, really wrong, that is rude, and Mrs. Gannett was not so unrealistic as to expect a high-school girl, even a country high-school girl, to answer, "Yes, ma'am," as the old maids did in her mother's kitchen; but there was often in Alva's tone an affected ease, a note of exaggerated carelessness and agreeability that was all the more irritating because Mrs. Gannett could not think of any way to object to it. At any rate it stopped her giggling; her tanned, painted face grew suddenly depressed and sober.

"The potato salad," she said. "Aspic and tongue. Don't forget to heat the rolls. Did you peel the tomatoes? Fine—Oh, look Alva, I don't think those radishes look awfully attractive, do you? You better slice them—Jean used to do roses, you know the way they cut petals around—they used to look lovely."

Alva began clumsily to cut radishes. Mrs. Gannett walked around the kitchen, frowning, sliding her fingertips along the blue and coral counters. She was wearing her hair pulled up into a topknot, showing her neck very thin, brown and rather sun-coarsened; her deep tan made her look sinewy and dried. Nevertheless Alva, who was hardly tanned at all because she spent the hot part of the day in the house, and who at seventeen was thicker than she would have liked in the legs and the waist, envied her this brown and splintery ele-

gance; Mrs. Gannett had a look of being made of entirely
synthetic and superior substances.

"Cut the angel food with a string, you know that, and I'll tell
you how many sherbet and how many maple mousse. Plain
vanilla for Mr. Gannett, it's in the freezer—There's plenty of
either for your own dessert—Oh, Derek, you monster!" Mrs.
Gannett ran out to the patio, crying, "Derek, Derek!" in tones
of shrill and happy outrage. Alva, who knew that Derek was
Mr. Vance, a stockbroker, just remembered in time not to peer
out the top of the Dutch door to see what was happening. That
was one of her difficulties on Sundays, when they were all
drinking, and becoming relaxed and excited; she had to remember that it was not permissible for her to show a little
relaxation and excitement too. Of course. she was not drinking,
except out of the bottoms of glasses when they were brought
back to the kitchen—and then only if it was gin, cold, and
sweetened.

But the feeling of unreality, of alternate apathy and reckless-
ness, became very strong in the house by the middle of afternoon. Alva would meet people coming from the bathroom,
absorbed and melancholy, she would glimpse women in the
dim bedrooms swaying towards their reflections in the mirror,
very slowly applying their lipstick, and someone would have
fallen asleep on the long chesterfield in the den. By this time
the drapes would have been drawn across the glass walls of
living room and dining room, against the heat of the sun; those
long, curtained and carpeted rooms, with their cool colours,
seemed floating in an underwater light. Alva found it already
hard to remember that the rooms at home, such small rooms,
could hold so many things; here were such bland unbroken
surfaces, such spaces—a whole long, wide passage empty,
except for two tall Danish vases standing against the farthest
wall, carpet, walls and ceiling all done in blue variants of grey;
Alva, walking down this hallway, not making any sound,

wished for a mirror, or something to bump into; she did not know if she was there or not.

Before she carried the lunch out to the patio she combed her hair at a little mirror at the end of the kitchen counter, pushing curls up around her face. She retied her apron, pulling its wide band very tight. It was all she could do; the uniform had belonged to Jean, and Alva had asked, the first time she tried it on, if maybe it was too big; but Mrs. Gannett did not think so. The uniform was blue, the predominant kitchen colour; it had white cuffs and collar and scalloped apron. She had to wear stockings too, and white Cuban-heeled shoes that clomped on the stones of the patio—making, in contrast to the sandals and pumps, a heavy, purposeful, plebian sound. But nobody looked around at her, as she carried plates, napkins, dishes of food to a long wrought-iron table. Only Mrs. Gannett came, and rearranged things. The way Alva had of putting things down on a table always seemed to lack something, though there, too, she did not make any real mistakes.

While they were eating she ate her own lunch, sitting at the kitchen table, looking through an old copy of *Time*. There was no bell, of course, on the patio; Mrs. Gannett called, "All right, Alva!" or simply, "Alva!" in tones as discreet and penetrating as those of the bell. It was queer to hear her call this, in the middle of talking to someone, and then begin laughing again; it seemed as if she had a mechanical voice, even a button she pushed, for Alva.

At the end of the meal they all carried their own dessert plates and coffee cups back to the kitchen. Mrs. Vance said the potato salad was lovely; Mr. Vance, quite drunk, said lovely, lovely. He stood right behind Alva at the sink, so very close she felt his breath and sensed the position of his hands; he did not quite touch her. Mr. Vance was very big, curly-haired, high-coloured; his hair was grey, and Alva found him alarming, because he was the sort of man she was used to being respectful to. Mrs. Vance talked all the time, and seemed, when talking to Alva, more unsure of herself, yet warmer, than any of the other women. There was some instability in the situation of the Vances; Alva was not sure what it was; it might have been just that they had not so much money as the others. At any rate they were always being very entertaining, very enthusiastic, and Mr. Vance was always getting too drunk.

"Going up north, Alva, up to Georgian Bay?" Mr. Vance said, and Mrs. Vance said, "Oh, you'll love it, the Gannetts have a lovely place," and Mr. Vance said, "Get some sun on you up there, eh?" and then they went away. Alva, able to move now, turned around to get some dirty plates and noticed that Mr. Gannett's cousin, or whoever he was, was still there. He was thin and leathery-looking, like Mrs. Gannett, though dark. He said, "You don't happen to have any more coffee here, do you?" Alva poured him what there was, half a cup. He stood and drank it, watching her stack the dishes. Then he said, "Lots of fun, eh?" and when she looked up, laughed, and went out.

Alva was free after she finished the dishes; dinner would be late. She could not actually leave the house; Mrs. Gannett might want her for something. And she could not go outside; they were out there. She went upstairs; then, remembering that Mrs. Gannett had said she could read any of the books in the den, she went down again to get one. In the hall she met Mr. Gannett, who looked at her very seriously, attentively, but seemed about to go past without saying anything; then he said, "See here, Alva—see here, are you getting enough to eat?"

It was not a joke, since Mr. Gannett did not make them. It was, in fact, something he had asked her two or three times before. It seemed that he felt a responsibility for her, when he saw her in his house; the important thing seemed to be, that she should be well fed. Alva reassured him, flushing with annoyance; was she a heifer? She said, "I

was going to the den to get a book. Mrs. Gannett said it
would be all right—"

"Yes, yes, any book you like," Mr. Gannett said, and he
unexpectedly opened the door of the den for her and led
her to the bookshelves, where he stood frowning. "What
book would you like?" he said. He reached toward the shelf
of brightly jacketed mysteries and historical novels, but Alva
said, "I've never read *King Lear*."

"*King Lear*," said Mr. Gannett. "Oh." He did not know
where to look for it, so Alva got it down herself. "Nor *The
Red and the Black*," she said. That did not impress him so
much, but it was something she might really read; she could
not go back to her room with just *King Lear*. She went out of
the room feeling well-pleased; she had shown him she did
something besides eat. A man would be more impressed by
King Lear than a woman. Nothing could make any difference
to Mrs. Gannett; a maid was a maid.

But in her room, she did not want to read. Her room was
over the garage, and very hot. Sitting on the bed rumpled
her uniform, and she did not have another ironed. She could
take it off and sit in her slip, but Mrs. Gannett might call
her, and want her at once. She stood at the window, looking
up and down the street. The street was a crescent, a wide
slow curve, with no sidewalks; Alva had felt a little con-
spicuous, the once or twice she had walked along it; you
never saw people walking. The houses were set far apart, far
back from the street, behind brilliant lawns and rockeries
and ornamental trees; in this area in front of the houses,
no one ever spent time but the Chinese gardeners; the lawn
furniture, the swings and garden tables were set out on the
back lawns, which were surrounded by hedges, stone walls,
pseudo-rustic fences. The street was lined with parked cars
this afternoon; from behind the houses came sounds of conversation and a great deal of laughter. In spite of the heat,

there was no blur on the day, up here; everything—the stone and white stucco houses, the flowers, the flower-coloured cars—looked hard and glittering, exact and perfect. There was no haphazard thing in sight. The street, like an advertisement, had an almost aggressive look of bright summer spirits; Alva felt dazzled by this, by the laughter, by people whose lives were relevant to the street. She sat down on a hard chair in front of an old-fashioned child's desk—all the furniture in this room had come out of other rooms that had been redecorated; it was the only place in the house where you could find things unmatched, unrelated to each other, and wooden things that were not large, low and pale. She began to write a letter to her family.

—and the houses, all the others too, are just tremendous, mostly quite modern. There isn't a weed in the lawns, they have a gardener spend a whole day every week just cleaning out what looks to be perfect already. I think the men are rather sappy, the fuss they make over perfect lawns and things like that. They do go out and rough it every once in a while but that is all very complicated and everything has to be just so. It is like that with everything they do and everywhere they go.

Don't worry about me being lonesome and downtrodden and all that maid sort of thing. I wouldn't let anybody get away with anything like that. Besides I'm not a maid really, it's just for the summer. I don't feel lonesome, why should I? I just observe and am interested. Mother, of course I can't eat with them. Don't be ridiculous. It's not the same thing as a hired girl at all. Also I prefer to eat alone. If you wrote Mrs. Gannett a letter she wouldn't know what you were talking about, and I don't mind. *So don't!*

Also I think it would be better when Marion comes down if I took my afternoon off and met her downtown. I don't want particularly to have her come here. I'm not sure how maids' relatives come. Of course it's all right if she wants to. I can't always tell how Mrs. Gannett will react, that's all, and I try to take it easy around her without letting her get away with anything. She is all right though.

In a week we will be leaving for Georgian Bay and of course
I am looking forward to that. I will be able to go swimming
every day, she (Mrs. Gannett) says and—

Her room was really too hot. She put the unfinished letter
under the blotter on the desk. A radio was playing in Margaret's room. She walked down the hall towards Margaret's
door, hoping it would be open. Margaret was not quite fourteen; the difference in age compensated for other differences,
and it was not too bad to be with Margaret.

The door was open, and there spread out on the bed were
Margaret's crinolines and summer dresses. Alva had not
known she had so many.

"I'm not really packing," Margaret said. "I know it would
be crazy. I'm just seeing what I've got. I hope my stuff is all
right," she said. "I hope it's not too—"

Alva touched the clothes on the bed, feeling a great delight
in these delicate colours, in the smooth little bodices, expen-
sively tucked and shaped, the crinolines with their crisp and
fanciful bursts of net; in these clothes there was a very pretty
artificial innocence. Alva was not envious; no, this had
nothing to do with her; this was part of Margaret's world,
that rigid pattern of private school (short tunics and long
black stockings), hockey, choir, sailing in summer, parties,
boys who wore blazers—

"Where are you going to wear them?" Alva said.

"To the Ojibway. The hotel. They have dances every
weekend, everybody goes down in their boats. Friday night
is for kids and Saturday night is for parents and other people
—That is I *will* be going," Margaret said rather grimly, "if
I'm not a social flop. Both the Davis girls are."

"Don't worry," Alva said a little patronizingly. "You'll be
fine."

"I don't really like dancing," Margaret said. "Not the way
I like sailing, for instance. But you have to do it."

"You'll get to like it," Alva said. So there would be

dances, they would go down in the boats, she would see them going and hear them coming home. All these things, which she should have expected—

Margaret sitting cross-legged on the floor, looked up at her with a blunt, clean face, and said, "Do you think I ought to start to neck this summer?"

"Yes," said Alva. "*I* would," she added almost vindictively. Margaret looked puzzled; she said, "I heard that's why Scotty didn't ask me at Easter—"

There was no sound, but Margaret slipped to her feet. "Mother's coming," she said with her lips only, and almost at once Mrs. Gannett came into the room, smiled with a good deal of control, and said, "Oh, Alva. This is where you are."

Margaret said, "I was telling her about the Island, Mummy."

"Oh. There are an awful lot of glasses sitting around down there Alva, maybe you could whisk them through now and they'd be out of the way when you want to get dinner— And Alva, do you have a fresh apron?"

"The yellow is so too tight, Mummy, I tried it on—"

"Look, darling, it's no use getting all that fripfrap out yet, there's still a week before we go—"

Alva went downstairs, passed along the blue hall, heard people talking seriously, a little drunkenly, in the den, and saw the door of the sewing-room closed softly, from within, as she approached. She went into the kitchen. She was thinking of the Island now. A whole island that they owned; nothing in sight that was not theirs. The rocks, the sun, the pine trees, and the deep, cold water of the Bay. What would she do there, what did the maids do? She could go swimming, at odd hours, go for walks by herself, and sometimes—when they went for groceries, perhaps—she would go along in the boat. There would not be so much work to do as there was here, Mrs. Gannett had said. She said the maids always enjoyed it. Alva thought of the other maids, those more talented, more accommodating girls; did they really enjoy it? What kind of freedom or content had they found, that she had not?

She filled the sink, got out the draining rack again and began to wash glasses. Nothing was the matter, but she felt heavy, heavy with the heat and tired and uncaring, hearing all around her an incomprehensible faint noise—of other people's lives, of boats and cars and dances—and seeing this street, that promised island, in a harsh and continuous dazzle of sun. She could not make a sound here, not a dint.

She must remember, before dinner time, to go up and put on a clean apron.

She heard the door open; someone came in from the patio. It was Mrs. Gannett's cousin.

"Here's another glass for you," he said. "Where'll I put it?"

"Anywhere," said Alva.

"Say thanks," Mrs. Gannett's cousin said, and Alva turned around wiping her hands on her apron, surprised, and then in a very short time not surprised. She waited, her back to the counter, and Mrs. Gannett's cousin took hold of her lightly, as in a familiar game, and spent some time kissing her mouth.

"She asked me up to the Island some weekend in August," he said.

Someone on the patio called him, and he went out, moving with the graceful, rather mocking stealth of some slight people. Alva stood still with her back to the counter.

This stranger's touch had eased her; her body was simply grateful and expectant, and she felt a lightness and confidence she had not known in this house. So there were things she had not taken into account, about herself, about them, and ways of living with them that were not so unreal. She would not mind thinking of the Island now, the bare sunny rocks and the black little pine trees. She saw it differently now; it was even possible that she wanted to go there. But things always came together; there was something she would not explore yet—a tender spot, a new and still mysterious humiliation.

A Trip to the Coast

The place called Black Horse is marked on the map but there is nothing there except a store and three houses and an old cemetery and a livery shed which belonged to a church that burned down. It is a hot place in summer, with no shade on the road and no creek nearby. The houses and the store are built of red brick of a faded, gingery colour, with a random decoration of grey or white bricks across the chimneys and around the windows. Behind them the fields are full of milk-weed and goldenrod and big purple thistles. People who are passing through, on their way to the Lakes of Muskoka and the northern bush, may notice that around here the bountiful landscape thins and flattens, worn elbows of rock appear in the diminishing fields and the deep, harmonious woodlots of elm and maple give way to a denser, less hospitable scrub-forest of birch and poplar, spruce and pine—where in the heat of the afternoon the pointed trees at the end of the road turn blue, transparent, retreating into the distance like a company of ghosts.

May was lying in a big room full of boxes at the back of the store. That was where she slept in the summer, when it got too hot upstairs. Hazel slept in the front room on the chesterfield and played the radio half the night; her grand-mother still slept upstairs, in a tight little room full of big furniture and old photographs that smelled of hot oilcloth and old women's woollen stockings. May could not tell what time it was because she hardly ever woke up this early. Most mornings when she woke up there was a patch of hot sun on the floor at her feet and the farmers' milk trucks were rattling past on the highway and her grandmother was scuttling back and forth from the store to the kitchen, where she had put a pot of coffee and a pan of thick bacon on the stove. Passing the old porch couch where May slept (its cushions still smelled faintly of mould and pine) she would twitch automatically at the sheet, saying, "Get up now, *get* up, do you think you're going to sleep till dinner-time? There's a man wants gas."

And if May did not get up but clung to the sheet, muttering angrily, her grandmother would come through next time with a little cold water in a dipper, which she dumped in passing on her granddaughter's feet. Then May would jump up, pushing her long switch of hair back from her face, which was sulky with sleepiness but not resentful; she accepted the rule of her grandmother as she accepted a rain squall or a stomach ache, with a tough, basic certainty that such things would pass. She put on all her clothes under her nightgown, with her arms underneath free of the sleeves; she was eleven years old and had entered a period of furious modesty during which she refused to receive a vaccination on her buttocks and screamed with rage if Hazel or her grandmother came into a room where she was dressing—which they did, she thought, for their own amusement and to ridicule the very idea of her privacy. She would go out and put gas in the car and come back wide awake, hungry; she would eat for breakfast four or five toast sandwiches with marmalade, peanut butter and bacon.

But this morning when she woke up it was just beginning to be light in the back room; she could just make out the printing on the cardboard boxes. Heinz Tomato Soup, she read, Golden Valley Apricots. She went through a private ritual of dividing the letters into threes; if they came out evenly it meant she would be lucky that day. While she was doing this she thought she heard a noise, as if someone was moving in the yard; a marvellous uneasiness took hold of her body at the soles of her feet and made her curl her toes and stretch her legs until she touched the end of the couch. She had a feeling through her whole body like the feeling inside her head when she was going to sneeze. She got up as quietly as she could and walked carefully across the bare boards of the back room, which felt sandy and springy underfoot, to the rough kitchen linoleum. She was wearing an old cotton nightgown of Hazel's, which billowed out in a soft, ghostly way behind her.

The kitchen was empty; the clock ticked watchfully on the shelf above the sink. One of the taps dripped all the time and the dishcloth was folded into a little pad and placed underneath it. The face of the clock was almost hidden by a yellow tomato, ripening, and a can of powder that her grandmother used on her false teeth. Twenty to six. She moved towards the screen door; as she passed the breadbox one hand reached in of its own accord and came out with a couple of cinnamon buns which she began to eat without looking at them; they were a little dry.

The back yard at this time of day was strange, damp and shadowy; the fields were grey and all the cobwebbed, shaggy bushes along the fences thick with birds; the sky was pale, cool, smoothly ribbed with light and flushed at the edges, like the inside of a shell. It pleased her that her grandmother and Hazel were out of this, that they were still asleep. Nobody had spoken for this day yet; its purity astonished her. She had a delicate premonition of freedom and danger, like a streak of dawn across that sky. Around the corner of the house where the woodpile was she heard a small dry clattering sound.

"Who's there?" said May in a loud voice, first swallowing a mouthful of cinnamon bun. "I know you are there," she said.

Her grandmother came around the house carrying a few sticks of kindling wrapped in her apron and making private unintelligible noises of exasperation. May saw her come, not really with surprise but with a queer let-down feeling that seemed to spread thinly from the present moment into all areas of her life, past and future. It seemed to her that any place she went her grandmother would be there beforehand: anything she found out her grandmother would know already, or else could prove to be of no account.

"I thought it was somebody in the yard," she said defensively. Her grandmother looked at her as if she were a stovepipe and came ahead into the kitchen.

"I didn't think you would of got up so early," May said. "What'd you get up so early for?"

Her grandmother didn't answer. She heard everything you said to her but she didn't answer unless she felt like it. She set to work making a fire in the stove. She was dressed for the day in a print dress, a blue apron rubbed and dirty across the stomach, an unbuttoned, ravelling, no-colour sweater that had belonged once to her husband, and a pair of canvas shoes. Things dangled on her in spite of her attempts to be tidy and fastened up; it was because there was no reasonable shape to her body for clothes to cling to; she was all flat and narrow, except for the little mound of her stomach like a four-months' pregnancy that rode preposterously under her skinny chest. She had knobby fleshless legs and her arms were brown and veined and twisted like whips. Her head was rather big for her body and with her hair pulled tightly over her skull she had the look of an under-nourished but maliciously intelligent baby.

"You go on back to bed," she said to May. May went instead to the kitchen mirror and began combing her hair and twisting it around her finger to see if it would go into a page-boy. She had remembered that it was today Eunie Parker's cousin was coming. She would have taken Hazel's curlers and done her hair up, if she thought she could do that without her grandmother knowing.

Her grandmother closed the door of the front room where Hazel was asleep. She emptied out the coffee pot and put in water and fresh coffee. She got a pitcher of milk out of the icebox, sniffed at it to make sure it was still all right and lifted two ants out of the sugar bowl with her spoon. She rolled herself a cigarette on a little machine she had. Then she sat at the table and read yesterday's newspaper. She did not speak another word to May until the coffee had perked and she had dampered the fire and the room was almost as light as day.

"You get your own cup if you want any," she said.

Usually she said May was too young to drink coffee. May got herself a good cup with green birds on it. Her grandmother didn't say anything. They sat at the table drinking coffee, May in her long nightgown feeling privileged and ill at ease. Her grandmother was looking around the kitchen with its stained walls and calendars as if she had to keep it all in sight; she had a rather sly abstracted look.

May said conversationally, "Eunie Parker has her cousin coming today. Her name is Heather Sue Murray."

Her grandmother did not pay any attention. Presently she said, "Do you know how old I am?"

May said, "No."

"Well take a guess."

May thought and said, "Seventy?"

Her grandmother did not speak for so long that May thought this was only another of her conversational blind alleys. She said, informatively, "This Heather Sue Murray has been a Highland dancer ever since she was three years old. She dances in competitions and all."

"Seventy-eight," her grandmother said. "Nobody knows that, I never told. No birth certificate. Never took the pension. Never took relief." She thought a while and said, "Never was in a hospital. I got enough in the bank to cover burial. Any headstone will have to come out of charity or bad conscience of my relatives."

"What do you want a headstone for?" May said sullenly, picking at the oilcloth at a spot where it was worn through. She did not like this conversation; it reminded her of a rather mean trick her grandmother had played on her about three years ago. She had come home from school and found her grandmother lying on that same couch in the back room where she slept now. Her grandmother lay with her hands dropped at her sides, her face the colour of curdled milk, her eyes closed; she wore an expression of pure and unassailable indifference. May had tried saying "Hello" first and then "Grandma" more or less in her everyday voice; her grandmother did not flick a muscle in her usually live and agitated face. May said again, more respectfully, "Grandma" and bending over did not hear the shallowest breath. She put out her hand to touch her grandmother's cheek, but was checked by something remote and not reassuring in that cold shabby hollow. Then she started to cry, in the anxious, bitten-off way of someone who is crying with no one to hear them. She was afraid to say her grandmother's name again; she was afraid to touch her, and at the same time afraid to take her eyes off her. However, her grandmother opened her eyes. Without lifting her arms or moving her head she looked up at May with a contrived, outrageous innocence and a curious spark of triumph. "Can't a person lay down around here?" she said. "Shame to be such a baby."

"I never said I *wanted* one," her grandmother said. "Go and get some clothes on," she said coldly, as May experimentally stuck one shoulder up through the loose neck of her nightgown. "Unless you think you are one of them Queens of Egypt."

"What?" said May looking at her shoulder splotched unpleasantly with peeling sunburn.

"Oh, one of them Queens of Egypt I understand they got at the Kinkaid Fair."

When May came back to the kitchen her grandmother was still drinking coffee and looking at the want-ad section of the city paper, as if she had no store to open or breakfast to cook or anything to do all day. Hazel had got up and was ironing a dress to wear to work. She worked in a store in Kinkaid which was thirty miles away and she had to leave for work early. She tried to persuade her mother to sell the store and go and live in Kinkaid which had two movie theatres, plenty of stores and restaurants and a Royal Dance Pavilion; but the old woman would not budge. She told Hazel to go and live where she liked but Hazel for some reason did not go. She was a tall drooping girl of thirty-three, with bleached hair, a long wary face and on oblique resentful expression emphasized by a slight cast, a wilful straying of one eye. She had a trunk full of embroidered pillowcases and towels and silverware. She bought a set of dishes and a set of copper-bottomed pots and put them away in her trunk; she and the old woman and May continued to eat off chipped plates and cook in pots so battered they rocked on the stove.

"Hazel's got everything she needs to get married but she just lacks one thing," the old woman would say.

Hazel drove all over the country to dances with other girls who worked in Kinkaid or taught school. On Sunday morning she got up with a hangover and took coffee with aspirin and put on her silk print dress and drove off down the road to sing in the choir. Her mother, who said she had no religion, opened up the store and sold gas and ice cream to tourists.

Hazel hung over the ironing-board yawning and tenderly

rubbing her blurred face and the old woman read out loud, "Tall industrious man, thirty-five years old, desires make acquaintance woman of good habits, non-smoker or drinker, fond of home life, no triflers please."

"Aw, Mom," Hazel said.

"What's triflers?" May said.

"Man in prime of life," the old woman read relentlessly, "desires friendship of healthy woman without encumbrances, send photograph first letter."

"Aw cut it out, Mom," Hazel said.

"What's encumbrances?" May said.

"Where would you be if I did get married?" Hazel said gloomily with a look on her face of irritable satisfaction.

"Any time you want to get married you can get."

"I got you and May."

"Oh, go on."

"Well I have."

"Oh, go on," the old woman said with disgust. "I look after my ownself. I always have." She was going to say a lot more, for this speech was indeed a signpost in her life, but the moment after she had energetically summoned up that landscape which was coloured vividly and artlessly like a child's crayon drawing, and presented just such magical distortions, she shut her eyes as if oppressed by a feeling of unreality, a reasonable doubt that any of this had ever existed. She tapped with her spoon on the table and said to Hazel, "Well you never had such a dream as I had last night."

"I never do dream anyway," Hazel said.

The old woman sat tapping her spoon and looking with concentration at nothing but the front of the stove.

"Dreamt I was walking down the road," she said. "I was walking down the road past Simmonses' gate and I felt like a cloud was passing over the sun, felt cold, like. So I looked up and I seen a big bird, oh, the biggest bird you ever saw, black as that stove top there, it was right over me between me and the sun. Did you ever dream a thing like that?"

"I never dream anything," Hazel said rather proudly.

"Remember that nightmare I had when I was sleeping in the front room after I had the red measles?" May said. "Remember that nightmare?"

"I'm not talking about any nightmare," the old woman said.

"I thought there was people in coloured hats going round and round in that room. Faster and faster so all their hats was blurred together. All the rest of them was invisible except they had on these coloured hats."

Her grandmother put her tongue out to lick off some specks of dry tobacco that were stuck to her lips, then got up and lifted the stove lid and spat into the fire. "I might as well talk to a barn wall," she said. "May, put a coupla sticks in that fire I'll fry us some bacon. I don't want to keep the stove on today any longer'n I can help."

"It's going to be hotter today than it was yesterday," Hazel said placidly. "Me and Lois have a bargain on not to wear any stockings. Mr. Peebles says a word to us we're going to say what do you think they hired you for, going around looking at everybody's legs? He gets *embarrassed*," she said. Her bleached head disappeared into the skirt of her dress with a lonesome giggle like the sound of a bell rung once by accident, then caught.

"Huh," the old woman said.

May and Eunie Parker and Heather Sue Murray sat in the afternoon on the front step of the store. The sun had clouded over about noon but it seemed the day got even hotter then. You could not hear a cricket or a bird, but there was a low wind; a hot, creeping wind came through the country grass. Because it was Saturday hardly anyone stopped at the store; the local cars drove on past, heading for town.

Heather Sue said, "Don't you kids ever hitch a ride?"

"No," May said.

Eunie Parker her best friend for two years said, "Oh, May wouldn't even be allowed. You don't know her grandmother. She can't do anything."

May scuffed her feet in the dirt and ground her heel into an ant hill. "Neither can you," she said.

"I can so," Eunie said. "I can do what I like." Heather Sue looked at them in her puzzled company way and said, "Well what is there to do here? I mean what do you kids *do*?"

Her hair was cut short all around her head; it was coarse, black, and curly. She had that Candy Apples lipstick on and it looked as if she shaved her legs.

"We go to the cemetery," May said flatly. They did, too. She and Eunie went and sat in the cemetery almost every afternoon because there was a shady corner there and no younger children bothered them and they could talk speculatively without any danger of being overheard.

"You go *where*?" Heather Sue said, and Eunie scowling into the dirt at their feet said, "Oh, we do not. I hate that stupid cemetery," she said. Sometimes she and May had spent a whole afternoon looking at the tombstones and picking out names that interested them and making up stories about the people who were buried there.

"Gee, don't give me the creeps like that," Heather Sue said. "It's awfully hot, isn't it? If I was at home this afternoon, I guess me and my girl friend would be going to the pool."

"We can go and swim at Third Bridge," Eunie said.

"Where is that?"

"Down the road, it's not far. Half a mile."

"In this heat?" Heather Sue said.

Eunie said, "I'll ride you on my bike." She said to May

in an overly gay and hospitable voice, "You get your bike too, come on."

May considered a moment and then got up and went into the store, which was always dark in the daytime, hot too, with a big wooden clock on the wall and bins full of little sweet crumbling cookies, soft oranges, onions. She went to the back where her grandmother was sitting on a stool beside the ice-cream freezer, under a big baking-powder sign that had a background of glittering foil, like a Christmas card.

May said, "Can I go swimming with Eunie and Heather Sue?"

"Where you going to go swimming?" her grandmother said, almost neutrally. She knew there was only one place you could go.

"Third Bridge."

Eunie and Heather Sue had come in and were standing by the door. Heather Sue smiled with delicacy and politeness in the direction of the old woman.

"No, no you can't."

"It's not deep there," May said.

Her grandmother grunted enigmatically. She sat bent over, her elbow on her knee and her chin pressed down on her thumb. She would not bother looking up.

"Why can't I?" May said stubbornly.

Her grandmother did not answer. Eunie and Heather Sue watched from the door.

"Why can't I?" she said again. "*Grandma*, why can't I?"

"You know why."

"Why?"

"Because that's where all the boys go. I told you before. You're getting too big for that." Her mouth shut down hard; her face set in the lines of ugly and satisfied secrecy; now she looked up at May and looked at her until she brought up a flush of shame and anger. Some animation came into her own face. "Let the rest of them chase after the boys, see what it gets them." She never once looked at Eunie and Heather Sue but when she said this they turned and fled out of the store. You could hear them running past the gas pumps and breaking into wild, somewhat desperate, whoops of laughter. The old woman did not let on she heard.

May did not say anything. She was exploring in the dark a new dimension of bitterness. She had a feeling that her grandmother did not *believe* in her own reasons any more, that she did not care, but would go on pulling these same reasons out of the bag, flourishing them nastily, only to see what damage they could do. Her grandmother said, "Heather-miss-what's-her-name. I *seen* her, stepping out of the bus this morning."

May walked out of the store straight through the back room and through the kitchen to the back yard. She went and sat down by the pump. An old wooden trough, green with decay, ran down from the spout of the pump to an island of cool mud in the dry clumps of grass. She sat there and after a while she saw a big toad, rather an old and tired one she thought, flopping around in the grass; she trapped it in her hands.

She heard the screen door shut; she did not look. She saw her grandmother's shoes, her incredible ankles moving towards her across the grass. She held the toad in one hand and with the other she picked up a little stick; methodically she began to prod it in the belly.

"You quit that," her grandmother said. May dropped the stick. "Let that miserable thing go," she said, and very slowly May opened her fingers. In the close afternoon she could smell the peculiar flesh smell of her grandmother who stood over her; it was sweetish and corrupt like the smell of old apple peel going soft, and it penetrated and prevailed over the more commonplace odours of strong soap and dry ironed cotton and tobacco which she always carried around with her.

"I bet you don't know," her grandmother said loudly. "I bet you don't know what's been going through my head in there in the store." May did not answer but bent down and began to pick with interest at a scab on her leg.

"I been thinking I might sell the store," her grandmother said in this same loud monotonous voice as if she were talking to a deaf person or some larger power. Standing looking at the ragged pine-blue horizon, holding her apron down in an old woman's gesture with her flat hands, she said, "You and me could get on the train and go out and see Lewis." It was her son in California, whom she had not seen for about twenty years.

Then May had to look up to see if her grandmother was playing some kind of trick. The old woman had always said that the tourists were fools to think one place was any better than another and that they would have been better off at home.

"You and me could take a trip to the coast," her grandmother said. "Wouldn't cost so much, we could sit up nights and pack some food along. It's better to pack your own food, you know what you're getting."

"You're too old," May said cruelly. "You're seventy-eight."

"People my age are travelling to the Old Country and all over, you look in the papers."

"You might have a heart attack," May said.

"They could put me in that car with the lettuce and tomatoes," the old woman said, "and ship me home cold." Meanwhile May could see the coast; she saw a long curve of sand like the beach at the lake only longer and brighter; the very words, *The Coast*, produced a feeling of coolness and delight in her. But she did not trust them, she could not understand; when in her life had her grandmother promised her any fine thing before?

There was a man standing at the front of the store drinking a lemon-lime. He was a small middle-aged man with a puffy, heat-shiny face; he wore a white shirt, not clean, a pale silk tie. The old woman had moved her stool up to the front counter and she sat there talking to him. May stood with her back to both of them looking out the front door. The clouds were dingy; the world was filled with an old, dusty unfriendly light that seemed to come not from the sky alone but from the flat brick walls, the white roads, the grey bush-leaves rustling and the metal signs flapping in the hot, monotonous wind. Ever since her grandmother had followed her into the back yard she had felt as if something had changed, something had cracked; yes, it was that new light she saw in the world. And she felt something about herself—like power, like the unsuspected still unexplored power of her own hostility, and she meant to hold it for a while and turn it like a cold coin in her hand.

"What company are you travelling for?" her grandmother said. The man said, "Rug Company."

"Don't they let a man go home to his family on the weekend?"

"I'm not travelling on business right now," the man said. "At least I'm not travelling on rug business. You might say I'm travelling on private business."

"Oh well," the old woman said, in the tone of one who does not meddle with anybody's private business. "Does it look to you like we're going to have a rain?"

"Could be," the man said. He took a big drink of lemon-lime and put the bottle down and wiped his mouth neatly with his handkerchief. He was the sort who would talk about his private business anyway; indeed he would not talk about anything else. "I'm on my way to see an acquaintance of mine, he's staying at his summer cottage," he said. "He has insomnia so bad he hasn't had a good night's rest in seven years."

"Oh well," the old woman said.

"I'm going to see if I can cure him of it. I've had pretty good success with some insomnia cases. Not one hundred per cent. Pretty good."

"Are you a medical man too?"

"No, I'm not," the little man said agreeably. "I'm a hypnotist. An amateur. I don't think of myself as anything but an amateur."

The old woman looked at him for several moments without saying anything. This did not displease him; he moved around the front of the store picking things up and looking at them in a lively and self-satisfied way. "I'll bet you never saw anybody that said he was a hypnotist before in your life," he said in a joking way to the old woman. "I look just like anybody else, don't I? I look pretty tame."

"I don't believe in any of that kind of thing," she said.

He just laughed. "What do you mean you don't *believe* in it?"

"I don't believe in any superstitious kind of thing."

"It's not superstition, lady, it's a living fact."

"I know what it is."

"Well now a lot of people are of your opinion, a surprising lot of people. Maybe you didn't happen to read an article that was published about two years ago in the *Digest* on this same subject? I wish I had it with me," he said. "All I know is I cured a man of drinking. I cured people of all sorts of itches and rashes and bad habits. Nerves. I don't claim I can cure everbody of their nervous habits but some people I can tell you have been very grateful to me. Very grateful."

The old woman put her hands up to her head and did not answer.

"What's the matter, lady, aren't you feeling well. You got a headache?"

"I feel all right."

"How did you cure those people?" May said boldly, though

her grandmother had always told her: don't let me catch you talking to strangers in the store.

The little man swung round attentively. "Why I hypnotize them, young lady. I hypnotize them. Are you asking me to explain to you what hypnotism is?"

May who did not know what she was asking flushed red and had no idea what to say. She saw her grandmother looking straight at her. The old woman looked out of her head at May and the whole world as if they had caught fire and she could do nothing about it, she could not even communicate the fact to them.

"She don't know what she's talking about," her grandmother said.

"Well it's very simple," the man said directly to May, in a luxuriantly gentle voice he must think suitable for children. "It's just like you put a person to sleep. Only they're not really asleep, do you follow me honey? You can talk to them. And listen—listen to this—you can go way deep into their minds and find out things they wouldn't even remember when they were awake. Find out their hidden worries and anxieties that's causing them the trouble. Now isn't that an amazing thing?"

"You couldn't do that with me," the old woman said. "I would know what was going on. You couldn't do that with me."

"I bet he could," May said, and was so startled at herself her mouth stayed open. She did not know why she had said that. Time and again she had watched her grandmother's encounters with the outside world, not with pride so much as a solid, fundamental conviction that the old woman would get the better of it. Now for the first time it seemed to her she saw the possibility of her grandmother's defeat; in her grandmother's face she saw it and not in the little man who must be crazy, she thought, and who made her want to laugh. The idea filled her with dismay and with a painful, irresistible excitement.

"Well you never can tell till you give it a try," the man said, as if it were a joke. He looked at May. The old woman made

up her mind. She said scornfully, "It don't matter to me."
She put her elbows on the counter and held her head between
her two hands, as if she were pressing something in. "Pity to
take your time," she said.

"You really ought to lay down so you can relax better."

"Sitting down—" she said, and seemed to lose her breath a
moment—"sitting down's good enough for me."

Then the man took a bottle-opener off a card of knick-
knacks they had in the store and he walked over to stand in
front of the counter. He was not in any hurry. When he spoke
it was in a natural voice but it had changed a little; it had
grown mild and unconcerned. "Now I know you're resisting
this idea," he said softly. "I know you're resisting it and I
know why. It's because you're afraid." The old woman made
a noise of protest or alarm and he held up his hand, but gently.
"You're afraid," he said, "and all I want to show you, all I
mean to show you, is that there is nothing to be afraid of. Nothing to be afraid of. Nothing. Nothing to be afraid of, I just
want you to keep your eyes on this shiny metal object I'm holding in my hand. That's right, just keep your eyes on this shiny
metal object here in my hand. Just keep your eyes on it. Don't
think. Don't worry. Just say to yourself, there's nothing to be
afraid of, nothing to be afraid of, nothing to be afraid of—"
His voice sank; May could not make out the words. She stayed
pressed against the soft-drink cooler. She wanted to laugh, she
could not help it, watching the somehow disreputable back of
this man's head and his white, rounded, twitching shoulders.
But she did not laugh because she had to wait to see what her
grandmother would do. If her grandmother capitulated it
would be as unsettling an event as an earthquake or a flood; it
would crack the foundations of her life and set her terrifyingly
free. The old woman stared with furious unblinking obedience
at the bottle-opener in the man's hand.

"Now I just want you to tell me," he said, "if you can still
see—if you can still see—" He bent forward to look into her

face. "I just want you to tell me if you can still see—" The old woman's face with its enormous cold eyes and its hard ferocious expression was on a level with his own. He stopped; he drew back.

"Hey what's the matter?" he said, not in his hypnotizing but his ordinary voice—in fact a sharper voice than ordinary, which made May jump. "What's the matter, lady, come on, wake up. Wake up," he said, and touched her shoulder to give her a little shake. The old woman with a look of intemperate scorn still on her face fell forwards across the counter with a loud noise, scattering several packages of Kleenex, bubble gum, and cake decorations over the floor. The man dropped the bottle-opener and giving May an outraged look and crying, "I'm not responsible—it never happened before," he ran out of the store to his car. May heard his car start and then she ran out after him, as if she wanted to call something, as if she wanted to call "Help" or "Stay." But she did not call anything, she stood with her mouth open in the dust in front of the gas pumps, and he would not have heard her anyway; he gave one wildly negative wave out the window of his car and roared away to the north.

May stood outside the store and no other cars went by on the highway, no one came. The yards were empty in Black Horse. It had begun to rain a little while before and the drops of rain fell separately around her, sputtering in the dust. Finally she went back and sat on the step of the store where the rain fell too. It was quite warm and she did not mind. She sat with her legs folded under her looking out at the road where she might walk now in any direction she liked, and the world which lay flat and accessible and full of silence in front of her. She sat and waited for that moment to come when she could not wait any longer, when she would have to get up and go into the store where it was darker than ever now on account of the rain and where her grandmother lay fallen across the counter dead, and what was more, victorious.

The Peace of Utrecht

I.

I have been at home now for three weeks and it has not been a success. Maddy and I, though we speak cheerfully of our enjoyment of so long and intimate a visit, will be relieved when it is over. Silences disturb us. We laugh immoderately. I am afraid—very likely we are both afraid—that when the moment comes to say goodbye, unless we are very quick to kiss, and fervently mockingly squeeze each other's shoulders, we will have to look straight into the desert that is between us and acknowledge that we are not merely indifferent; at heart we reject each other, and as for that past we make so much of sharing we do not really share it at all, each of us keeping it jealously to herself, thinking privately that the other has turned alien, and forfeited her claim.

At night we often sit out on the steps of the verandah, and drink gin and smoke diligently to defeat the mosquitoes and postpone until very late the moment of going to bed. It is hot; the evening takes a long time to burn out. The high brick house, which stays fairly cool until midafternoon, holds the heat of the day trapped until long after dark. It was always like this, and Maddy and I recall how we used to drag our mattress downstairs onto the verandah, where we lay counting falling stars and trying to stay awake till dawn. We never did, falling asleep each night about the time a chill drift of air came up off the river, carrying a smell of reeds and the black ooze of the riverbed. At half-past ten a bus goes through the town, not slowing much; we see it go by at the end of our street. It is the same bus I used to take when I came home from college, and I remember coming into Jubilee on some warm night, seeing the earth bare around the massive roots of the trees, the drinking fountain surrounded by little puddles of water on the main street, the soft scrawls of blue and red and orange light that said BILLIARDS and CAFE; feeling as I recognized these signs a queer kind of oppression and release, as I exchanged the whole holiday world of school, of friends and, later on, of love, for the dim world of continuing disaster, of home. Maddy making the same journey four years earlier must have felt the same thing. I want to ask her: is it possible that children growing up as we did lose the ability to believe in—to be at home in—any ordinary and peaceful reality? But I don't ask her; we never talk about any of that. No exorcising here, says Maddy in her thin, bright voice with the slangy quality I had forgotten, we're not going to depress each other. So we haven't.

One night Maddy took me to a party at the Lake, which is about thirty miles west of here. The party was held in a cottage a couple of women from Jubilee had rented for the week. Most of the women there seemed to be widowed, single, separated or divorced; the men were mostly young and unmarried —those from Jubilee so young that I remember them only as little boys in the lower grades. There were two or three older men, not with their wives. But the women—they reminded me surprisingly of certain women familiar to me in my childhood, though of course I never saw their party-going personalities, only their activities in the stores and offices, and not infrequently in the Sunday schools, of Jubilee. They differed from the married women in being more aware of themselves in the world, a little brisker, sharper and coarser (though I can think of only one or two whose respectability was ever in question).

They wore resolutely stylish though matronly clothes, which tended to swish and rustle over their hard rubber corsets, and they put perfume, quite a lot of it, on their artificial flowers. Maddy's friends were considerably modernized; they had copper rinses on their hair, and blue eyelids, and a robust capacity for drink.

Maddy I thought did not look one of them, with her slight figure and her still carelessly worn dark hair; her face has grown thin and strained without losing entirely its girlish look of impertinence and pride. But she speaks with the harsh twang of the local accent, which we used to make fun of, and her expression as she romped and drank was determinedly undismayed. It seemed to me that she was making every effort to belong with these people and that shortly she would succeed. It seemed to me too that she wanted me to see her succeeding, to see her repudiating that secret, exhilarating, really monstrous snobbery which we cultivated when we were children together, and promised ourselves, of course, much bigger things than Jubilee.

During the game in which all the women put an article of clothing—it begins decorously with a shoe—in a basket, and then all the men come in and have a race trying to fit things on to their proper owners, I went out and sat in the car, where I felt lonely for my husband and my friends and listened to the hilarity of the party and the waves falling on the beach and presently went to sleep. Maddy came much later and said, "For heaven's sake!" Then she laughed and said airily like a lady in an English movie, "You find these goings-on distasteful?" We both laughed; I felt apologetic, and rather sick from drinking and not getting drunk. "They may not be much on intellectual conversation but their hearts are in the right place, as the saying goes." I did not dispute this and we drove at eighty miles an hour from Inverhuron to Jubilee. Since then we have not been to any more parties.

But we are not always alone when we sit out on the steps.

Often we are joined by a man named Fred Powell. He was at the party, peaceably in the background remembering whose liquor was whose and amiably holding someone's head over the rickety porch railing. He grew up in Jubilee as we did but I do not remember him, I suppose because he went through school some years ahead of us and then went away to the war. Maddy surprised me by bringing him home to supper the first night I was here and then we spent the evening, as we have spent many since, making this strange man a present of our childhood, or of that version of our childhood which is safely preserved in anecdote, as in a kind of mental cellophane. And what fantasies we build around the frail figures of our child-selves, so that they emerge beyond recognition incorrigible and gay. We tell stories together well. "You girls have got good memories," Fred Powell says, and sits watching us with an air of admiration and something else—reserve, embarrass-ment, deprecation—which appears on the faces of these mild deliberate people as they watch the keyed-up antics of their entertainers.

Now thinking of Fred Powell I admit that my reaction to this—this *situation* as I call it—is far more conventional than I would have expected; it is even absurd. And I do not know what situation it really is. I know that he is married. Maddy told me so, on the first evening, in a merely informative voice. His wife is an invalid. He has her at the Lake for the summer, Maddy says, he's very good to her. I do not know if he is Maddy's lover and she will never tell me. Why should it mat-ter to me? Maddy is well over thirty. But I keep thinking of the way he sits on our steps with his hands set flat on his spread knees, his mild full face turned almost indulgently toward Maddy as she talks; he has an affable masculine look of being diverted but unimpressed. And Maddy teases him, tells him he is too fat, will not smoke his cigarettes, involves him in private, nervous, tender arguments which have no meaning and no end. He allows it. (And this is what frightens me, I know it now: he allows it; *she needs it.*) When she is a little drunk she says in tones of half-pleading mockery that he is her only real friend. He speaks the same language, she says. Nobody else does. I have no answer to that.

Then again I begin to wonder: *is* he only her friend? I had forgotten certain restrictions of life in Jubilee—and this holds good whatever the pocket novels are saying about small towns —and also what strong, respectable, never overtly sexual friendships can flourish within these restrictions and be fed by them, so that in the end such relationships may consume half a life. This thought depresses me (unconsummated relationships depress outsiders perhaps more than anybody else) so much that I find myself wishing for them to be honest lovers.

The rhythm of life in Jubilee is primitively seasonal. Deaths occur in the winter; marriages are celebrated in the summer. There is good reason for this; the winters are long and full of hardship and the old and weak cannot always get through them. Last winter was a catastrophe, such as may be expected every ten or twelve years; you can see how the pavement in the streets is broken up, as if the town had survived a minor bombardment. A death is dealt with then in the middle of great difficulties; there comes time now in the summer to think about it, and talk. I find that people stop me in the street to talk about my mother. I have heard from them about her funeral, what flowers she had and what the weather was like on that day. And now that she is dead I no longer feel that when they say the words "your mother" they deal a knowing, cunning blow at my pride. I used to feel that; at those words I felt my whole identity, that pretentious adolescent construction, come crumbling down.

Now I listen to them speak of her, so gently and ceremoniously, and I realize that she became one of the town's possessions and oddities, its brief legends. This she achieved in spite of us, for we tried, both crudely and artfully, to keep her at home, away from that sad notoriety; not for her sake, but for ours, who suffered such unnecessary humiliation at the sight of her eyes rolling back in her head in a temporary paralysis of the eye muscles, at the sound of her thickened voice, whose embarrassing pronouncements it was our job to interpret to outsiders. So bizarre was the disease she had in its effects that it made us feel like crying out in apology (though we stayed stiff and white) as if we were accompanying a particularly tasteless sideshow. All wasted, our pride; our purging its rage in wild caricatures we did for each other (no, not caricatures, for she was one herself; imitations). We should have let the town have her; it would have treated her better.

About Maddy and her ten-year's vigil they say very little; perhaps they want to spare my feelings, remembering that I was the one who went away and here are my two children to show for it, while Maddy is alone and has nothing but that discouraging house. But I don't think so; in Jubilee the feelings are not spared this way. And they ask me point-blank why I did not come home for the funeral; I am glad I have the excuse of the blizzard that halted air travel that week, for I do not know if I would have come anyway, after Maddy had written so vehemently urging me to stay away. I felt strongly that she had a right to be left alone with it, if she wanted to be, after all this time.

After all this time. Maddy was the one who stayed. First, she went away to college, then I went. You give me four years, I'll give you four years, she said. But I got married. She was not surprised; she was exasperated at me for my wretched useless feelings of guilt. She said that she had always meant to stay. She said that Mother no longer "bothered" her. "Our Gothic Mother," she said, "I play it out now, I let her be. I don't keep trying to make her *human* any more. You know." It would simplify things so much to say that Maddy was religious, that she felt the joys of self-sacrifice, the strong, mystical appeal of total rejection. But about Maddy who could say that? When we were in our teens, and our old aunts, Aunt Annie and Auntie Lou, spoke to us of some dutiful son or daughter who had given up everything for an ailing parent, Maddy would quote impiously the opinions of modern psychiatry. Yet she stayed. All I can think about that, all I have ever been able to think, to comfort me, is that she may have been able and may even have chosen to live without time and in perfect imaginary freedom as children do, the future untampered with, all choices always possible.

To change the subject, people ask me what it is like to be back in Jubilee. But I don't know, I am still waiting for something to tell me, to make me understand that I am back. The day I drove up from Toronto with my children in the back seat of the car I was very tired, on the last lap of a twenty-five-hundred-mile trip. I had to follow a complicated system of highways and sideroads, for there is no easy way to get to Jubilee from anywhere on earth. Then about two o'clock in the afternoon I saw ahead of me, so familiar and unexpected, the gaudy, peeling cupola of the town hall, which is no relation to any of the rest of the town's squarely-built, dingy grey-and-red-brick architecture. (Underneath it hangs a great bell, to be rung in the event of some mythical disaster.) I drove up the main street—a new service station, new stucco front on the Queen's Hotel—and turned into the quiet, decaying side streets where old maids live, and have birdbaths and blue delphiniums in their gardens. The big brick houses that I knew, with their wooden verandahs and gaping, dark-screened windows, seemed to me plausible but unreal. (Anyone to whom I have mentioned the dreaming, sunken feeling of these streets wants to take me out to the north side of town where there is a new soft-drink bottling plant, some new ranch-style houses and a Tastee-Freez.) Then I parked my car in a little splash of shade in front of the house where I used to live. My little girl, whose name is Margaret, said neutrally yet with some disbelief, "Mother, is that your house?"

And I felt that my daughter's voice expressed a complex disappointment—to which, characteristically, she seemed resigned, or even resigned *in advance;* it contained the whole flatness and strangeness of the moment in which is revealed the source of legends, the unsatisfactory, apologetic and persistent reality. The red brick of which the house is built looked harsh and hot in the sun and was marked in two or three places by long grimacing cracks; the verandah, which always had the air of an insubstantial decoration, was visibly falling away. There was—there *is*—a little blind window of coloured glass beside the front door. I sat staring at it with a puzzled lack of emotional recognition. I sat and looked at the house and the window shades did not move, the door did not fly open, no one came out on the verandah; there was no one at home. This was as I had expected, since Maddy works now in the office of the town clerk, yet I was surprised to see the house take on such a closed, bare, impoverished look, merely by being left empty. And it was brought home to me, as I walked across the front yard to the steps, that after all these summers on the Coast I had forgotten the immense inland heat, which makes you feel as if you have to carry the whole burning sky on your head.

A sign pinned to the front door announced, in Maddy's rather sloppy and flamboyant hand: VISITORS WELCOME, CHILDREN FREE, RATES TO BE ARRANGED LATER (YOU'LL BE SORRY) WALK IN. On the hall table was a bouquet of pink phlox whose velvety scent filled the hot air of a closed house on a summer afternoon. "Upstairs!" I said to the children, and I took the hand of the little girl and her smaller brother, who had slept in the car and who rubbed against me, whimpering, as he walked. Then I paused, one foot on the bottom step, and turned to greet, matter-of-factly, the reflection of a thin, tanned, habitually watchful woman, recognizably a Young

Mother, whose hair, pulled into a knot on top of her head, exposed a jawline no longer softly fleshed, a brown neck rising with a look of tension from the little sharp knobs of the collarbone—this in the hall mirror that had shown me, last time I looked, a commonplace pretty girl, with a face as smooth and insensitive as an apple, no matter what panic and disorder lay behind it.

But this was not what I had turned for; I realized that I must have been waiting for my mother to call, from her couch in the dining-room, where she lay with the blinds down in the summer heat, drinking cups of tea which she never finished, eating—she had dispensed altogether with mealtimes, like a sickly child—little bowls of preserved fruit and crumblings of cake. It seemed to me that I could not close the door behind me without hearing my mother's ruined voice call out to me, and feeling myself go heavy all over as I prepared to answer it. Calling, *Who's there?*

I led my children to the big bedroom at the back of the house, where Maddy and I used to sleep. It has thin, almost worn-out white curtains at the windows and a square of linoleum on the floor; there is a double bed, a washstand which Maddy and I used as a desk when we were in high school, and a cardboard wardrobe with little mirrors on the inside of the doors. As I talked to my children I was thinking—but carefully, not in a rush—of my mother's state of mind when she called out *Who's there?* I was allowing myself to hear—as if I had not dared before—the cry for help—undisguised, oh, shamefully undisguised and raw and supplicating—that sounded in her voice. A cry repeated so often, and, things being as they were, so uselessly, that Maddy and I recognized it only as one of those household sounds which must be dealt with, so that worse may not follow. *You go and deal with Mother,* we would say to each other, or *I'll be out in a minute, I have to deal with Mother.*

It might be that we had to perform some of the trivial and

unpleasant services endlessly required, or that we had to supply five minutes' expediently cheerful conversation, so remorselessly casual that never for a moment was there a recognition of the real state of affairs, never a glint of pity to open the way for one of her long debilitating sieges of tears. But the pity denied, the tears might come anyway; so that we were defeated, we were forced—to stop that noise—into parodies of love. But we grew cunning, unfailing in cold solicitude; we took away from her our anger and impatience and disgust, took all emotion away from our dealings with her, as you might take away meat from a prisoner to weaken him, till he died.

We would tell her to read, to listen to music and enjoy the changes of season and be grateful that she did not have cancer. We added that she did not suffer any pain, and that is true—if imprisonment is not pain. While she demanded our love in every way she knew, without shame or sense, as a child will. And how could we have loved her, I say desperately to myself, the resources of love we had were not enough, the demand on us was too great. Nor would it have changed anything.

"Everything has been taken away from me," she would say. To strangers, to friends of ours whom we tried always unsuccessfully to keep separate from her, to old friends of hers who came guiltily infrequently to see her, she would speak like this, in the very slow and mournful voice that was not intelligible or quite human; we would have to interpret. Such theatricality humiliated us almost to death; yet now I think that without that egotism feeding stubbornly even on disaster she might have sunk rapidly into some dim vegetable life. She kept herself as much in the world as she could, not troubling about her welcome; restlessly she wandered through the house and into the streets of Jubilee. Oh, she was not resigned; she must have wept and struggled in that house of stone (as I can, but will not, imagine) until the very end.

But I find the picture is still not complete. Our Gothic
Mother, with the cold appalling mask of the Shaking Palsy
laid across her features, shuffling, weeping, devouring attention wherever she can get it, eyes dead and burning, fixed
inward on herself; this is not all. For the disease is erratic and
leisurely in its progress; some mornings (gradually growing
fewer and fewer and farther apart) she wakes up better; she
goes out to the yard and straightens up a plant in such a
simple housewifely way; she says something calm and lucid
to us; she listens attentively to the news. She has wakened out
of a bad dream; she tries to make up for lost time, tidying the
house, forcing her stiff trembling hands to work a little while
at the sewing machine. She makes us one of her specialties,
a banana cake or a lemon meringue pie. Occasionally since
she died I have dreams of her (I never dreamt of her when she
was alive) in which she is doing something like this, and I
think, why did I exaggerate so to myself, see, she is all right,
only that her hands are trembling—

At the end of these periods of calm a kind of ravaging
energy would come over her; she would make conversation
insistently and with less and less coherence; she would demand
that we rouge her cheeks and fix her hair; sometimes she might
even hire a dressmaker to come in and make clothes for her,
working in the dining room where she could watch—spending
her time again more and more on the couch. This was
extravagant, unnecessary from any practical point of view
(for why did she need these clothes, where did she wear them?)
and nerve-racking, because the dressmaker did not understand what she wanted and sometimes neither did we. I
remember after I went away receiving from Maddy several
amusing, distracted, quietly overwrought letters describing
these sessions with the dressmaker. I read them with sympathy
but without being able to enter into the once-familiar atmosphere of frenzy and frustration which my mother's demands
could produce. In the ordinary world it was not possible to

re-create her. The picture of her face which I carried in my mind seemed too terrible, unreal. Similarly the complex strain of living with her, the feelings of hysteria which Maddy and I once dissipated in a great deal of brutal laughter, now began to seem partly imaginary; I felt the beginnings of a secret, guilty estrangement.

I stayed in the room with my children for a little while because it was a strange place, for them it was only another strange place to go to sleep. Looking at them in this room I felt that they were particularly fortunate and that their life was safe and easy, which may be what most parents think at one time or another. I looked in the wardrobe but there was nothing there, only a hat trimmed with flowers from the five-and-ten, which one of us must have made for some flossy Easter. When I opened the drawer of the washstand I saw that it was crammed full of pages from a loose-leaf notebook. I read: "The Peace of Utrecht, 1713, brought an end to the War of the Spanish Succession." It struck me that the handwriting was my own. Strange to think of it lying here for ten years— more; it looked as if I might have written it that day.

For some reason reading these words had a strong effect on me; I felt as if my old life was lying around me, waiting to be picked up again. Only then for a few moments in our old room did I have this feeling. The brown halls of the old High School (a building since torn down) were re-opened for me, and I remembered the Saturday nights in spring, after the snow had melted and all the country people crowded into town. I thought of us walking up and down the main street, arm in arm with two or three other girls, until it got dark, then going in to Al's to dance, under a string of little coloured lights. The windows in the dance hall were open; they let in the raw spring air with its smell of earth and the river; the hands of farm boys crumpled and stained our white blouses when we danced. And now an experience which seemed not at all memorable at the time (in fact Al's was a dismal place and the ritual of walking up and down the street to show ourselves off we thought crude and ridiculous, though we could not resist it) had been transformed into something curiously meaningful for me, and complete; it took in more than the girls dancing and the single street, it spread over the whole town, its rudimentary pattern of streets and its bare trees and muddy yards just free of the snow, over the dirt roads where the lights of cars appeared, jolting towards the town, under an immense pale wash of sky.

Also: we wore ballerina shoes, and full black taffeta skirts, and short coats of such colours as robin's egg blue, cerise red, lime green. Maddy wore a great funereal bow at the neck of her blouse and a wreath of artificial daisies in her hair. These were the fashions, or so we believed, of one of the years after the war. Maddy; her bright skeptical look; my sister.

I ask Maddy, "Do you ever remember what she was like before?"
"No," says Maddy. "No, I can't."
"I sometimes think I can," I say hesitantly. "Not very often."
Cowardly tender nostalgia, trying to get back to a gentler truth.
"I think you would have to have been away," Maddy says, "You would have to have been away these last—quite a few—years to get those kind of memories."

It was then she said: No exorcising.

And the only other thing she said was, "She spent a lot of time sorting things. All kinds of things. Greeting cards. Buttons and yarn. Sorting and putting them into little piles. It would keep her quiet by the hour."

II.

I have been to visit Aunt Annie and Auntie Lou. This is the third time I have been there since I came home and each time they have been spending the afternoon making rugs out of dyed rags. They are very old now. They sit in a hot little porch that is shaded by bamboo blinds; the rags and the half-finished rugs make an encouraging, domestic sort of disorder around them. They do not go out any more, but they get up early in the mornings, wash and powder themselves and put on their shapeless print dresses trimmed with rickrack and white braid. They make coffee and porridge and then they clean the house, Aunt Annie working upstairs and Auntie Lou down. Their house is very clean, dark and varnished, and it smells of vinegar and apples. In the afternoon they lie down for an hour and then put on their afternoon dresses, with brooches at the neck, and sit down to do hand work.

They are the sort of women whose flesh melts or mysteriously falls away as they get older. Auntie Lou's hair is still black, but it looks stiff and dry in its net as the dead end of hair on a ripe ear of corn. She sits straight and moves her bone-thin arms in very fine, slow movements; she looks like an Egyptian, with her long neck and small sharp face and greatly wrinkled, greatly darkened skin. Aunt Annie, perhaps because of her gentler, even coquettish manner, seems more humanly fragile and worn. Her hair is nearly all gone, and she keeps on her head one of those pretty caps designed for young wives who wear curlers to bed. She calls my attention to this and asks if I do not think it is becoming. They are both adept at these little ironies, and take a mild delight in pointing out whatever is grotesque about themselves. Their company manners are exceedingly lighthearted and their conversation with each other falls into an accomplished pattern of teasing and protest. I have a fascinated glimpse of Maddy and myself, grown old, caught back in the web of sisterhood after everything else has disappeared, making tea for some young, loved, and essentially unimportant relative—and exhibiting just such a polished relationship; what will anyone ever know of us? As I watch my entertaining old aunts I wonder if old people play such stylized

and simplified roles with us because they are afraid that anything more honest might try our patience; or if they do it out
of delicacy—to fill the social time—when in reality they feel
so far away from us that there is no possibility of communi-
cating with us at all.

At any rate I felt held at a distance by them, at least until
this third afternoon when they showed in front of me some
signs of disagreement with each other. I believe this is the
first time that has happened. Certainly I never saw them argue
in all the years when Maddy and I used to visit them, and we
used to visit them often—not only out of duty but because we
found the atmosphere of sense and bustle reassuring after the
comparative anarchy, the threatened melodrama, of our
house at home.

Aunt Annie wanted to take me upstairs to show me something. Auntie Lou objected, looking remote and offended, as
if the whole subject embarrassed her. And such is the feeling
for discretion, the tradition of circumlocution in that house,
that it was unthinkable for me to ask them what they were
talking about.

"Oh, let her have her tea," Auntie Lou said, and Aunt
Annie said, "Well. When she's *had* her tea."

"Do as you like then. That upstairs is hot."

"Will you come up, Lou?"

"Then who's going to watch the children?"

"Oh, the children. I forgot."

So Aunt Annie and I withdrew into the darker parts of the
house. It occurred to me, absurdly, that she was going to give
me a five-dollar bill. I remembered that sometimes she used
to draw me into the front hall in this mysterious way and open
her purse. I do not think that Auntie Lou was included in that
secret either. But we went on upstairs, and into Aunt Annie's
own bedroom, which looked so neat and virginal, papered with
timid flowery wallpaper, the dressers spread with white
scarves. It was really very hot, as Auntie Lou had said.

"Now," Aunt Annie said, a little breathless. "Get me down that box on the top shelf of the closet."

I did, and she opened it and said with her wistful conspirator's gaiety, "Now I guess you wondered what became of all your mother's clothes?"

I had not thought of it. I sat down on the bed, forgetting that in this house the beds were not to be sat on; the bedrooms had one straight chair apiece, for that. Aunt Annie did not check me. She began to lift things out, saying, "Maddy never mentioned them, did she?"

"I never asked her," I said.

"No. Nor I wouldn't. I wouldn't say a word about it to Maddy. But I thought I might as well show you. Why not? Look," she said. "We washed and ironed what we could and what we couldn't we sent to the cleaners. I paid the cleaning myself. Then we mended anything needed mending. It's all in good condition, see?"

I watched helplessly while she held up for my inspection the underwear which was on top. She showed me where things had been expertly darned and mended and where the elastic had been renewed. She showed me a slip which had been worn, she said, only once. She took out nightgowns, a dressing gown, knitted bed-jackets. "This was what she had on the last time I saw her," she said. "I think it was. Yes." I recognized with alarm the peach-coloured bed-jacket I had sent for Christmas.

"You can see it's hardly used. Why, it's hardly used at all."

"No," I said.

"Underneath is her dresses." Her hands rummaged down through those brocades and flowered silks, growing yearly more exotic, in which my mother had wished to costume herself. Thinking of her in these peacock colours, even Aunt Annie seemed to hesitate. She drew up a blouse. "I washed this by hand, it looks like new. There's a coat hanging up in the closet. Perfectly good. She never wore a coat. She wore it when she went into the hospital, that was all. Wouldn't it fit you?"

"No," I said. "*No*." For Aunt Annie was already moving towards the closet. "I just got a new coat. I have several coats. Aunt Annie!"

"But why should you go and buy," Aunt Annie went on in her mild stubborn way, "when there are things here as good as new."

"I would rather buy," I said, and was immediately sorry for the coldness in my voice. Nevertheless I continued, "When I need something, I do go and buy it." This suggestion that I was not poor any more brought a look of reproach and aloofness into my aunt's face. She said nothing. I went and looked at a picture of Aunt Annie and Auntie Lou and their older brothers and their mother and father which hung over the bureau. They stared back at me with grave accusing Protestant faces, for I had run up against the simple unprepossessing materialism which was the rock of their lives. Things must be used; everything must be used up, saved and mended and made into something else and used again; clothes were to be worn. I felt that I had hurt Aunt Annie's feelings and that furthermore I had probably borne out a prediction of Auntie Lou's, for she was sensitive to certain attitudes in the world that were too sophisticated for Aunt Annie to bother about, and she had very likely said that I would not want my mother's clothes.

"She was gone sooner than anybody would have expected," Aunt Annie said. I turned around surprised and she said, "Your mother." Then I wondered if the clothes had been the main thing after all; perhaps they were only to serve as the introduction to a conversation about my mother's death, which Aunt Annie might feel to be a necessary part of our visit. Auntie Lou would feel differently; she had an almost superstitious dislike of certain rituals of emotionalism; such a conversation could never take place with her about.

"Two months after she went into the hospital," Aunt Annie said. "She was gone in two months." I saw that she was crying distractedly, as old people do, with miserable scanty tears. She pulled a handkerchief out of her dress and rubbed at her face.

"Maddy told her it was nothing but a check-up," she said. "Maddy told her it would be about three weeks. Your mother went in there and she thought she was coming out in three weeks." She was whispering as if she was afraid of us being overheard. "Do you think she wanted to stay in there where nobody could make out what she was saying and they wouldn't let her out of her bed? She wanted to come home!"

"But she was too sick," I said.

"No, she wasn't, she was just the way she'd always been, just getting a little worse and a little worse as time went on. But after she went in there she felt she would die, everything kind of closed in around her, and she went down so fast."

"Maybe it would have happened anyway," I said. "Maybe it was just the time."

Aunt Annie paid no attention to me. "I went up to see her," she said. "She was so glad to see me because I could tell what she was saying. She said Aunt Annie, they won't keep me in here for good, will they? And I said to her, No. I said, No.

"And she said, Aunt Annie ask Maddy to take me home again or I'm going to die. She didn't want to die. Don't you ever think a person wants to die, just because it seems to every-body else they have got no reason to go on living. So I told Maddy. But she didn't say anything. She went to the hospital every day and saw your mother and she wouldn't take her home. Your mother told me Maddy said to her, I won't take you home."

"Mother didn't always tell the truth," I said. "Aunt Annie, you know that."

"*Did you know your mother got out of the hospital?*"

"No," I said. But strangely I felt no surprise, only a vague physical sense of terror, a longing not to be told—and beyond this a feeling that what I would be told I already knew, I had always known.

"Maddy, didn't she tell you?"

"No."

"Well she got *out*. She got out the side door where the ambulance comes in, it's the only door that isn't locked. It was at night when they haven't so many nurses to watch them. She got her dressing gown and her slippers on, the first time she ever got anything on herself in years, and she went out and there it was January, snowing, but she didn't go back in. She was away down the street when they caught her. After that they put the board across her bed."

The snow, the dressing gown and slippers, the board across the bed. It was a picture I was much inclined to resist. Yet I had no doubt that this was true, all this was true and exactly as it happened. It was what she would do; all her life as long as I had known her led up to that flight.

"Where was she going?" I said, but I knew there was no answer.

"I don't know. Maybe I shouldn't have told you. Oh, Helen, when they came after her she tried to run. She tried to *run*."

The flight that concerns everybody. Even behind my aunt's soft familiar face there is another, more primitive old woman, capable of panic in some place her faith has never touched.

She began folding the clothes up and putting them back in the box. "They nailed a board across her bed. I saw it. You can't blame the nurses. They can't watch everybody. They haven't the time.

"I said to Maddy after the funeral, Maddy, may it never happen like that to you. I couldn't help it, that's what I said." She sat down on the bed herself now, folding things and putting them back in the box, making an effort to bring her voice back to normal—and pretty soon succeeding, for having lived this long who would not be an old hand at grief and self-control?

"We thought it was hard," she said finally. "Lou and I thought it was hard."

Is this the last function of old women, beyond making rag rugs and giving us five-dollar bills—making sure the haunts we have contracted for are with us, not one gone without?

She was afraid of Maddy—through fear, had cast her out for good. I thought of what Maddy had said: nobody speaks the same language.

When I got home Maddy was out in the back kitchen making a salad. Rectangles of sunlight lay on the rough linoleum. She had taken off her high-heeled shoes and was standing there in her bare feet. The back kitchen is a large untidy pleasant room with a view, behind the stove and the drying dishtowels, of the sloping back yard, the CPR station and the golden, marshy river that almost encircles the town of Jubilee. My children who had felt a little repressed in the other house immediately began to play under the table.

"Where have you been?" Maddy said.

"Nowhere. Just to see the Aunts."

"Oh, how are they?"

"They're fine. They're indestructible."

"Are they? Yes I guess they are. I haven't been to see them for a while. I don't actually see that much of them any more."

"Don't you?" I said, and she knew then what they had told me.

"They were beginning to get on my nerves a bit, after the funeral. And Fred got me this job and everything and I've been so busy—" She looked at me, waiting for what I would say, smiling a little derisively, patiently.

"Don't be guilty, Maddy," I said softly. All this time the children were running in and out and shrieking at each other between our legs.

"I'm not guilty," she said. "Where did you get that? I'm not guilty." She went to turn on the radio, talking to me over her shoulder. "Fred's going to eat with us again since he's alone. I got some raspberries for dessert. Raspberries are almost over for this year. Do they look all right to you?"

"They look all right," I said. "Do you want me to finish this?"

"Fine," she said. "I'll go and get a bowl."

She went into the dining room and came back carrying a pink cut-glass bowl, for the raspberries.

"I couldn't go on," she said. "I wanted my life."

She was standing on the little step between the kitchen and the dining room and suddenly she lost her grip on the bowl, either because her hands had begun to shake or because she had not picked it up properly in the first place; it was quite a heavy and elaborate old bowl. It slipped out of her hands and she tried to catch it and it smashed on the floor.

Maddy began to laugh. "Oh, hell," she said. "Oh, hell, oh *Hel*-en," she said, using one of our old foolish ritual phrases of despair. "Look what I've done now. In my bare feet yet. Get me a broom."

"Take your life, Maddy. Take it."

"Yes I will," Maddy said. "Yes I will."

"Go away, don't stay here."

"Yes I will."

Then she bent down and began picking up the pieces of broken pink glass. My children stood back looking at her with awe and she was laughing and saying, "It's no loss to me. I've got a whole shelf full of glass bowls. I've got enough glass bowls to do me the rest of my life. Oh, don't stand there looking at me, go and get me a broom!" I went around the kitchen looking for a broom because I seemed to have forgotten where it was kept and she said, "But why can't I, Helen? *Why can't I?*"

Dance of the Happy Shades

Miss Marsalles is having another party. (Out of musical integrity, or her heart's bold yearning for festivity, she never calls it a recital.) My mother is not an inventive or convincing liar, and the excuses which occur to her are obviously second-rate. The painters are coming. Friends from Ottawa. Poor Carrie is having her tonsils out. In the end all she can say is: Oh, but won't all that be too much trouble, *now*? *Now* being weighted with several troublesome meanings; you may take your choice. Now that Miss Marsalles has moved from the brick and frame bungalow on Bank Street, where the last three parties have been rather squashed, to an even smaller place— if she has described it correctly—on Bala Street. (Bala Street, where is that?) Or: now that Miss Marsalles' older sister is in bed, following a stroke; now that Miss Marsalles herself—as my mother says, we must face these things—is simply getting *too old*.

Now? asks Miss Marsalles, stung, pretending mystification, or perhaps for that matter really feeling it. And she asks how her June party could ever be too much trouble, at any time, in any place? It is the only entertainment she ever gives any more (so far as my mother knows it is the only entertainment she ever has given, but Miss Marsalles' light old voice, undismayed, indefatigably social, supplies the ghosts of tea parties,

private dances, At Homes, mammoth Family Dinners). She
would suffer, she says, as much disappointment as the children,
if she were to give it up. Considerably more, says my mother
to herself, but of course she cannot say it aloud; she turns her
face from the telephone with that look of irritation—as if she
had seen something messy which she was unable to clean up
—which is her private expression of pity. And she promises to
come; weak schemes for getting out of it will occur to her
during the next two weeks, but she knows she will be there.

She phones up Marg French who like herself is an old pupil
of Miss Marsalles and who has been having lessons for her
twins, and they commiserate for a while and promise to go
together and buck each other up. They remember the year
before last when it rained and the little hall was full of rain-
coats piled on top of each other because there was no place to
hang them up, and the umbrellas dripped puddles on the dark
floor. The little girls' dresses were crushed because of the
way they all had to squeeze together, and the living room
windows would not open. Last year a child had a nosebleed.

"Of course that was not Miss Marsalles' fault."

They giggle despairingly. "No. But things like that did
not use to happen."

And that is true; that is the whole thing. There is a feeling
that can hardly be put into words about Miss Marsalles'
parties; things are getting out of hand, anything may happen.
There is even a moment, driving in to such a party, when the
question occurs: will anybody else be there? For one of the
most disconcerting things about the last two or three parties
has been the widening gap in the ranks of the regulars, the old
pupils whose children seem to be the only new pupils Miss
Marsalles ever has. Every June reveals some new and surely
significant dropping-out. Mary Lambert's girl no longer
takes; neither does Joan Crimble's. What does this mean?
think my mother and Marg French, women who have moved
to the suburbs and are plagued sometimes by a feeling that

they have fallen behind, that their instincts for doing the right thing have become confused. Piano lessons are not so important now as they once were; everybody knows that. Dancing is believed to be more favourable to the development of the whole child—and the children, at least the girls, don't seem to mind it as much. But how are you to explain that to Miss Marsalles, who says, "All children need music. All children love music in their hearts"? It is one of Miss Marsalles' indestructible beliefs that she can see into children's hearts, and she finds there a treasury of good intentions and a natural love of all good things. The deceits which her spinster's sentimentality has practised on her original good judgment are legendary and colossal; she has this way of speaking of children's hearts as if they were something holy; it is hard for a parent to know what to say.

In the old days, when my sister Winifred took lessons, the address was in Rosedale; that was where it had always been. A narrow house, built of soot-and-raspberry-coloured brick, grim little ornamental balconies curving out from the second-floor windows, no towers anywhere but somehow a turreted effect; dark, pretentious, poetically ugly—the family home. And in Rosedale the annual party did not go off too badly. There was always an awkward little space before the sandwiches, because the woman they had in the kitchen was not used to parties and rather slow, but the sandwiches when they did appear were always very good: chicken, asparagus rolls, wholesome, familiar things—dressed-up nursery food. The performances on the piano were, as usual, nervous and choppy or sullen and spiritless, with the occasional surprise and interest of a lively disaster. It will be understood that Miss Marsalles' idealistic view of children, her tender- or simple-mindedness in that regard, made her almost useless as a teacher; she was unable to criticize except in the most delicate and apologetic way and her praises were unforgivably dishonest; it took an unusually conscientious pupil to come through with anything like a creditable performance.

But on the whole the affair in those days had solidity, it had tradition, in its own serenely out-of-date way it had style. Everything was always as expected; Miss Marsalles herself, waiting in the entrance hall with the tiled floor and the dark, church-vestry smell, wearing rouge, an antique hairdo adopted only on this occasion, and a floor-length dress of plum and pinkish splotches that might have been made out of old upholstery material, startled no one but the youngest children. Even the shadow behind her of another Miss Marsalles, slightly, older, larger, grimmer, whose existence was always forgotten from one June to the next, was not discomfiting—though it was surely an arresting fact that there should be not one but two faces like that in the world, both long, gravel-coloured, kindly and grotesque, with enormous noses and tiny, red, sweet-tempered and shortsighted eyes. It must finally have come to seem like a piece of luck to them to be so ugly, a protection against life to be marked in so many ways, *impossible*, for they were gay as invulnerable and childish people are; they appeared sexless, wild and gentle creatures, bizarre yet domestic, living in their house in Rosedale outside the complications of time.

In the room where the mothers sat, some on hard sofas, some on folding chairs, to hear the children play "The Gypsy Song," "The Harmonious Blacksmith" and the "Turkish March," there was a picture of Mary, Queen of Scots, in velvet, with a silk veil, in front of Holyrood Castle. There were brown misty pictures of historical battles, also the Harvard Classics, iron firedogs and a bronze Pegasus. None of the mothers smoked, nor were ashtrays provided. It was the same room, exactly the same room, in which they had performed themselves; a room whose dim impersonal style (the flossy bunch of peonies and spirea dropping petals on the piano was Miss Marsalles' own_touch and not entirely happy) was at the same time uncomfortable and reassuring. Here they found themselves year after year—a group of busy, youngish women who had eased their cars impatiently through the archaic streets of Rosedale, who had complained for a week previously about the time lost, the fuss over the children's dresses and, above all, the boredom, but who were drawn together by a rather implausible allegiance—not so much to Miss Marsalles as to the ceremonies of their childhood, to a more exacting pattern of life which had been breaking apart even then but which survived, and unaccountably still survived, in Miss Marsalles' living room. The little girls in dresses with skirts as stiff as bells moved with a natural awareness of ceremony against the dark walls of books, and their mothers' faces wore the dull, not unpleasant look of acquiescence, the touch of absurd and slightly artificial nostalgia which would carry them through any lengthy family ritual. They exchanged smiles which showed no lack of good manners, and yet expressed a familiar, humorous amazement at the sameness of things, even the selections played on the piano and the fillings of the sandwiches; so they acknowledged the incredible, the wholly unrealistic persistence of Miss Marsalles and her sister and their life.

After the piano-playing came a little ceremony which always caused some embarrassment. Before the children were allowed to escape to the garden—very narrow, a town garden, but still a garden, with hedges, shade, a border of yellow lilies—where a long table was covered with crepe paper in infants' colours of pink and blue, and the woman from the kitchen set out plates of sandwiches, ice cream, prettily tinted and tasteless sherbet, they were compelled to accept, one by one, a year's-end gift, all wrapped and tied with ribbon, from Miss Marsalles. Except among the most naive new pupils this gift caused no excitement of anticipation. It was apt to be a book, and the question was, where did she find such books? They were of the vintage found in old Sunday-school libraries, in attics and the basements of second-hand stores, but they were all stiff-backed, unread, brand new. *Northern Lakes and Rivers, Knowing the Birds, More Tales by Grey-Owl, Little Mission Friends*. She also gave pictures: "Cupid Awake and Cupid Asleep," "After the Bath," "The Little Vigilantes"; most of these seemed to feature that tender childish nudity which our sophisticated prudery found most ridiculous and disgusting. Even the boxed games she gave us proved to be insipid and unplayable —full of complicated rules which allowed everybody to win.

The embarrassment the mothers felt at this time was due not so much to the presents themselves as to a strong doubt whether Miss Marsalles could afford them; it did not help to remember that her fees had gone up only once in ten years (and even when that happened, two or three mothers had quit). They always ended up by saying that she must have other resources. It was obvious—otherwise she would not be living in this house. And then her sister taught—or did not teach any more, she was retired but she gave private lessons, it was believed, in French and German. They must have enough, between them. If you are a Miss Marsalles your wants are simple and it does not cost a great deal to live.

But after the house in Rosedale was gone, after it had given way to the bungalow on Bank Street, these conversations about Miss Marsalles' means did not take place; this aspect of Miss Marsalles' life had passed into that region of painful subjects which it is crude and unmannerly to discuss.

"I will die if it rains," my mother says. "I will die of depression at this affair if it rains." But the day of the party it does not rain and in fact the weather is very hot. It is a hot gritty summer day as we drive down into the city and get lost, looking for Bala Street.

When we find it, it gives the impression of being better than we expected, but that is mostly because it has a row of trees, and the other streets we have been driving through, along the railway embankment, have been unshaded and slatternly. The houses here are of the sort that are divided in half, with a sloping wooden partition in the middle of the front porch; they have two wooden steps and a dirt yard. Apparently it is in one of these half-houses that Miss Marsalles lives. They are red brick, with the front door and the window trim and the porches painted cream, grey, oily-green and yellow. They are neat, kept-up. The front part of the house next to the one where Miss Marsalles lives has been turned into a little store; it has a sign that says: GROCERIES AND CONFECTIONERY.

The door is standing open. Miss Marsalles is wedged between the door, the coatrack and the stairs; there is barely room to get past her into the living room, and it would be impossible, the way things are now, for anyone to get from the living room upstairs. Miss Marsalles is wearing her rouge, her hairdo and her brocaded dress, which it is difficult not to tramp on. In this full light she looks like a character in a masquerade, like the feverish, fancied-up courtesan of an unpleasant Puritan imagination. But the fever is only her rouge; her eyes, when we get close enough to see them, are the same as ever, red-rimmed and merry and without apprehension. My mother and I are kissed—I am greeted, as always, as if I were around five years old—and we get past. It seemed to me that Miss Marsalles was looking beyond us as she kissed us; she was looking up the street for someone who has not yet arrived.

The house has a living room and a dining room, with the oak doors pushed back between them. They are small rooms. Mary Queen of Scots hangs tremendous on the wall. There is no fireplace so the iron firedogs are not there, but the piano is, and even a bouquet of peonies and spirea from goodness knows what garden. Since it is so small the living room looks crowded, but there are not a dozen people in it, including children. My mother speaks to people and smiles and sits down. She says to me, Marg French is not here yet, could she have got lost too?

The woman sitting beside us is not familiar. She is middle-aged and wears a dress of shot taffeta with rhinestone clips; it smells of the cleaners. She introduces herself as Mrs. Clegg, Miss Marsalles' neighbour in the other half of the house. Miss Marsalles has asked her if she would like to hear the children play, and she thought it would be a treat; she is fond of music in any form.

My mother, very pleasant but looking a little uncomfortable, asks about Miss Marsalles' sister; is she upstairs?

"Oh, yes, she's upstairs. She's not herself though, poor thing."

That is too bad, my mother says.

"Yes it's a shame. I give her something to put her to sleep for the afternoon. She lost her powers of speech, you know. Her powers of control generally, she lost." My mother is warned by a certain luxurious lowering of the voice that more lengthy and intimate details may follow and she says quickly again that it is too bad.

"I come in and look after her when the other one goes out on her lessons."

"That's very kind of you. I'm sure she appreciates it."

"Oh well I feel kind of sorry for a couple of old ladies like them. They're a couple of babies, the pair."

My mother murmurs something in reply but she is not looking at Mrs. Clegg, at her brick-red healthy face or the—to me —amazing gaps in her teeth. She is staring past her into the dining room with fairly well-controlled dismay.

What she sees there is the table spread, all ready for the party feast; nothing is lacking. The plates of sandwiches are set out, as they must have been for several hours now; you can see how the ones on top are beginning to curl very slightly at the edges. Flies buzz over the table, settle on the sandwiches and crawl comfortably across the plates of little iced cakes brought from the bakery. The cut-glass bowl, sitting as usual in the centre of the table, is full of purple punch, without ice apparently and going flat.

"I tried to tell her not to put it all out ahead of time," Mrs. Clegg whispers, smiling delightedly, as if she were talking about the whims and errors of some headstrong child. "You know she was up at five o'clock this morning making sandwiches. I don't know what things are going to taste like Afraid she wouldn't be ready I guess. Afraid she'd forget something. They hate to forget."

"Food shouldn't be left out in the hot weather," my mother says.

"Oh, well I guess it won't poison us for once. I was only thinking what a shame to have the sandwiches dry up. And when she put the ginger-ale in the punch at noon I had to laugh. But what a waste."

My mother shifts and rearranges her voile skirt, as if she has suddenly become aware of the impropriety, the hideousness even, of discussing a hostess's arrangements in this way in her own living room. "Marg French isn't here," she says to me in a hardening voice. "She did say she was coming."

"I am the oldest girl here," I say with disgust.

"Shh. That means you can play last. Well. It won't be a very long programme this year, will it?"

Mrs. Clegg leans across us, letting loose a cloud of warm unfresh odour from between her breasts. "I'm going to see if she's got the fridge turned up high enough for the ice cream. She'd feel awful if it was all to melt."

My mother goes across the room and speaks to a woman she knows and I can tell that she is saying, Marg French *said* she was *coming*. The women's faces in the room, made up some time before, have begun to show the effects of heat and a fairly general uneasiness. They ask each other when it will begin. Surely very soon now; nobody has arrived for at least a quarter of an hour. How mean of people not to come, they say. Yet in this heat, and the heat is particularly dreadful down here, it must be the worst place in the city—well you can almost see their point. I look around and calculate that there is no one in the room within a year of my age.

The little children begin to play. Miss Marsalles and Mrs. Clegg applaud with enthusiasm; the mothers clap two or three times each, with relief. My mother seems unable, although she makes a great effort, to take her eyes off the dining-room table and the complacent journeys of the marauding flies. Finally she achieves a dreamy, distant look, with her eyes focused somewhere above the punch-bowl, which makes it possible for her to keep her head turned in that direction and yet does not in any positive sense give her away. Miss Marsalles as well has trouble keeping her eyes on the performers; she keeps looking towards the door. Does she expect that even now some of the unexplained absentees may turn up? There are far more than half a dozen presents in the inevitable box beside the piano, wrapped in white paper and tied with silver ribbon—not real ribbon, but the cheap kind that splits and shreds.

It is while I am at the piano, playing the minuet from *Berenice*, that the final arrival, unlooked-for by anybody but Miss Marsalles, takes place. It must seem at first that there has been some mistake. Out of the corner of my eye I see a whole procession of children, eight or ten in all, with a red-haired woman in something like a uniform, mounting the front step. They look like a group of children from a private school on an excursion of some kind (there is that drabness and sameness about their clothes) but their progress is too scrambling and disorderly for that. Or this is the impression I have; I cannot really look. Is it the wrong house, are they really on their way to the doctor for shots, or to Vacation Bible Classes? No, Miss Marsalles has got up with a happy whisper of apology; she has gone to meet them. Behind my back there is a sound of people squeezing together, of folding chairs being opened, there is an inappropriate, curiously unplaceable giggle.

And above or behind all this cautious flurry of arrival there is a peculiarly concentrated silence. Something has happened, something unforeseen, perhaps something disastrous; you can feel such things behind your back. I go on playing. I fill the first harsh silence with my own particularly dogged and lumpy interpretation of Handel. When I get up off the piano bench I almost fall over some of the new children who are sitting on the floor.

One of them, a boy nine or ten years old, is going to follow me. Miss Marsalles takes his hand and smiles at him and there is no twitch of his hand, no embarrassed movement of her head to disown this smile. How peculiar; and a boy, too. He turns his head towards her as he sits down; she speaks to him encouragingly. But my attention has been caught by his profile as he looks up at her—the heavy, unfinished features, the abnormally small and slanting eyes. I look at the children seated on the floor and I see the same profile repeated two or three times; I see another boy with a very large head and fair shaved hair, fine as a baby's; there are other children whose features are regular and unexceptional, marked only by an infantile openness and calm. The boys are dressed in white shirts and short grey pants and the girls wear dresses of grey-green cotton with red buttons and sashes.

"Sometimes that kind is quite musical," says Mrs. Clegg.

"Who are they?" my mother whispers, surely not aware of how upset she sounds.

"They're from that class she has out at the Greenhill School. They're nice little things and some of them quite musical but of course they're not all there."

My mother nods distractedly; she looks around the room and meets the trapped, alerted eyes of the other women, but no decision is reached. There is nothing to be done. These children are going to play. Their playing is no worse—not much worse—than ours, but they seem to go so slowly, and then there is nowhere to look. For it is a matter of politeness surely not to look closely at such children, and yet where else can you look during a piano performance but at the performer? There is an atmosphere in the room of some freakish inescapable dream. My mother and the others are almost audible saying to themselves: *No, I know it is not right to be repelled by such children and I am not repelled, but nobody told me I was going to come here to listen to a procession of little—little idiots for that's what they are*—WHAT KIND OF A PARTY IS THIS? Their applause however has increased, becoming brisk, let-us-at-least-get-this-over-with. But the programme shows no signs of being over.

Miss Marsalles says each child's name as if it were a cause for celebration. Now she says, "Dolores Boyle!" A girl as big as I am, a long-legged, rather thin and plaintive-looking girl with blonde, almost white, hair uncoils herself and gets up off the floor. She sits down on the bench and after shifting around a bit and pushing her long hair back behind her ears she begins to play.

We are accustomed to notice performances, at Miss Marsalles' parties, but it cannot be said that anyone has ever expected music. Yet this time the music establishes itself so effortlessly, with so little demand for attention, that we are hardly even surprised. What she plays is not familiar. It is something fragile, courtly and gay, that carries with it the freedom of a great unemotional happiness. And all that this girl does—but this is something you would not think could ever be done—is to play it so that this can be felt, all this can be felt, even in Miss Marsalles' living-room on Bala Street on a preposterous afternoon. The children are all quiet, the ones from Greenhill School and the rest. The mothers sit, caught with a look of protest on their faces, a more profound anxiety than before, as if reminded of something that they had forgotten they had forgotten; the white-haired girl sits ungracefully at the piano with her head hanging down, and the music is carried through the open door and the windows to the cindery summer street.

Miss Marsalles sits beside the piano and smiles at everybody in her usual way. Her smile is not triumphant, or modest. She does not look like a magician who is watching people's faces to see the effect of a rather original revelation; nothing like that. You would think, now that at the very end of her life she has found someone whom she can teach—whom she must teach—to play the piano, she would light up with the importance of this discovery. But it seems that the girl's playing like this is something she always expected, and she finds it natural and satisfying; people who believe in miracles do not make much fuss when they actually encounter one. Nor does it seem that she regards this girl with any more wonder than the other children from Greenhill School, who love her, or the rest of us, who do not. To her no gift is unexpected, no celebration will come as a surprise.

The girl is finished. The music is in the room and then it is gone and naturally enough no one knows what to say. For the moment she is finished it is plain that she is just the same as before, a girl from Greenhill School. Yet the music was not imaginary. The facts are not to be reconciled. And so after a few minutes the performance begins to seem, in spite of its innocence, like a trick—a very successful and diverting one, of course, but perhaps—how can it be said?—perhaps not altogether *in good taste*. For the girl's ability, which is undeniable but after all useless, out-of-place, is not really something that anybody wants to talk about. To Miss Marsalles such a thing is acceptable, but to other people, people who live in the world, it is not. Never mind, they must say something and so they speak gratefully of the music itself, saying how lovely, what a beautiful piece, what is it called?

"The Dance of the Happy Shades," says Miss Marsalles. *Danse des ombres heureuses*, she says, which leaves nobody any the wiser.

But then driving home, driving out of the hot red-brick streets and out of the city and leaving Miss Marsalles and her no longer possible parties behind, quite certainly forever, why is it that we are unable to say—as we must have expected to say—*Poor Miss Marsalles?* It is the Dance of the Happy Shades that prevents us, it is that one communiqué from the other country where she lives.

FOR THE BEST IN PAPERBACKS, LOOK FOR THE 🐧

In every corner of the world, on every subject under the sun, Penguin represents quality and variety – the very best in publishing today.

For complete information about books available from Penguin – including Puffins, Penguin Classics and Arkana – and how to order them, write to us at the appropriate address below. Please note that for copyright reasons the selection of books varies from country to country.

In the United Kingdom: Please write to *Dept E.P., Penguin Books Ltd, Harmondsworth, Middlesex, UB7 0DA.*

If you have any difficulty in obtaining a title, please send your order with the correct money, plus ten per cent for postage and packaging, to *PO Box No 11, West Drayton, Middlesex*

In the United States: Please write to *Dept BA, Penguin, 299 Murray Hill Parkway, East Rutherford, New Jersey 07073*

In Canada: Please write to *Penguin Books Canada Ltd, 2801 John Street, Markham, Ontario L3R 1B4*

In Australia: Please write to the *Marketing Department, Penguin Books Australia Ltd, P.O. Box 257, Ringwood, Victoria 3134*

In New Zealand: Please write to the *Marketing Department, Penguin Books (NZ) Ltd, Private Bag, Takapuna, Auckland 9*

In India: Please write to *Penguin Overseas Ltd, 706 Eros Apartments, 56 Nehru Place, New Delhi, 110019*

In the Netherlands: Please write to *Penguin Books Netherlands B.V., Postbus 195, NL–1380AD Weesp*

In West Germany: Please write to *Penguin Books Ltd, Friedrichstrasse 10–12, D–6000 Frankfurt/Main 1*

In Spain: Please write to *Alhambra Longman S.A., Fernandez de la Hoz 9, E–28010 Madrid*

In Italy: Please write to *Penguin Italia s.r.l., Via Como 4, I-20096 Pioltello (Milano)*

In France: Please write to *Penguin Books Ltd, 39 Rue de Montmorency, F-75003 Paris*

In Japan: Please write to *Longman Penguin Japan Co Ltd, Yamaguchi Building, 2–12–9 Kanda Jimbocho, Chiyoda-Ku, Tokyo 101*

A CHOICE OF PENGUIN FICTION

The Captain and the Enemy   Graham Greene

The Captain always maintained that he won Jim from his father at a game of backgammon...'It is good to find the best living writer ... still in such first-rate form' – Francis King in the *Spectator*

The Book and the Brotherhood   Iris Murdoch

'Why should we go on supporting a book which we detest?' Rose Curtland asks. 'The brotherhood of Western intellectuals versus the book of history,' Jenkin Riderhood suggests. 'A thoroughly gripping, stimulating and challenging fiction' – *The Times*

The King of the Fields   Isaac Bashevis Singer

His profound and magical excursion into prehistory. '*The King of the Fields* reaps an abundant harvest ... it has a deceptive biblical simplicity and carries the poetry of narrative to rare heights. At eighty-five, Isaac Bashevis Singer has lost none of his incomparable wonder-working power' – *Sunday Times*

The Enigma of Arrival   V. S. Naipaul

'For sheer abundance of talent, there can hardly be a writer alive who surpasses V. S. Naipaul. Whatever we want in a novelist is to be found in his books' – Irving Howe in *The New York Times Book Review*

Lewis Percy   Anita Brookner

'Anita Brookner shines again ... [a] tender and cruel, funny and sad novel about an innocent idealist, whose gentle rearing by his widowed mother causes him to take too gallant a view of women' – *Daily Mail*. 'Vintage Brookner' – *The Times*

A CHOICE OF PENGUIN FICTION

Humboldt's Gift Saul Bellow

Bellow's classic story of the writer's life in America is an exuberant tale of success and failure. 'Sharp, erudite, beautifully measured ... One of the most gifted chroniclers of the Western world alive today' – *The Times*

Incline Our Hearts A. N. Wilson

'An account of an eccentric childhood so moving, so private and personal, and so intensely funny that it bears inescapable comparison with that greatest of childhood novels, *David Copperfield*' – *Daily Telegraph*

The Lyre of Orpheus Robertson Davies

'The lyre of Orpheus opens the door of the underworld', wrote E. T. A. Hoffmann; and his spirit, languishing in limbo, watches over, and comments on, the efforts of the Cornish Foundation as its Trustees decide to produce an opera. 'A marvellous finale' (*Sunday Times*) to Robertson Davies's Cornish Trilogy.

The New Confessions William Boyd

The outrageous, hilarious autobiography of John James Todd, a Scotsman born in 1899 and one of the great self-appointed (and failed) geniuses of the twentieth century. 'Brilliant ... a Citizen Kane of a novel' – *Daily Telegraph*

The Blue Gate of Babylon Paul Pickering

'Like Ian Fleming gone berserk, the writing is of supreme quality, the humour a taste instantly acquired' – *Mail on Sunday*. 'Brilliantly exploits the fluently headlong manner of Evelyn Waugh's early black farces' – *Sunday Times*

FOR THE BEST IN PAPERBACKS, LOOK FOR THE 🐧

A CHOICE OF PENGUIN FICTION

A Far Cry From Kensington Muriel Spark

'Pure delight' – Claire Tomalin in the *Independent*. 'A 1950s Kensington of shabby-genteel bedsitters, espresso bars and A-line dresses ... irradiated with sudden glows of lyricism she can so beautifully effect' – Peter Kemp in the *Sunday Times*

Love in the Time of Cholera Gabriel García Márquez

The Number One international bestseller. 'Admirers of *One Hundred Years of Solitude* may find it hard to believe that García Márquez can have written an even better novel. But that's what he's done' – *Newsweek*

Enchantment Monica Dickens

The need to escape, play games, fantasize, is universal. But for some people it is everything. To this compassionate story of real lives Monica Dickens brings her unparalleled warmth, insight and perception. 'One of the tenderest souls in English fiction' – *Sunday Times*

My Secret History Paul Theroux

'André Parent saunters into the book, aged fifteen ... a creature of naked and unquenchable ego, greedy for sex, money, experience, *another life* ... read it warily; read it twice, and more; it is darker and deeper than it looks' – *Observer*. 'On his best form since *The Mosquito Coast*' – *Time Out*

Decline and Fall Evelyn Waugh

A comic yet curiously touching account of an innocent plunged into the sham, brittle world of high society. Evelyn Waugh's first novel brought him immediate public acclaim and remains a classic of its kind.

A CHOICE OF PENGUIN FICTION

A Natural Curiosity   Margaret Drabble

Moving effortlessly from black comedy to acute social observation, Margaret Drabble picks up the thread of the characters and stories of *The Radiant Way*, as her engrossing panorama of the way we are today shifts to the north of England. 'Confident and marvellously accomplished' – *London Review of Books*

Summer's Lease   John Mortimer

'It's high summer, high comedy too, when Molly drags her amiably bickering family to a rented Tuscan villa for the hols ... With a cosy fluency of wit, Mortimer charms us into his urbane tangle of clues...' – *Mail on Sunday*. 'Superb' – Ruth Rendell

Nice Work   David Lodge

'The campus novel meets the industrial novel ... compulsive reading' – David Profumo in the *Daily Telegraph*. 'A work of immense intelligence, informative, disturbing and diverting ... one of the best novelists of his generation' – Anthony Burgess in the *Observer*

S.   John Updike

'John Updike's very funny satire not only pierces the occluded hocus-pocus of Lego religion which exploits the gullible and self-deluded ... but probes more deeply and seriously the inadequacies on which superstitious skulduggery battens' – *The Times*

The Counterlife   Philip Roth

'Roth has now surpassed himself' – *Washington Post*. 'A breathtaking *tour de force* of wit, wisdom, ingenuity and sharply-honed malice' – *The Times*

The Moons of Jupiter

'A remarkable writer whose characters emerge in shining clarity ... A major talent is at work here' – *Los Angeles Times*

In these eleven stories Alice Munro's women discover that love is rarely honest, kind or reliable (although they keep trying); that people are not puzzles to be 'arbitrarily solved' (although they continue to search the past and present for clues).

'Alice Munro has been compared with Proust, short-listed for the Booker prize, and remains (though dazzling) quite unperturbed and unaffected, her writing smooth and supple' – *Financial Times*

Something I've Been Meaning to Tell You

'A spellbinding tour through a world of love, menace and surprise' – *Los Angeles Times*

Alice Munro's territory is the secrets which crackle beneath the façade of ordinary lives. Rooted in small towns or urban desolations, her stories open up a whole geography of pain, desire and bruised acceptance and unerringly expose the innermost depths of the female heart.

The Beggar Maid

'Wonderful! Whether *The Beggar Maid* is a collection of stories or a new kind of novel I'm not quite sure, but whatever it is, it's wonderful' – John Gardner, author of *Grendel*

As a child Rose had a hard life. Born into the back streets of a small Canadian town, she battled incessantly with her practical and shrewd stepmother, who cowed her with tales of her own past and warnings of the dangerous world outside. But Rose was ambitious – she won a scholarship and left for Toronto where she married Patrick; for him she was his Beggar Maid, 'meek and voluptuous, with her shy white feet', and he was her knight, content to sit and adore her . . .

'A work of great brilliance and depth . . . Munro's power of analysis, of sensations and thoughts, is almost Proustian in its sureness' – Alan Hollinghurst in the *New Statesman*

Lives of Girls and Women

Del Jordan's scrapbook of memories records a young girl changing from childhood to adolescence. Through the women and men she encounters – her mother courageously selling encyclopedias, gaining her freedom almost imperceptibly; her Aunts Elspeth and Grace, two lives devoted to Uncle Craig; Garnet her first bittersweet taste of love; and best friend Naomi relentlessly pursuing marriage – Del becomes aware of her own potential and the excitement of an unknown independence . . .

'A superb account of complex childhood perceptions and experiences' – *Guardian*